PRAISE FOR DEVEREAUX'S DIME STORE MYSTERIES

Dying for a Cupcake

"Swanson cooks up a delectable treat with *Dying for a Cupcake.* When former resident Kizzy Cutler arrives back in town and hosts a cupcake competition where her assistant dies under mysterious circumstances and Kizzy has several near misses, Deveraux Sinclair has to run her five-and-dime store and figure out who could be mad enough at Kizzy to want her dead. With a plentiful cast of suspects, this was a fast-paced page-turner of a mystery that I couldn't put down. A fun, lively, and thoroughly engaging mystery with sprinkles on top!"

—*New York Times* bestselling author Jenn McKinlay

Dead Between the Lines

"Much to enjoy." —Kings River Life Magazine

"Another great story from Denise Swanson. . . . This series is filled with very interesting characters, and I can't wait to see where the author takes them next. The possibilities seem endless."

—Escape with Dollycas into a Good Book

Nickeled-and-Dimed to Death

"Delightful. . . . Readers will look forward to seeing more of the quick-witted Dev." —*Publishers Weekly*

continued . . .

"A fabulously entertaining read. The pace is quick, the prose is snappy, and the dialogue is sharp."

—The Maine Suspect

"Peopled with unique characters, Ms. Swanson's books are always entertaining." —Fresh Fiction

"Quite the caper. [Swanson] is masterful in her storytelling." —*Romantic Times*

Little Shop of Homicide

"Swanson puts just the right amount of sexy sizzle in her latest engaging mystery." —*Chicago Tribune*

"Veteran author Swanson debuts a spunky new heroine with a Missouri stubborn streak."

—*Library Journal* (starred review)

"A new entertaining mystery series that her fans will appreciate. . . . With a touch of romance in the air, readers will enjoy this delightful cozy."

—Genre Go Round Reviews

"Swanson has a gift for portraying small-town life, making it interesting, and finding both the ridiculous and the satisfying parts of living in one. I wish Dev a long and happy shelf life." —AnnArbor.com

"A top-notch new mystery . . . all the right ingredients for another successful series." —*Romantic Times*

PRAISE FOR THE *NEW YORK TIMES* BESTSELLING SCUMBLE RIVER MYSTERY SERIES

"Endearing . . . quirky . . . a delight." —*Chicago Tribune*

"Bounces along with gently wry humor and jaunty twists and turns. The quintessential amateur sleuth: bright, curious, and more than a little nervy."
—Agatha Award–winning author Earlene Fowler

"[A] lively, light, and quite insightful look at small-town life." —*The Hartford Courant*

"A fun and fast-paced mystery. . . . Reading about Scumble River is as comfortable as being in your own hometown." —The Mystery Reader

"Top-notch storytelling, with truly unique and wonderful characters." —*CrimeSpree Magazine*

"Smartly spins on a solid plot and likable characters."
—*South Florida Sun-Sentinel*

"Denise Swanson keeps getting better and better . . . unforgettable reads!" —Roundtable Reviews

"A magnificent tale written by a wonderful author."
—*Midwest Book Review*

"Denise Swanson hits all the right notes in this brisk and witty peek at small-town foibles and foul play."
—*Romantic Times* (top pick)

Also by Denise Swanson

DEVEREAUX'S DIME STORE MYSTERIES

Dead Between the Lines
Little Shop of Homicide
Nickeled-and-Dimed to Death

SCUMBLE RIVER MYSTERIES

Murder of a Needled Knitter
Murder of a Stacked Librarian
Murder of the Cat's Meow
Novella: *"Dead Blondes Tell No Tales"*
Murder of a Creped Suzette
Murder of a Bookstore Babe
Murder of a Wedding Belle
Murder of a Royal Pain
Murder of a Chocolate-Covered Cherry
Murder of a Botoxed Blonde
Murder of a Real Bad Boy
Murder of a Smart Cookie
Murder of a Pink Elephant
Murder of a Barbie and Ken
Murder of a Snake in the Grass
Murder of a Sleeping Beauty
Murder of a Sweet Old Lady
Murder of a Small-Town Honey

Dying for a Cupcake

A Devereaux's Dime Store Mystery

Denise Swanson

AN OBSIDIAN MYSTERY

OBSIDIAN
Published by the Penguin Group
Penguin Group (USA) LLC, 375 Hudson Street,
New York, New York 10014

USA | Canada | UK | Ireland | Australia | New Zealand | India | South Africa | China
penguin.com
A Penguin Random House Company

First published by Obsidian, an imprint of New American Library,
a division of Penguin Group (USA) LLC

First Printing, March 2015

ISBN 978-0-451-41889-0

Printed in the United States of America
10 9 8 7 6 5 4 3 2 1

In memory of my great aunt, Margaret Pierard. Born February 18, 1911, and passed away December 10, 2013. She was an amazing woman who saw 102 years of world changes.

CHAPTER 1

Attendance at the Saturday Night Prayer Circle was at an all-time high, and despite our group's nickname, it wasn't because any of us had suddenly gotten religion. We met to gripe about our problems, and although an occasional Hail Mary might be muttered under our breath, no one brought rosary beads or dropped to their knees—unless they fell off their stiletto heels.

"Poppy Kincaid."

"Here."

"Veronica Ksiazak."

"Here."

"Devereaux Sinclair."

"I'm sitting right in front of you, Winnie," I grumbled. "What's with this roll call crap anyway?"

"You'll see." She smiled mysteriously. "It's a surprise."

I generally found Winnie Todd amusing, but for various reasons, not the least of which was my messed-up love life, I was in a bad mood tonight. I probably should have stayed home, but the chance to avoid my grandmother's questions along with the lure of alcohol had overcome my better judgment.

The fishbowl-size margaritas and endless bottles of wine that appeared miraculously in front of us whenever our glasses came close to being empty eased a lot of our group's woes. The prompt service could be due to the large tips we always left, but more likely it was because my best friend and fellow circle member, Poppy Kincaid, owned the joint.

Her nightclub, Gossip Central, was the most popular watering hole in Shadow Bend, Missouri—population four thousand twenty-eight. Strictly speaking, Poppy's place wasn't inside the city limits; it was a quarter mile across the line. Although I had never asked her about it, my guess was that she had deliberately chosen a location just outside her police chief father's jurisdiction.

No grown woman wanted her daddy showing up every time the authorities were called to break up a fight at her bar—especially since Poppy wasn't on speaking terms with her dad. In fact, Poppy's issues with her father were one of the main reasons she was a member of our little underground society.

My motives for participating went by the names Deputy U.S. Marshal Jake Del Vecchio and Dr. Noah Underwood—two smoking-hot guys who claimed to be interested in me, but who tended to disappear from my life at regular intervals. True, I was having a hard time deciding which guy I really loved, and thus was seeing them both. But seriously, if either of them cared for me as much as they said they did, wouldn't they be spending more time in my company than at their jobs? I mean, I understood long hours and hard work, but it had been weeks since I'd had a date with either man.

I mentally slapped myself. I had vowed not to think about Jake—or Noah—tonight or my dilemma in trying to figure out which one was the right man for me. Instead, I was going to enjoy being with my friends and maybe even figuring out how to keep my dime store in the black for another quarter. Besides wanting to partake in a glass or three of wine, and the chance to dodge my grandmother's curiosity about my love life, my presence at the Saturday Night Prayer Circle was largely due to the text from Ronni Ksiazak saying that during the gathering, she planned to present an idea of how to bring tourists into Shadow Bend.

Tourists meant cash. And extra cash was something that I was sure that nearly everyone attending the evening's meeting could use. Ronni needed to fill her huge old Italianate-style Victorian bed-and-breakfast with paying guests if she was going to repay the loan that her family had given her to buy and renovate the place. Poppy had a serious fashion addiction to support, and Winnie was continuously fund-raising for various charities that constantly had their hands out for additional donations.

Although I didn't know the fifth woman seated across the cocktail table, I was fairly certain she wouldn't object to making a little spare change on the side, either. Harlee Ames was thirty-seven, eight years older than I was, and had only recently returned to town after spending the last twenty years in the service. She'd moved home a few months ago and opened Forever Used, an upscale consignment shop aimed at Shadow Bend's affluent new arrivals.

Our community's population consisted of the locals—mostly farmers, ranchers, and factory workers who had lived in or around the town all their lives—and transplants from Kansas City who had relocated to the area for the fresh air and the cheap land. A huge chasm separated the two groups, and I worried that Harlee's store would widen the gap between the haves and have-nots all the more. Even secondhand, the designer clothing and accessories her shop specialized in cost more than a lot of the original Shadow Benders earned in a week.

But I couldn't put my finger on whether that was what bothered me about Harlee, or if it was something else. As I mused about my reaction to our group's newest member, Ronni brought our gathering to order.

Raising her drink, the B & B owner said, "Here's to the Saturday Sisterhood. May we all make a lot of moola." Ronni was nearly as driven and competitive as I was, so I wasn't surprised when she added, "And may we also leave our male competitors in the dust."

"Hear, hear!" Winnie Todd clanked her wineglass with mine. "Ronni's idea will put my cooking school on the map. Especially since she's arranged media coverage."

Ah, that was why Winnie was playing teacher. She was opening a cooking school. Considering that she had come of age in the sixties, and was rumored to be growing pot in her basement, I wondered if her specialty would be "magic" brownies. Maybe the weed was for her culinary classes rather than for her personal consumption.

Certainly, Winnie's wardrobe looked as if she were living in Haight-Ashbury. Tonight she had on a white vinyl minidress with a cutout midriff. The metal chains that fastened the bodice to the skirt rattled every time she took a deep breath. It was like sitting next to the ghost of Psychedelic Christmas Past.

"How many of you know who Kizzy Cutler is?" Ronni asked, breaking into my musings about Winnie's fashion choice.

The name sounded familiar, but a face didn't immediately come to my mind. Poppy was silent, and Winnie had a similarly puzzled expression, as if she, too, was trying to dredge up an elusive memory. Harlee was the only one who spoke up.

"Kizzy was in my class in high school. Why?"

"She lives in Chicago now and she owns the über-successful Kizzy Cutler's Cupcakes," Ronni explained. "She was a client of the advertising firm I used to work for and I was a part of the team that handled her account. She's the one who first told me about Shadow Bend." Ronni took a swallow of her martini. "Kizzy always spoke so fondly of her hometown that when I decided I'd had enough of city life, I took a look at what was available here."

"I always wondered how you ended up in our little burg," Poppy commented.

"Me, too," I said, sipping my wine. I loved Shadow Bend, but was curious why someone without any friends or relatives here had chosen to relocate and open a business in our small community. Ronni didn't seem the type to have moved for the open spaces or the air quality.

"Seems like a lot of people end up here for various reasons." Winnie winked at me. "Like your hunky marshal."

Grrr! I forced a smile. Winnie was harmless, and I didn't want to snap at her a second time tonight, but I had just started to relax and now that she mentioned Jake, the conversation he and I had had that afternoon popped into my mind. I'd been so happy to see his picture on my cell phone's screen. Contact with him when he was on the job was sporadic at best, and his current case—tracking down a serial killer in St. Louis called the Doll Maker who had kidnapped Jake's ex-wife, Meg—was even more intense than his usual assignments. Too bad his news hadn't been what I was hoping to hear. Instead of reporting that his team was making progress in finding Meg, Jake had said that the

Doll Maker was still running him around with promises and threats.

Ronni interrupted my brooding. "Kizzy and I still keep in touch, and when she mentioned that she was starting a new themed cupcake line called the Flavors of Your Life, I suggested that she should kick it off with a contest to find the most original cupcake flavor. I recommended that because she currently distributes in the Midwest and South, the competition should be limited to those regions, and—"

"And Kizzy agreed to hold the final rounds of baking and judging here in Shadow Bend!" Winnie shouted.

Ronni shot Winnie an exasperated look, clearly unhappy that the older woman had blurted out the news before she could make the announcement. Then she gave a tiny shrug and said, "I told Kizzy I could provide accommodations for the judges and media at my B and B, and that the contestants can stay at the Cattlemen's Motel." Ronni consulted her notes. "We can use Winnie's cooking school for the actual baking and I thought that Poppy could handle the evening entertainment here at Gossip Central."

"Sure." Poppy's expression turned serious as she grabbed a pen from her pocket and started scribbling on a paper napkin. "How many people and what kinds of events are we talking about?"

"There are ten finalists, three judges, and the Dessert Channel has said they'd be interested in covering the contest, so we'd need to include whatever crew they send. Plus Kizzy, her partner, and her executive assistant." Ronni ticked the attendees off on her fingers. "And if we get the buzz we hope for, there should be lots of day-trippers here to join in the fun, so we want to keep it family-friendly."

"Isn't this the coolest thing you've ever heard of?"

ing uninvited up the steps and zeroing her malevolent gaze on me.

Gwen had quite a crush on Noah, and that he preferred to date me, someone she considered inferior in both looks and social status, drove Gwen bat-shit crazy. I could have told her that even if I was out of the picture, she wouldn't have a chance in hell with the handsome doctor. The problem wasn't that she was a few years older than he was; it was that she was too much like his mother—a high-maintenance snob.

"I'm hardly alone." I swept my arm around the group. "Oh, that's right. You don't consider other women people, do you? To you they're just rivals."

"Gwen." Poppy slid from her stool and took the intruder's arm. "I'm afraid I'm going to have to ask you to go back down to the bar. You know the Hayloft is a restricted area."

"What's the big secret?" Gwen narrowed her color-contact-lens-enhanced blue eyes. "Are you witches stirring up trouble in your cauldron?"

The witch reference was Gwen's favorite metaphor when attacking me—although generally, she pronounced the *b* instead of the *w*—so going along with her theme, I said, "Yes, we are. We're brewing up love potions, and from what I hear about your lack of beaux, perhaps you'd like to put in an order."

"You little—" Gwen interrupted herself, then smiled spitefully. "But of course you really aren't little, are you? Have you gone up a size . . . or two since the last time I saw you? Not that you were ever exactly slim. What did my cousin tell me they use to call you in high school? Stay Puft Marshmallow Girl, wasn't it?"

Her cruel words took me back thirteen years to the end of my sophomore year. I'd always been a size 12—and sometimes a 14—in a size 2 world, but until my family went from prosperous and respected to poor and humble, that hadn't bothered me and no one had teased me about my weight. However, once my family's circumstances changed, the mean girls had sensed weakness and descended on me like vampires on the last bag of plasma in the blood bank. That was one of the problems with living in the same town you had grown up in—there was no hiding from your past.

Coming back to the present, I gathered my wits and retorted, "You're right, Gwen." I ran my hands down my hips. "I've always been on the curvy side. Then again, the men in this town seem to prefer rounded to scrawny." I put a suggestive purr into my voice. "At least Jake and Noah seem to."

Gwen's plastic-surgery-smoothed face turned an unbecoming shade of magenta. It was always dangerous to stand up to someone like her, someone who thought she was better than the rest of us. She'd never been one to be able to handle what she dished out, and even as she snatched a half-full bottle of wine from the table and swung it at my head, I knew she was plotting an even worse retaliation.

As I tried to scramble out of Gwen's reach, Harlee leaped from the couch, and before I could blink, she had the Botoxed brunette flat on the floor. I'd never seen anyone move so fast—at least outside of an action movie.

How on earth had Harlee done that? She'd been a blur. To top it off, not a hair of her calico-colored spikes was out of place and there wasn't a drop of perspiration on her impassive face. Still waters may run deep, but clearly, consignment shopkeepers ran even deeper. What exactly had she done in the service? Were women allowed in the Special Forces? Maybe she'd been a Green Beret.

I glanced down at Gwen, who was threatening to have Harlee arrested for assault, and I shivered, remembering that Noah's previous girlfriend had been murdered. It seemed that a lot of women wanted to be Mrs. Dr. Underwood, and didn't hesitate to get violent in pursuit of the position.

At that moment, Gwen glared at me with such venom that I wondered if I might become the next victim in the battle to walk down the aisle with Noah. Which would really suck since I hadn't even decided if I wanted to marry him yet.

CHAPTER 2

A loud thump from overhead rattled the glasses lined up on the shelf behind the soda fountain. I cringed, then smiled apologetically at the two older ladies who were seated on stools in front of me. They were trying to enjoy their hot fudge sundaes, but the transformation of my second story for the cupcake contest was interfering with their Tuesday afternoon treat.

Slightly more than three weeks had passed since I'd agreed to the remodeling, and the noise level seemed to increase with every passing day, as did my worry that I had made a bad decision. The deposit that Kizzy Cutler's Cupcakes had given me for the rent was substantial, and the terms of their leasing contract were generous, but I didn't want to lose my regulars.

That morning, both the Quilting Queens and the Scrapbooking Scalawags had cut their weekly meetings short, complaining about the racket. I had an agreement with several of the local craft groups that in exchange for my providing them with a meeting space, they bought the materials for their projects from me and contracted for refreshments. As a bonus, the members often also picked up other bits and pieces that caught their eye while walking through the shop to get to their alcove. Upsetting valuable customers like my hobbyists was not a smart business move.

Ronni had promised me that the renovations were almost finished, and I hoped she was right. I couldn't afford to have any of the clubs that met at my store decide to find a new location.

After another thunderous bang from above, the elderly women abandoned their remaining ice cream and nearly ran out the front door. Sighing, I cleaned up the soda fountain and headed over to the old kitchen table I used as a workbench. It was located in the space behind the register, and from that vantage point, I could see the entrance. Not that I was expecting any shoppers. The hours after lunch were usually slow. Often, I didn't see a single customer from one to three, which made it the perfect time to work on my sideline—custom-made, personalized gift baskets.

When I bought the dime store, I'd known I would need something besides the sale of merchandise in order to stay profitable, so I'd added the baskets. That part of my enterprise was extremely lucrative since I was selling my creativity more than the actual items included in the basket, and I wished I had even more time to devote to promoting it.

I had one steady customer, Oakley Panigrahi, who bought upwards of twenty thank-you gifts a month. Noah had introduced me to the Kansas City real estate tycoon a few months ago and I'd been providing him with premium baskets ever since. Oakley sold luxury properties and was a demanding client, but he paid top dollar, and I wanted to complete his contract before the cupcake contest started.

I also had a request for one of my special creations that I needed to finish before the late-afternoon crowd showed up. I usually made that kind of basket before the store opened, but this client hadn't placed his order until nine that morning and was paying extra to have it ready for him to pick up at six p.m.

Swallowing the last bite of my lunch—a ham and cheese sandwich on Gran's homemade bread—I put the final touch on the basket in front of me. Each design included my trademark—the perfect book for both the occasion and the person receiving the gift. This thank-you present was intended for a municipal judge, and I carefully positioned a beautiful copy of *To Kill a Mockingbird* in the exact center of the basket. Months ago, I had found a first book club edition at an estate sale for fifty dollars, and I'd been saving it for just the right recipient.

I took a quick picture of the finished product for my store's Web site and Facebook page, then moved on to the anniversary basket, which was my next project. The guy who had ordered the rush job had forgotten that he and his bride had walked down the aisle five years ago today. And when his wife had handed him a beautiful package at breakfast, he'd panicked and said her gift was a big surprise that she'd receive that evening. His problem was that his wife was the kind of person who went out and bought something if she wanted it, so he was stumped as to what to get her.

Looking over his questionnaire—half of which he'd been in too much of a hurry to complete—I frowned. He was fortunate that I had an extensive stock of items that would please any woman or he'd be out of luck, because he hadn't left me any time to order additional products.

As I gathered the supplies, "Torn Between Two Lovers" started to play from somewhere beneath the mountain of stuff on my worktable. I dug hastily through the piles until I located my cell phone. Then I touched the speaker icon and said, "Hello."

"Are you busy?" Jake's sensual baritone sent a delightful shiver down my spine.

"Nope." I could picture his deep blue eyes smiling into mine, his silky black hair against my fingertips, and the feel of his muscled arms holding me close.

The chemistry between Jake and me was so strong that I could feel the pull through the telephone. Which should have been enough to make me choose him as the man I wanted in my life. But Noah was more the steady good guy that I could depend on to be home every night rather than off chasing criminals. In short, Noah was someone I could actually see myself marrying, while it was difficult to picture Jake waiting for me as I walked toward him in a wedding dress.

The irony was that before Jake had entered my life and Noah had reentered it, I'd seldom dated, and the thought of settling down rarely crossed my mind. Now it was always lurking in the back of my head. Which guy could I visualize in a tuxedo at the front of the church waiting for me?

"I have some news," Jake said, breaking into my inner debate.

"You're coming home?" Technically Shadow Bend wasn't Jake's home. He had an apartment in St. Louis. But I hoped his permanent residence was about to change, because just before his ex-wife was abducted, he'd submitted his resignation to the marshal service and taken his great-uncle's offer to manage the family cattle ranch just outside of town.

"Not yet." Jake sighed. "However, we finally have a lead on the Doll Maker."

"That's great," I said, my breath catching at the discouragement I heard in his voice.

I couldn't blame him for feeling disheartened. More than six weeks had passed since his ex-wife was kidnapped, and as hard as it was for any of us to acknowledge, odds were she was dead. I knew how horrible this whole situation was for Jake. While Meg had divorced him when he was injured in the line of duty, Jake was the kind of guy who would never turn his back on someone who needed him.

Despite Meg's callous treatment of him when it looked as if he'd never walk again, Jake would feel as though it was his duty to save her from the Doll Maker's ghastly clutches. Which meant that Jake was pretty much trapped in St. Louis at the beck and call of a madman, because every three or four days, the Doll Maker demanded that unless Jake showed up at a specific spot, he'd receive pieces of Meg in the next mail delivery.

Nope. I couldn't blame Jake for trying to rescue her. He was a true hero. Someone who did what had to be done regardless of the consequences to himself. But it was his sense of duty that made me question whether he and I could ever have a life together in Shadow Bend. The kind of life that I could have with Noah.

"Yeah," Jake agreed, bringing me back to the conversation. "He's been communicating with me via burner phones, but our forensic team thinks they've figured out the general area where he's been buying them. We've got eyes on the three most likely stores where we think he'll get the next one."

"So you just have to wait." I tried to keep the impatience out of my tone. "Any idea when he'll get in touch with you again?"

"If he keeps true to his pattern, it'll be tomorrow or the next day." Jake blew out a frustrated breath. "He never goes more than five days between calls and always seems to know exactly where I am and how long it will take me to get to his chosen location."

"Do you think he's watching you?" I wanted to tell him to be careful, but that was just plain silly. I knew he'd be as careful as he could, but if it came to giving his life to save that of an innocent bystander, he'd sacrifice his own. That was what a U.S. Marshal did, and nothing I said would change his instinct to serve and protect. So I bit my tongue and tried to inject encouragement into my tone as I said, "I'm sure you guys will nail him."

"So, what's happening in Shadow Bend?" Jake said, ignoring both my question and my attempt to play cheerleader. "How are the cupcake contest preparations going?"

Before I could answer, a deafening boom came from upstairs. Startled, I knocked the phone off the table. As I searched the cluttered tabletop for my cell, the string of curses cascading down from above made me glad there weren't any kids sitting at the soda fountain.

By the time I retrieved my phone, there was a thread of anxiety running through Jake's voice when he demanded, "What happened?"

"The crew working on my second floor must have dropped something," I said. "Either that or the ceiling is about to fall down on my head."

"Are you sorry you agreed to the remodeling and rental?" Jake asked.

"I guess not." I continued to work on the basket, placing a tube of strawberry-flavored Skin Honey against the folds of a red satin kimono. According to the package, the gel was an edible personal lubricant that would soften your skin and liven up your libido. The instructions said to smooth it on wherever you wanted to be kissed. Picturing Jake next to me, I could think of several locations where his lips would be welcome.

"So you're not having second thoughts?" Jake asked, clearly detecting the hesitation in my tone. "It must be distracting having the construction guys there."

"A little." I kept working on my special order. In twenty minutes, when summer school was dismissed for the day, a swarm of starving teenagers would take over the store, and I wouldn't have time to do anything but serve them ice cream, candy, and sodas. "But with the construction crew removing several walls, I now have a nice open area where I can put shelves and display cases. And they left one office suite intact so I can still rent it to someone."

"Then you're good?" Jake didn't sound convinced.

"Ronni says they'll be done today, tomorrow at the latest." That didn't exactly answer his question, but it was as close as I was willing to admit that I might have made a bad decision. "Kizzy and her entourage arrive Thursday afternoon and the contest activities start bright and early Friday morning."

"That means a lot of strangers are about to pour into Shadow Bend," Jake said. "Did the cupcake company hire any security?"

"I doubt it." Chuckling, I added, "Seriously, what do you think will happen? A food fight?"

"Just be careful," Jake ordered. "Make sure you aren't alone with anyone you don't know."

"Okay." I stretched the word out. Why was Jake being so paranoid? Oh. Yeah. He was a marshal. Most law enforcement officers tended to think that in any given situation, the worst would happen.

After a long pause, Jake asked, "How's your father adjusting?"

My father had recently been released from a long prison sentence. Although he *had* committed the crime of which he'd been convicted, it wasn't his fault. At the time, someone who had been attempting to frame him for embezzlement roofied him. Only recently had that person admitted to having drugged my father. After the other guy's confession, Dad had been paroled rather than pardoned, because despite the fact that he hadn't willingly taken the Rohypnol, he had run over and accidently killed a woman while under the drug's influence. He might have been able to get the conviction overturned, but taking parole had been cheaper and quicker than a new trial.

"It's hard to say." I considered adding a pair of Turn Me On vibrating panties to the basket, but since I didn't know what size the guy's wife wore, I reluctantly put them aside. It was a shame since the bikinis contained a secret pocket that held a wireless vibrating bullet operated by remote control—an item I thought might be just the right anniversary gift for the woman who had everything.

"Oh?" Jake's voice broke into my thoughts. "Haven't you two been talking?"

"Of course we talk." Since I couldn't include the panties, I nestled a pink Lipstick Vibe next to a Good Girl Bad Girl blindfold. "Dad decided against taking back his old position at the bank, but he does have a job."

"Where?"

"Here." I stepped back to admire my creation and chewed my thumbnail. Something was missing. "He's taking Xylia's shifts." I'd recently lost my weekend clerk and hadn't had a chance to hire a permanent replacement.

"How's that working out?" Jake's tone was wary.

"I'm treading delicately." I rummaged through my "naughty" box and found the perfect touch for the anniversary basket, a pink-and-black feather spanker. One end was adorned with marabou and the other with a small leather paddle. I briefly wondered which spouse would be wielding the plaything and I suspected it wouldn't be the husband. "It's not as if I can give my dad orders or yell at him if he does something wrong, so I have to be a lot more diplomatic than I prefer to be in an employer/employee relationship."

Jake's husky laugh made me reconsider giving the sex toy away. Maybe I had a better use for it. Before I could ask Jake's opinion of the matter, I heard a phone ring on his end and he put me on hold. While I waited for him to return, I completed the basket with a copy of Sylvia Day's naughty novel *Bared to You*, the first in her popular Crossfire series.

When Jake got back on the line a few seconds later, his voice was tense as he said, "That was the Doll Maker. He gave me ten minutes to make it to Busch Stadium and I'm at least nine minutes away. I'll call when I have a chance."

He hung up as I struggled for something to say, and I stared at my cell, wondering if I would ever get used to dating a man with such a dangerous and all-consuming occupation. I'd never know if our "so long" was really "good-bye forever." With his job always coming first, he'd never be completely mine.

Jake and Noah had agreed I could date them both until I decided which one I loved. But Jake had been gone almost since the instant that arrangement went into effect. Of course, Noah hadn't been around much, either. His mother's fake illnesses were keeping him occupied, and any of his time that she didn't claim, his medical practice did. The whole situation with both guys was as messed up as a pile of clothes hangers. Maybe I needed to forget about Jake and Noah and find someone with a nine-to-five job and a less complicated life.

CHAPTER 3

Thursday morning, I savored the silence of a completely empty building. No hammering. No swearing. And best of all, no boots stomping back and forth over my head. For the next few hours, Devereaux's Dime Store was back to being mine and mine alone.

As promised, the workmen had finished up Tuesday night and the decorator had descended with her team on Wednesday to perform their magic. Both crews had done a good job. Removing the partition between two of the office suites had produced a large, open area that would be perfect for viewing and judging the cupcakes that the finalists produced at Winnie's cooking school.

The interior designer had chosen a soft teal for the walls with brown curlicue accents stenciled near the ceiling. A raised dais in the front of the room contained two metal stands to exhibit the cupcakes—a five-foot-tall pink Ferris wheel and an equally large yellow roller coaster. Wrought-iron bistro tables and chairs were scattered around the rest of the space.

Although I typically wasn't happy when the store was deserted, today I knew it was the lull before the storm and I was thrilled to have the place to myself while I got ready for the baking competition. During the chaos of renovation, I hadn't been able to concentrate, so now, hoping for impulse buys, I arranged cupcake-themed merchandise on all the end-cap displays and on the shelves near the cash register. While I fussed with the layout, I thought about the coming weekend.

Anticipating big crowds, I had arranged for my part-time clerk, Hannah Freeman, and my father to work all three days of the contest. Hannah's previous schedule—a part of her vocational ed program at the high school—had been four mornings and one afternoon a week. However, she'd graduated last month and was leaving for college in the fall, so I needed to start interviewing for her position.

I also had to find out if my father planned to continue working weekends for me or if I should be looking for two new employees instead of one. How to put the question to him tactfully, so he didn't feel I was pushing him away, was the tricky part. Like my mother, who had run off to California the minute Dad was sentenced, I hadn't trusted his innocence when he was falsely accused of embezzlement. And during the twelve years he was in jail, I'd gone to see him only once.

I had no excuse for the former, and my reason for the latter wasn't much better since he probably didn't truly believe that I had developed a sort of claustrophobia after my first trip to the prison. Strangely enough, the phobia was because I had loved him so much, not because I didn't care about him. I'd always been a daddy's girl, and when he'd been convicted, I was shattered by both what I perceived as his betrayal of our family and his absence from my life. I missed him like crazy, but seeing him handcuffed and behind a steel-reinforced window made me feel as if I couldn't breathe. I had actually fainted the one and only time I'd visited.

Now that he was out of jail, I had a chance to try to make up for my lack of faith and, worse, my lack of visits. But I hadn't quite figured out how yet. Shoving that problem out of my mind, I continued to fuss with a display that contained flip-flops, rubber clogs, slippers, and tennis shoes—all imprinted with brightly colored cupcakes. As I was finishing up, I heard the sound of sleigh bells jingling. I hurriedly shoved the last pink sneaker into place and glanced toward the front of the store.

Noah was standing in the entrance, scanning the shop. When he spotted me, he waved and let the door close behind him. I waved back and hurried toward him. It had been several weeks since we were able to coordinate our schedules to spend more than a few minutes together, and at least ten days since we'd been face-to-face. I had missed him and my heart sped up at the sight of him.

As I got closer, I saw that he looked exhausted. Although his dark blond hair was flawlessly styled, I noticed that instead of tapering neatly to the collar of his crisp Dolce & Gabbana dress shirt, it curled over the starched white cotton. He'd obviously had to skip his biweekly trim. The deep lines of fatigue bracketing his mouth and the dark circles under his gray eyes gave the impression of too little sleep and too much responsibility.

"Hi." Noah drew me into his arms and rested his forehead against mine. "I have an hour between appointments and figure this might be the last time this weekend you have a minute to call your own."

"You're probably right about that." As I caressed his cheek, a sense of peace I felt with no one else stole over me. "Any luck finding your mother a home health aide that she'll accept?"

"Cross your fingers." Noah took my hand and stroked his thumb against my palm. "I finally took your advice, and on Monday, I hired a young, attractive male aide." Noah wrinkled his brow. "I should have done it when you first suggested it, but the idea was so unnerving that I couldn't make myself consider it."

"I told you that he'd just be eye candy." I tapped Noah's perfect nose. "You know darn well Nadine wouldn't dream of having an affair with the hired help, but with the right guy, she'll enjoy some harmless flirtation and keep him around for the attention."

"So far, so good." Noah smiled ruefully. "It's been three days and she hasn't fired him yet. The previous record was twelve hours."

"That sounds hopeful." I slipped my arms around his neck, enjoying the strength of his embrace. "Maybe Monday, once this cupcake contest is over, we can actually spend some time together."

"I wish I could, but . . ." He trailed off, refusing to meet my eyes.

"But what?" Stepping back from him, I tilted my head. "I thought you texted me that Dr. Rodriguez was starting full-time this week."

After attending the combined B.A. and M.D. program at the University of Missouri's School of Medicine and completing a three-year residency in family medicine, Noah had returned to Shadow Bend and opened the Underwood Clinic. The only medical center in a forty-mile radius, it was always packed with patients. Until recently, because of the long hours and low pay, he'd been unable to entice another physician into joining his practice, but last month he'd finally found an altruistic doctor who was willing to move to a small town, work ten-hour days, and settle for less money.

"She did." Noah was still avoiding my gaze. "But now that Elexus is on board and it appears that I've got Mother's situation under control, I need to keep a promise that I made to one of my professors."

"Oh?" I did not like where this conversation was heading, which seemed to be in a direction what would take Noah away from Shadow Bend.

"My med school mentor, Dr. Johnston, asked all of us to pledge to do a tour of duty every year with Disaster Doctors."

"Which is?" I asked.

I had no intention of making this easy for Noah. It felt too much like the last time he'd walked out on me, which had been back in high school when my father went to prison. Recently, I had learned that I might have misinterpreted Noah's actions at the time. A few months ago, he'd told me that when we were teenagers he'd broken up with me to protect my grandmother from his mother, who had threatened to have her arrested as an accomplice to my father's suspected embezzlement. He'd also claimed that he'd tried to get back together with me. But I still wasn't sure I believed his assertions or fully trusted him. Which was a big part of why I was still trying to decide between him and Jake.

With Noah's past betrayal in mind, even though I knew I was being petty, I hardened my expression and waited for an explanation. I'd been patient about his mother and his work, so now that he had some free time, I wasn't happy that he wouldn't be spending even a minute—or at least a couple of weeks—of it with me.

What was it with him and Jake? Intellectually, I understood they were both principled guys with commitments they were honor-bound to fulfill, but emotionally it felt as if I was always last on their priority list.

"Disaster Doctors is an organization that sends medical teams into places that have recently experienced either a natural or man-made disaster," Noah explained. "Health care personnel sign up for one or two weeks, bring their own equipment and supplies, and take care of the victims of hurricanes, tornadoes, floods, and—"

"And war, right?" I'd been thinking about what a man-made disaster might be, and combat was the only logical one that came to mind.

"Yes, DD goes into battle zones." He tried to pull me into a hug.

"Where are you going?" I moved out of his reach. This was not a discussion that I wanted to have while I was distracted by his touch. The chemistry between Noah and me might not have been quite as hot as the one between Jake and me, but he still could make me sizzle.

"Léogâne, Haiti," Noah answered with a smile. "And there's no war there."

"Great." I couldn't keep the sarcasm out of my voice. "So instead of agonizing that you might be shot at or blown up, I can worry about you contracting cholera or AIDS. What a relief."

"I've had my cholera vaccination and I'll double-glove, always wear scrubs, masks, and protective eyewear," Noah assured me.

"But the cholera vaccine doesn't provide a hundred percent immunity." I watched a lot of *National Geographic* on television, and there had been a recent series on Haiti and its many diseases. "And gloves get punctured."

"I'm aware of that, and I'll take all the necessary precautions."

"There's no way I can talk you out of this?" I asked, even though I knew the answer.

"I'll be home a week from tomorrow." Noah put his arms around me. "And I promise to be extra careful."

"Humph." I stepped out of his embrace. "It's not so much that I don't want you to keep your promise to your mentor, but I don't understand why you have to rush off the minute you get a little free time. Time we could finally spend together."

"Two reasons." Noah put his arms around me again and drew me close. "One, I haven't fulfilled my promise of a week a year since graduating." He smoothed his hand down my hair. "And two, the doctor who was originally scheduled had to drop out because of a death in his family. Without me, the team is one man short. It makes the whole operation more dangerous without the full quota of medical personnel because then everyone is more rushed and might get careless." He leaned back and looked me in the eye. "As you pointed out, there are a lot of serious communicable diseases in Haiti."

"Fine," I conceded. "But I'm still not happy that the first free time you get, you aren't spending it with me."

"Will you save that Saturday night after I get back for me?"

"We'll see." I shivered when his hands tunneled under my T-shirt and stroked my bare skin. Smiling, I relented and said, "It's a date."

"Good." He dipped his head. "You know, I've been daydreaming about doing this all morning." He pressed his lips to mine.

His kiss was slow and thoughtful, as if he was savoring every moment. I felt myself melting. We really were good together. I wondered why it was so hard for me to decide between Noah and Jake. It all came down to whether I preferred floating on a cloud or riding a roller coaster. Did I want the prince or the cowboy?

All too soon, Noah said, "I have to get back to the clinic for my next appointment."

"My late-afternoon rush will be starting soon, too." I sighed. Both of us were always so busy. I was sick of snatching a kiss here and a hug there. We needed time together so I could decide if Noah was Mr. Right.

Before I could move out of his arms, Noah wound a stray strand of my hair around his finger and said, "You know, I've always loved the color of your hair. It reminds me of cinnamon. My favorite spice."

"Aw." I smoothed my ponytail. "That's so sweet of you."

"And the blue-green of your eyes is going to haunt me while I'm gone."

"Good." I never thought of myself as attractive, but it was nice to hear that Noah did.

"I might not be able to call while I'm in Haiti. I don't know if my cell phone will work there or not, so don't be concerned if you don't hear from me." Noah stepped away from me, walked to the front door, and opened it.

"Okay." I followed him, kissed his cheek, and watched him disappear down the sidewalk.

Terrific. Now both the guys I cared for were willingly putting themselves in dangerous situations. I scowled. Maybe I needed to start dating less noble men.

CHAPTER 4

A few hours later, as I entered the Golden Dragon, Noah and Jake popped back into my mind. I'd had dates with both guys at this place, and wished at least one of them were with me tonight. But they weren't, and there was no use mooning over absent boyfriends, so I forced the men from my mind and followed the hostess as she led me to the small private dining room in the rear.

Ronni had arranged for the contest committee to have dinner with Kizzy Cutler and her entourage at Shadow Bend's only Chinese restaurant. My mouth watered at the smell of ginger and garlic, and my stomach growled, reminding me that lunch had been a very small sandwich eaten many hours ago.

I slid into one of four empty chairs, noticing that I was among the last to arrive. Ronni introduced me to the cupcake people. Kizzy was not at all how I had pictured her. Instead of a sophisticated twenty-first-century businesswoman, she looked like a nineteen-fifties housewife all dolled up for an evening out with her husband. She wore a baby blue voile shirtwaist dress with a full circle skirt, a pearl necklace, and blue pumps. A matching clutch lay on the table in front of her.

Suddenly, I was conscious of my own casual appearance. My summer work uniform was jeans, sneakers, and a polo shirt with DEVEREAUX'S DIME STORE embroidered on the pocket. In deference to meeting the cupcake tycoon for the first time, I'd exchanged the polo for a blue-and-green swirl-print tunic and the tennis shoes for navy sandals, but I'd kept on my Levi's. Seeing Kizzy's perfect blond French twist, I wished I had combed out my ponytail. Still, even if I had fixed my hair, I knew my feeble efforts would have been in vain. The cupcake CEO was stunningly beautiful.

After the waitress took our drink orders and left, Ronni said, "Kizzy, I hope your suite is okay."

"It's delightful, thank you," Kizzy said. "I love the little balcony."

"That's my favorite part of those suites, too," Ronni said. "Is your partner happy with hers?"

"Lee is easy to please," Kizzy answered. "She has simple tastes."

"That must make her pleasant to travel with." Ronni raised an eyebrow in my direction, then turned back to Kizzy and asked, "Is your assistant comfortable in her room? I'm sorry there wasn't anything larger available for her."

"Fallon's accommodations are fine for her station in life." Kizzy waved her hand, clearly dismissing her employee's need for luxury. "She came to me from a program for young people who had gotten caught up in the penal system due do drug crimes." Kizzy took a sip of water. "Fallon claimed she never was a user, but she spent a year in prison for bringing drug money across the border for her boyfriend." Kizzy put down her glass and tapped her nails against the plastic. "So you see how even the smallest bedroom in your B and B is a step up."

"Right," Ronni agreed, a bemused look on her face. Regrouping, she glanced around the table and frowned. "I wonder what's keeping Harlee."

"Oh. Sorry," I apologized. "I forgot to tell you that she called me and said that she isn't going to come after all. She tried to contact you and couldn't get through, so she asked me to pass on her regrets."

"Then we're all here except for your business partner and assistant," Ronni said to Kizzy. "Are they going to be able to make it?"

"They should have been right behind us." Kizzy checked her phone. "Just as we were leaving, I got a message from a delivery service saying they had a package for me and would be at the B and B in ten or fifteen minutes. Fallon volunteered to stay behind and sign for it, and Lee offered to wait with her so she wouldn't have to drive on unfamiliar roads alone."

"I hope they didn't get lost." Ronni glanced toward the door. "The one-way streets can be a little confusing around here."

"They'd have called if they needed directions." Kizzy shrugged. "Let's go ahead and order."

"I'm sure no one minds waiting for them," I said, ignoring my hunger pangs.

Kizzy bared her teeth in a fake smile; then when everyone around the table finished expressing their willingness to wait, she said, "Devereaux, how sweet of you to offer your opinion on the matter. I love that you have your own idea on the issue." Her smile faded and she narrowed her eyes. "I just don't want to hear it."

Seriously? Why was Kizzy so hostile? I'd never met her before, so it couldn't be a past grudge. Still, she was the star of our little weekend, so I bit my tongue and kept quiet.

Kizzy beckoned to a nearby waitress and said, "We're ready." After placing her order, Kizzy turned to Ronni and commented, "I'm sure Lee and Fallon will arrive soon. After all, what could happen to them here in Shadow Bend? It has to be one of the safest spots on earth."

I shivered and traded looks with Poppy, who raised a delicate eyebrow. Evidently, Kizzy didn't keep in touch with old friends from the area who could have filled her in on Shadow Bend's recent spate of crimes. She obviously didn't subscribe to her hometown paper, either. The *Banner* had made sure everyone was fully informed on all the gruesome details.

Ronni must not have told Kizzy that Shadow Bend wasn't the same little town that the cupcake mogul had moved away from so many years ago. Not that I blamed Ronni for withholding that little tidbit. No way would a shrewd businesswoman like Kizzy want to hold her big promotional kickoff in a place that had had two homicides in the past four months.

The table was still placing their orders when Lee Kimbrough arrived a few minutes later. She was an attractive woman in her mid- to late forties who reminded me of Lauren Bacall—tall, cool, and elegant. She even had Bacall's husky voice and languid mannerisms.

After Lee was introduced, and told the waitress what she wanted to eat, she explained, "The delivery service called and said that they'd be another ten or fifteen minutes, so Fallon offered to wait and told me to go on ahead."

"I wonder what's in the package." Kizzy frowned. "I'm not expecting anything."

"Maybe it's a good-luck gift from one of your friends," Lee suggested.

"Maybe," Kizzy agreed.

Just as our food was served, Kizzy got a call and answered it by pressing the speaker on her cell phone. We could all hear Fallon identify herself.

We listened as she said, "The delivery driver finally showed up, but now I don't feel well, so I'm not coming to the restaurant. I'm going to lie down and see if the nausea goes away."

"Fine." Kizzy's lack of interest in the conversation was evident in her voice.

"I have a really bad taste in my mouth," Fallon went on, even though Kizzy didn't encourage her. "I feel headachy and dizzy. Maybe I'm getting the flu."

"Uh-huh." Kizzy listened to all this with a distracted air, then said, "Whatever, dear." She quickly disconnected, gave the rest of us a bright smile, and said, "Let's eat."

I was a bit surprised that neither Kizzy nor Lee seemed concerned about their employee's health. On the other hand, perhaps Fallon tended to be hypochondriacal and her headaches were common occurrences.

Now that Fallon's whereabouts had been accounted for, we all relaxed. The food was delicious and Kizzy entertained us with the story of starting up her business. She took a sip of her lychee martini, then continued. "So when I finally was able to submit my resignation and devote my full attention to Kizzy Cutler's Cupcakes, the owner of the bakery said to me, 'Running your own company is a lot of work. You won't have time for a personal life. You know that money can't buy happiness.'"

"What did you say?" Ronni asked.

"I told her that whoever had started that vicious rumor simply didn't know where to shop." Kizzy laughed.

We all chuckled and I relaxed. There was a generally optimistic vibe about the success of the cupcake contest weekend and I felt hopeful that the event would be the financial boost we all were counting on.

The dinner meeting broke up around nine thirty, and by the time I got home, Gran was already asleep. The lights in Dad's apartment over the garage had been on, but I still wasn't comfortable enough with our relationship to stop by for a nightcap or a father-daughter chat. After twelve years apart, we were still tiptoeing around each other. We weren't at ease enough for the casual rapport we used to have, but we had too much history to act as reserved as we truly felt. It was an odd situation to be in and neither of us was sure where we stood with the other.

Shoving the issue of my precarious relationship with Dad aside, I headed to my bedroom. I was tired and it wouldn't be a bad idea to turn in early. Tomorrow would be a busy day—at least I hoped it would—and I wanted to be on my toes to handle the increased foot traffic in the store. The last thing I recalled after washing my face and changing into my nightshirt was slipping between the crisp sheets and briefly wondering if I had remembered to set my alarm.

I was having a wonderful dream involving Jake and Noah. The two men were fanning me with palm leaves, feeding me grapes, and assuring me they loved me enough to share me so I didn't have to choose just one of them, when the strains of the sickeningly sweet and thoroughly annoying "Cupcake Song" blared from my bedside table. Struggling to wake up, I swept the nightstand with my palm, trying to locate my cell phone and quiet the grating music.

Ronni had insisted that Poppy, Winnie, Harlee, and I make this cloying little ditty sung by Pinkie Pie of My

Little Pony fame the official emergency ringtone for the contest weekend. I pushed my hair out of my eyes and peered groggily at the glowing numerals of my clock radio. It was three a.m. Why was she calling me at this ungodly hour? The competition hadn't even started yet. What kind of crisis could there be before dawn? Had she butt-dialed her phone?

Fumbling my cell off the nightstand and sweeping my finger across the answer icon, I mumbled, "Hello."

"Oh, my God!" Ronni's voice screeched into my ear. "Thank goodness you answered. Fallon's dead! You have to get here right away."

"What?" I tried to clear my sleep-fogged brain. "Are you sure?" I sat on the edge of the mattress. "Have you called an ambulance?"

"Yes." Ronni drew in a deep breath, then said, "The EMTs came and were taking her to the hospital, but she died before they got there."

"That's awful." My mouth suddenly dry, I got up and stumbled into the bathroom in search of a drink of water. "But why do you need me to come over? There's nothing I can do about the poor girl's death."

"Kizzy is demanding an emergency meeting of the contest committee," Ronni explained. "I already got ahold of Poppy and Winnie, and they're on their way, but Harlee isn't answering her phone."

Ronni paused and I could hear a voice that sounded like Kizzy's shout, "Tell her to swing by Harlee's place and pick her up."

I put my cell on speaker and set it down next to the sink as I pulled on jeans and a T-shirt. "Doesn't Kizzy have to handle Fallon's death?" A part of me was appalled that the cupcake queen was able to think about the competition at a time like this. But another part of me, the one that wasn't as nice, understood what it took for a woman to prosper in a competitive business and admired Kizzy's single-minded pursuit of success.

"Lee is taking care of that end," Ronni answered, then whispered, "Kizzy didn't think anyone needed to go with the poor girl, but Lee grabbed the car keys and followed the ambulance. She's keeping us informed, but when I offered to drive Kizzy to the hospital to join her, our esteemed CEO nearly bit my head off."

"Informed about what?" I homed in on the important piece of info as I scraped my hair back into a ponytail. After it was secured, I snatched the phone from the bathroom counter, then dashed into the kitchen. I needed to leave Gran a note in case I wasn't home when she got up. She'd worry if I wasn't there for breakfast.

"We'll discuss all that when you get here." Ronni reeled off Harlee's address and added, "Hurry up. Kizzy is driving me insane."

Ten minutes later, I pounded on Harlee's front door. When she didn't answer, I tried again, but after the third round of knocking, I gave up, hopped in my car, and drove over to Ronni's place. Either Harlee slept like the dead or she wasn't at home, and I suspected that neither possibility would satisfy Kizzy.

When I arrived at the B & B, Winnie and Poppy were huddled around Ronni's kitchen table, cradling mugs of coffee. They barely acknowledged my presence as I took my seat. Both looked as if they had dressed in the dark, pulling on whatever clothing had been nearest their beds. Poppy had on a leather miniskirt, gray sweatshirt, and neon pink flip-flops. Instead of their usual artful disarray, her platinum curls stood out from her head like corkscrews and there were mascara smudges underneath her gorgeous amethyst eyes.

Winnie had on black yoga pants, some sort of polyester floral blouse, and bunny slippers. Her gray hair frizzed around her face like a dandelion gone to seed and she had tiny round glasses with lavender lenses perched on her nose. She must have been too groggy to put in her contacts. Winnie's expression reminded me of a child who had begged for a sip of her father's beer—reluctant to swallow the bitter brew, but unwilling to spit it out and admit she didn't like it. Clearly, the universe had let Winnie down.

Ronni was still wearing the dress she'd had on at the Golden Dragon. But instead of the nude patent leather Jimmy Choo platform pumps she'd worn at the restaurant, she was barefoot. Her chocolate brown waves were now knotted in a messy bun on the top of her head, and any vestige of the carefully applied makeup she'd had on at dinner was long gone. Her blue-gray eyes were bloodshot, and after she handed me a cup of coffee, she collapsed onto her chair as if all the bones in her body had instantly liquefied.

I took a sip of the hot ambrosia, then asked, "Where's Kizzy?"

"On the phone with Lee," Ronni answered. "Evidently, when someone who is apparently healthy dies suddenly, the cops are called. Since the ambulance was still within the city limits when Fallon passed, the Shadow Bend Police Department is in charge. Lee is waiting for Chief Kincaid to arrive at the hospital."

"Oh." I took another mouthful of caffeinated goodness, then said, "Tell me what happened." No one answered, and I prodded, "Start from the beginning. I know that Fallon said she had a headache when she called, but there really wasn't any indication that her illness was serious. When did she start to get so sick?"

"When we got home from the restaurant, Lee went to check on Fallon. She discovered her in the bathroom, vomiting." Ronni buried her face in her hands, and her voice was muffled as she continued. "Lee found me and asked the location of the closest urgent care center. I told her the nearest one was forty miles away at the county seat."

"That really is a problem." Winnie spoke for the first time, the social crusader inside her overcoming her shock. "Now that he's hired a second doctor, Noah needs to extend the hours of his clinic so the community has medical resources available within a reasonable time frame."

Ronni ignored Winnie's outburst, and continued. "When I went upstairs with Lee, Fallon was sweating and seemed sort of hyper. She also seemed really ticked off at us, but I couldn't figure out why. Then all of a sudden, she crumpled to the floor and started to have what I was pretty darn sure were convulsions. I ran downstairs and called nine-one-one, but by the time the EMTs got here, she was unconscious. They loaded her in the ambulance and took off for the hospital. When Lee arrived, the EMT told her that Fallon had died a few minutes after they left the B and B."

"Any idea what happened?" I put down my empty mug. "You said she was healthy. Did Kizzy or Lee tell you that or did you just assume it from her age and appearance? She could have had some sort of medical condition that wasn't apparent to the untrained eye."

"Kizzy said that all of her employees had just had their yearly physicals and Fallon had passed with flying colors," Ronni answered. "From the hyper way she was acting and the rest of her symptoms—the vomiting and sweating—my best guess would be some kind of drug overdose."

"Don't be ridiculous. All of the Kizzy Cutler's Cupcakes personnel are required to submit to monthly drug testing," Kizzy snapped as she stalked into the kitchen and glared at Ronni. "Whatever her past issues with drugs had been, Fallon was now clean and sober. She'd turned her life around. She was a fine, upstanding young woman. The company will mourn her loss."

"Of course," Ronni acquiesced. "I certainly didn't mean to imply otherwise."

"Good." Kizzy smiled insincerely. "I'm sure the pathologist will tell us it was some sort of undiagnosed medical condition. A tragedy, but unavoidable." Kizzy poured herself a cup of coffee, sat down at the table, and said, "Now let's discuss how we're going to handle the situation in light of the recent misfortune."

"Perhaps we should cancel the contest out of respect for Fallon's passing," I suggested, knowing full well that Kizzy would reject my recommendation, but wanting to see how she wiggled out of it without appearing like a coldhearted witch. "Or at least reschedule it. Right before Thanksgiving might work."

From her recent actions, it was clear that Kizzy was not about to inconvenience herself over something as inconsequential as an employee's death. And I'd bet money that she had no intention of postponing the big introduction of her new cupcake line.

"Fallon wouldn't want that," Kizzy assured me with a dismissive glance. "She was a trouper and would feel awful if everyone who put so much time and effort into making the cupcake contest weekend a huge success ended up losing money because of her."

"Right." I marveled at how confidently the cupcake magnate spoke for her dead assistant. "How silly of me to think otherwise."

Ronni shot me a silencing glare and I mimicked zipping my lips. Once I shut up, Kizzy outlined the story that would be given to the press and who would be responsible for the tasks previously assigned to Fallon.

For the next couple of hours we drank endless cups of coffee, nodding and taking notes as Kizzy talked and gave orders.

Ronni's grandfather clock had just chimed six times when the doorbell rang. The police had arrived in the form of Chief Eldridge Kincaid and two of his crime scene techs. Both Chief Kincaid's heavily starched khaki uniform and gray buzz cut made me itch to salute him, but I resisted the urge. He demanded flawlessness in himself and all the people around him, which was a problem when his daughter was the self-professed town bad girl. I imagined his obsession with perfection wasn't much fun for his officers, either.

The chief ignored Poppy and she returned the favor, but he greeted me and asked how my dad was doing. Once my father was paroled and released from prison, he and the chief had resumed their previous friendship, something for which I was eternally grateful. Most of the townspeople had accepted that Dad had gotten a bum rap, but there were enough who, despite the evidence, refused to believe that he had been framed. I was sure that the chief's public willingness to remain pals had helped those who were on the fence come down on my father's side of the issue.

Once it became clear that Poppy, Winnie, and I hadn't been at the B & B when Fallon got sick, and had never met the girl, the chief lost interest in us. He asked us a few questions, but since we didn't have any firsthand knowledge of the situation, he allowed us to leave. Actually, allowed wasn't the right word; he ordered us to go. It was clear he couldn't wait to get rid of us, especially his daughter, who had answered his inquiries with as few words as possible, glowering at him during the entire encounter.

As I was on my way out the door, I overheard the

chief say to one of his techs, "Make sure you get a sample of the victim's vomit and bag anything that she might have ingested." Chief Kincaid glanced at me as I stood in the foyer obviously eavesdropping and he said, "Dev, is there something you need?" I shook my head and he asked, "Something you want to add to your statement?"

"No."

He motioned toward the exit. "Then it's best if you leave. You don't want to get caught up in the investigation and be late opening up your store."

The chief had hit my Achilles' heel, so I nodded and hurried away. Since I'd already been a reluctant participant in two of his prior cases, the last thing I needed was to get involved in a situation concerning another dead body.

CHAPTER 5

With Fallon's death and the subsequent police investigation, the cupcake contest had gotten off to a rough start, but at least the weather was cooperating. July in Missouri could be a scorcher, so I was relieved that the thermometer on the Savings and Guaranty read a pleasant eighty-two degrees. The reasonable temperature was fortunate, since most of the townspeople and a good number of visitors were gathered in the village square. And that many people pressed together on a hot day would have been a recipe for disaster, not dessert.

The square was the heart of Shadow Bend. The businesses that were lucky enough to be located on the four blocks that edged the town common would have a huge advantage over any establishments that weren't in direct sight of the cupcake tourists. Thank goodness, my store was front and center. Little's Tea Room, Brewfully Yours, and the bakery—which of course was selling Kizzy Cutler's Cupcakes—would also benefit from the increased foot traffic.

My favorite part of the square was the gazebo. With its intricately carved arches that linked the eight white cast-iron columns, it was like a scene straight out of a Norman Rockwell painting. I could see why Kizzy had chosen it for the competition kickoff. It presented the perfect photo op for a company introducing a cupcake line called the Flavors of Your Life.

Speaking of the cupcake queen, where was she? The opening ceremony, followed by a luncheon for the contestants, judges, media, and committee members, was supposed to start at noon. It was now ten after twelve and I could hear the crowd getting restless. People were shifting from foot to foot and looking at their watches. Maybe Kizzy had forgotten that in a small town, being tardy wasn't considered fashionably late, but incredibly rude, and it often wasn't tolerated.

Had something happened since this morning? I hadn't heard from Ronni since leaving the B & B. After hurrying home, I'd taken a quick shower, filled in Gran and my father about Fallon's death, then rushed to the dime store. Since then, Dad, Hannah, and I had been busy with customers and I hadn't had time to check my cell. Fishing it from the pocket of my jeans, I saw that I hadn't missed any calls or texts.

Just as I was about to phone Ronni to see if there was a problem, Kizzy and her entourage swept through the crowd and climbed the steps to the gazebo. A portable sound system had been installed, and once they were all assembled, Kizzy spoke into the microphone.

"Welcome to the Kizzy Cutler's Cupcake Weekend. Before we get started, I have a sad announcement to make. My beloved assistant, Fallon Littlefield, passed away suddenly last night. Although I'm heartbroken and begged my business partner to call off the competition, Lee convinced me that because Fallon had worked so hard to make this event a success, she wouldn't have wanted to disappoint all of you. Fallon had no family, and in order to save the trees that would be used to make her casket and because embalming fluid contains harmful chemicals such as formaldehyde, methanol, and ethanol, which are not good for the environment, she wanted to be cremated. A private memorial service will be held when we return to Chicago." Kizzy paused, wiping away a tear. "After considering all of Fallon's wishes, it is with a heavy heart that I have agreed to go forward with the competition. We will be dedicating the contest to her memory."

Wow! Kizzy was good. Even though I knew the truth, she almost had me blubbering. I edged closer to the pavilion and peered at Lee Kimbrough, who was standing behind her partner. She was in the shadow, so I couldn't see her expression, but her posture was tense and she had her arms folded tightly across her chest. It looked to me as if everything wasn't hunky-dory in cupcake land.

After introducing the contestants, Kizzy waited for the applause to die down, then said, "Now please give a warm welcome to our esteemed celebrity judges." She gestured to a trio standing next to her, then put a hand on the shoulder of a woman dressed in an exquisite blue-and-white polka-dot sheath. "Thomasina Giancarlo is an award-winning pastry chef originally from Naples, Italy, and the owner of Something Sweeter Restaurant in Kansas City."

As Kizzy went on and on about Thomasina's accomplishments, I studied the tiny woman. I found it odd that someone who wore a size 2 was a pastry chef. Didn't she eat her own confections? Where did all the calories go? The only things large about her were her breasts and lips. From a certain angle, she looked like a blow-up doll.

I returned my attention to the gazebo when Kizzy

turned to the imposing woman next to Thomasina and said, "Next, we have Annalee Paulson. Annalee is the star of *Sugar and Spice*, the hit baking show on KC-MTV."

The local television station ran mostly reruns with an occasional cooking program and farm report to provide variety. I hadn't seen *Sugar and Spice*, but I knew my grandmother was a fan. Gran and her friend Frieda were somewhere in the crowd, and although I hadn't spotted them, I was sure that if she knew that Annalee was a judge, Gran was doubtlessly in the front row.

Kizzy paused as the audience finished clapping for Annalee, then indicated a handsome African-American man, and said, "Last, but not least, we have Vance Buddy. Mr. Buddy is a renowned cookbook author, blogger, and winner of the prestigious *New York Centennial* Best Cookbook of 2013 Award."

Vance resembled a thirtyish Denzel Washington and I could hear some of the women next to me murmuring that he could bake their bread anytime. I had to agree that I wouldn't kick him out of my kitchen, either.

As I was fantasizing about his buns, a girl standing next to me with the words BUTTERCREAM IS MY FAVORITE ACCESSORY embroidered on her pink T-shirt giggled and said, "I'm surprised Kizzy chose Vance as one of the judges."

I turned in time to see the teen's male companion roll his eyes, then paste an interested look on his face and ask, "Why are you surprised, Liza? It sounds like the guy has the creds to pick a winner."

"Because of what Vance wrote about her cupcakes on his blog."

"You read his blog?" the boyfriend asked, then muttered, "That explains a lot."

"Sure." Liza giggled again. "He always posts pictures of himself shirtless, eating whatever he's writing about. And, man, that dude is ripped."

"So, what did Mr. Centerfold say about the chick's cupcakes?"

"He said that the cake was dense and dry, like its creator, and the frosting was as bland as the company had grown to be in recent years."

The boyfriend cracked up. When he got his breath, he said, "Maybe the cupcake chick didn't see the blog."

"Oh, Kizzy saw it all right." Liza crossed her arms. "She sued Vance for defamation or libel or whatever. But he took down the blog, so the case never went to court."

"So they made up." The boyfriend shrugged, clearly bored with the conversation. "Maybe she asked him to be a judge to mend fences."

"Highly unlikely." Liza snickered. "Vance lost a lot of followers over his removal of that blog. His readers felt that he'd caved in and given up his First Amendment rights."

"Tragic." The boyfriend slung his arm around Liza's shoulders and the couple sauntered off.

I turned my attention back to the gazebo. Kizzy had just begun her closing remarks, thanking everyone and reminding them of all the planned activities, when the tornado siren started blaring. Both she and the audience froze. It was a beautiful day without a cloud in the sky. There were no warm and cold or dry and moist air masses to collide. In fact, no sign of any kind of storm at all. Kizzy said something to Lee, who threw her hands in the air.

Even though there was no indication of a twister, I was a little surprised that no one ran for cover. Everyone just stood their ground, gazing upward and babbling to their neighbor. This went on for several seconds, and I had just decided to try to herd as many people as I could persuade to come with me toward the city hall's shelter, when the siren abruptly stopped.

A moment later, Mayor Geoffrey Eggers pushed his way to the front of the gazebo, waving his cell phone in the air like a victory baton. At well over six feet six and weighing in at a mere hundred and seventy pounds, Eggers resembled a stick figure drawn by a kindergartener. Albeit a stick figure with scraggly eyebrows and a beaklike nose, wearing a thousand-dollar designer suit.

His honor tended to get petulant if he felt he wasn't being given his mayoral due, so Ronni had included him on the Cupcake Weekend committee. The best I could say about his contribution to the event was that he hadn't gotten in our way, which considering his usual modus operandi was a small miracle in itself.

Eggers grabbed the mike, and said, "Sorry, folks. Everything is fine. Our siren seems to have malfunctioned. There is no tornado."

Kizzy wrestled the microphone back from the mayor and announced, "The official luncheon, which is invitation only, will began in twenty minutes at the Ksiazak B and B. Afterward the contestants will be taken a tour of the kitchen facilities at the Todd Cooking School and be given time to make a practice batch of their entries. Tonight is the fashion show sponsored by Forever Used. Tickets for that event are for sale at the consignment shop and at Devereaux's Dime Store."

With that parting message, Kizzy and the rest of the group on the pavilion descended the steps and trooped toward a waiting minibus that would transport them to the various venues. I watched as they boarded the shuttle, noting that while Kizzy was the first one to embark, her partner, Lee, was the last. Was Lee deliberately keeping her distance from Kizzy or just in charge of rounding up the stragglers? Considering that Kizzy had painted Lee as the bad guy in her touching little speech about carrying on despite Fallon's death, I suspected it was probably the former.

Once the bus pulled away, I hurried to the dime store to help my father and Hannah serve all the customers I hoped would migrate from the square into the store. After slipping around the back of the building, I entered the storage room, where I took a second to refasten my ponytail and put on some lip gloss before heading into the store.

Finished with my minimal primping, I walked onto the sales floor and grinned. I was thrilled to see that the place was packed, and my heart swelled with pride. Regardless of my mood, the minute I walked into my shop, its old-fashioned charm made me smile. This store held some of the best memories of my childhood. My mom buying me a chocolate ice-cream cone from the soda fountain. Dad taking me for penny candy after church on Sunday. And Gran giving me a bottle of her favorite perfume, Evening in Paris, when I turned twelve to welcome me into the female sisterhood.

Seeing the dime store in all its vintage glory, bustling with customers, I knew I had made the right decision in buying it. When the Thornbee sisters, age ninety-one, had put the five-and-dime on the market, I was commuting to Kansas City every day for my job as a financial consultant at Stramp Investments. Making a six-figure salary was nice, an hour on the road each way not so much. So between Gran's doctor advising me that I needed to spend more time with her and my love for the store, I immediately put in an offer for the shop. The thought of the business being converted into one of the chain dollar stores and Gran having to go into an assisted-living facility had galvanized me into action.

The Thornbee twins' grandfather built the dime store when Shadow Bend was no more than a stagecoach stop, and the town had lost enough of its heritage when so much of the farmland and orchards had become housing developments for Kansas City commuters. Now instead of fresh fruit and fields of corn or soybeans, we had cookie-cutter houses, a fancy golf course, and a country club.

The excited voices of my customers drew me back from my reverie. There was no acoustical tile or cork matting to mute their lively conversations. Instead, the old tin ceiling and hardwood floors amplified the sound of people socializing with their neighbors and friends. Although I had doubled the interior space, installed Wi-Fi, and added the basket business, I had tried to keep the character of the original five-and-dime intact.

Noting that Hannah was behind the soda fountain and Dad was handling the register, I proceeded to the candy counter. I used the few minutes it took people to notice that I was there to study my father. Kern Sinclair was tall and lean, and held himself as erect as an army general.

Although I had inherited his height, I had gotten my mother's more voluptuous body type. Unfortunately, I hadn't been blessed with her willpower and never had been able to stick to her eight-hundred-calorie diet plan. My hair was a combination of Mom's blond and Dad's auburn color, but now that my father had a few strands of gray, our shades were closer than when he was a young man.

There were lines in my dad's face that hadn't been there before he went to prison, but all in all, I was relieved that he seemed to be adjusting well to his sudden freedom. From the expression in his bright green eyes as he chatted with the woman buying a pair of cupcake flip-flops and a Cupcake Weekend T-shirt, I suspected that he enjoyed working in the store and that he might become my permanent employee. How I felt about that possibility was still up for debate.

The shoppers finally noticed me and suddenly there was a line at the candy counter. For the next hour, I worked steadily, packing chocolate confections into little white pasteboard boxes. But as a young woman wavered between a hand-dipped hazelnut crunch truffle and this month's signature candy, a bonbon containing macadamia nuts, Cointreau, and white chocolate, I glanced over at Hannah as she filled soda fountain orders.

I would miss the quirky teenager when she left next month for college. Hannah's way of dressing fooled a lot of people into underestimating the girl, but I had come to recognize that she wasn't weird, just a limited edition.

Today Hannah wore an extremely tiny cream miniskirt trimmed in leather and chains, a teal tank that was cinched from her bustline to her hip and laced up the back, and plum leather wedge-heeled sneakers. Most adults figured anyone who sported such outrageous outfits was too bizarre to be perceptive. This assumption was a serious miscalculation on their part.

The line at the candy case had dwindled to a mother, daughter, and granddaughter trio, and as the young girl made her selections, I listened to the two older women discussing Fallon's death.

"I heard that they have no idea what caused that girl from the cupcake company to drop dead." The grandmother, busy pulling her short shorts from the crack of her butt, didn't bother to lower her voice. "One of the

EMTs' wives told me she was throwing up something fierce. Then suddenly she just keeled over, went stiff as a board, and started twitching and jerking like she was dancing the Watusi."

"A young woman like that, it was probably a drug overdose." The daughter flipped her bottle-blond curls over her shoulder and adjusted her halter top to display more cleavage. "I read an article in a magazine while I was waiting for my hair appointment and it listed all the symptoms of what they call club drugs."

"Well, not that I wish that poor girl any ill will, but I sure hope that it was the drugs." The grandmother shivered theatrically and pulled at the ruffles around the bottom of her cropped T-shirt. "I heard that she might have eaten something that had gone bad."

Shoot! I shot a startled look at the two women as I folded the top of the pink-and-brown-striped bag and secured it with a gold foil seal. Gossip that Fallon had consumed a toxic substance was all we needed. I debated correcting the women, but since I had no idea what the true cause of death was, I kept out of the discussion.

Instead, I handed the package to the granddaughter, and said, "Thank you. Please come again."

When the little girl smiled, I noticed she wore a jewel-encrusted gold grill across her teeth.

As the three generations of bimbos walked away, I heard the daughter state, "Food poisoning wouldn't be too bad. We can just be careful what we eat. But I heard that it might be something catching, like that flu that was going around last winter. If it's something contagious, maybe we should leave town before we're exposed to it."

Crap! Rumors of a disease were worse than ones of food poisoning.

The initial rush of customers had ebbed, so I started straightening displays and returning misplaced merchandise to its proper shelf. As I worked, I wondered if Chief Kincaid had figured out what happened to Fallon. I suspected that unless it was fairly obvious, it would take the lab a while to run the tests. In the meantime, the tittle-tattle could ruin the Cupcake Weekend.

I had been relieved when Kizzy announced that the luncheon was still going to take place at Ronni's. I'd been afraid that the police might have declared the B & B off-limits until they figured out what had caused Fallon's death. Evidently, the cops had been able to collect whatever evidence there was to gather, and hadn't had to cordon off the guesthouse, which was a good sign. Now if they would just announce that Fallon had died of natural causes, we could all relax.

Around three, I decided Dad and Hannah could handle the store on their own and headed to the B & B to find out if Ronni had any news to share regarding Fallon's death. I knew the luncheon would be over, but maybe there would be some food left. I hadn't had time for breakfast, and while my father and Hannah had taken lunch breaks, I hadn't and was starving. I only hoped that whatever the police had concluded about the young woman's demise didn't ruin my appetite.

CHAPTER 6

The Ksiazak B & B was on one of those narrow, not-quite-two-lane streets, common in the older parts of Shadow Bend. As I was approaching the guesthouse, a Swift Action Delivery truck appeared out of nowhere and hurtled toward me, nearly sideswiping my little Z4. At first, I was too shocked to react, but then words regarding the marital status of the driver's mother and what he could do to himself in the privacy of his own bedroom burst from my mouth like steam from a boiling teakettle.

Shakily, I pulled into the nearest parking spot and tried to calm my racing heart. I was so going to report that guy to his company. I hadn't gotten the license number of the van, but how many Swift Action deliverymen could there be servicing our little town?

When I finally calmed down enough to climb out of my car, I held my breath as I examined the Z4's fenders and the driver's-side door. The BMW was the only really expensive toy that I had kept after quitting my job with Stramp Investments. At the time, I rationalized that because of the poor economy I wouldn't get a good price for it if I sold it, but the honest truth was that I loved that car, and I knew there was more chance of me winning America's Next Top Model than ever owning a vehicle like it again.

After a thorough inspection, I blew out a sigh of relief. The sapphire black paint was still perfectly smooth. My sky-high insurance deductible meant that repairing cosmetic damage was out of the question. And call me superficial, but the idea of driving a dented vehicle made me cringe.

Satisfied that my baby was still in pristine condition, I strolled up the B & B's sidewalk, admiring the enormous Italianate-style mansion. Back in the mid–eighteen hundreds when this type of Victorian design had been popular, it had belonged to one of the town's five founding families. Rumor had it that the cupola in the center of the nearly flat roof, the ornamental brackets, and the wraparound porch made the wealthy residents feel as if they were living in a renaissance villa somewhere in Italy.

As I rang the doorbell, it occurred to me that everyone might already have gone over to the cooking school. Maybe I should have headed to Winnie's instead of coming here. Or at least called to find out the group's current location.

I was digging my cell phone out of my jeans' pocket when, like the great Oz, I saw Ronni's face materialize in the curved window of the double front door. She grinned, and a nanosecond later, she ushered me into the spacious foyer, then pulled me over to the reception area nestled inside the curve of a beautiful wooden staircase.

"Have a seat." She plopped down behind the desk and tapped a few keys on the laptop.

Once I was off my feet, I asked, "Has the cupcake menagerie all left for Winnie's?"

"About ten minutes ago." Ronni gestured to the computer. "I needed to get some work done, and since the cooking school's so small, I said that I'd skip the tour and catch up with them all at dinner."

"It was a brilliant idea to ask the various churches to host the meals." I stretched my legs out and rubbed my sore calves. Standing behind the candy counter for so long without moving was tough on the muscles. "They get to make some money for their organization and the cupcake committee gets a large enough space to feed the contestants, judges, media, and the rest of the crew without having to transport all of them to an out-of-town restaurant."

"At first I was stumped when I realized that Shadow Bend's dining options were limited to Little's Tea Room, the Golden Dragon, the diner by the highway, and the Dairy Queen," Ronni said, "because none of those could handle the number of people we would need to accommodate."

"St. Saggy's is tonight's location, right?" I was referring to St. Sagar. No one had any idea why Shadow Bend's Catholic church had been named for a martyred bishop from Turkey and, not surprisingly, the parishioners called it St. Saggy. "And then tomorrow's lunch is the Baptists, and the Presbyterians are doing the cookout in the square for dinner."

"Yes. Except for the people staying here, everyone is on their own for breakfast," Ronni answered, concentrating on the laptop's screen. "The Methodists won the lottery for the Sunday supper."

"Right." I nodded. "All the churches wanted that meal because it's when the cupcake winner will be announced."

"That one and the picnic were the most sought-after since they're the only meals open to the public and thus the most profitable." Ronni's fingers flew over the keyboard. "Which is why we finally just put all the churches into a hat and drew names for the various options."

"How did today's lunch go?" I asked. "Did all your helpers show up?"

"Sure." Ronni finished whatever she'd been working on and closed the laptop's lid. "Cody and his buddies did a great job. I was glad he was able to come up with enough local college friends of his for me to hire. This is the first time since I bought the B and B that it's at full capacity, and I couldn't prepare breakfast, serve it, and clean all the rooms by myself."

Cody Gomez did odd jobs for Ronni when he wasn't at college, and had volunteered to find the additional employees the B & B required for the Cupcake Weekend. Our community wasn't accustomed to needing so many workers. After the crowd at the dime store this afternoon, I just hoped that Dad, Hannah, and I could handle the customers because I doubted there were many jobless teenagers still in town for me to employ.

"Speaking of lunch, is there anything left?" I asked. "The shop was mobbed, so I didn't get a chance to eat anything and I'm famished." My stomach rumbled as if to reinforce my last statement.

"Sure." Ronni jumped to her feet. "Come on into the kitchen and I'll fix you a plate. It's all cold stuff, sandwiches, salads, and such. Since we ran out of churches willing to host meals, I had to come up with the food for today's lunch myself." She glanced over her shoulder and winked at me. "And none of the kids I hired know how to cook."

"Anything is fine." I followed her down the hall and took a seat at the table as she opened the fridge. "It's got to be better than my usual lunch of PB and J or a carton of Greek yogurt."

"Oh, it's good," Ronni assured me as she fixed me a plate. "I had Chapattis over in Sparkville cater it from their deli department."

"Yum." Chapattis was a tiny Italian market located on the outskirts of Shadow Bend's nearest neighbor. "Another great idea."

"Yep. I'm full of 'em." Ronni beamed, then, after pouring us both a glass of iced tea, joined me. "Let's just hope this baking competition turns out to be one of my good ideas and not one of my harebrained schemes." She ran her fingertip over the wood of the table. "What's the word on the street about Fallon's death?"

"Besides having you feed me, that's why I came over." I paused as I bit into a stuffed pepper shooter, moaning as the pickled cherry peppers filled with prosciutto ham wrapped around provolone cheese exploded on my taste buds. Then after swallowing, I told Ronni about the conversation I had overheard at the store. I finished with, "So I wondered if the cops had come to any conclusion about what caused Fallon to die so suddenly?"

"Not that they told me." Ronni tossed a black olive into her mouth. "Maybe you should give your buddy Chief Kincaid a call."

"I doubt he'd share information with me unless I had something to trade." I ate a bite of insalata caprese. After I savored the slices of mozzarella and tomatoes drizzled with extra-virgin olive oil and sprinkled with fresh basil leaves, I added, "You know the only time he's ever generous with info is when I can give him important facts in exchange."

"Shoot!" Ronni took a sip of her iced tea. "We really need to know in what direction the police's investigation is heading so we can nip the rumors in the bud before they scare away all the Cupcake Weekenders."

She paused. "Do you have any other contacts at the cop shop? One of the dispatchers?"

"Nobody I can come up with right this minute." I briefly considered the woman who had kept Jake up to date on the last case, but Nympho Barbie wouldn't spill the content of official reports to me. That is, unless I promised to gift wrap the hunky deputy marshal and put him under her Christmas tree, and I wasn't feeling quite that desperate yet.

"Can Poppy get anyone to talk?" Ronni asked as she spread a thin slice of Italian bread with Brie, fig jam, dried fruits, and pine nuts.

"Well . . ." I hesitated. It was a well-known fact that Poppy and her father didn't get along, but few people knew how deeply the rift actually ran. "I don't think she'd be willing to ask her dad for that kind of favor. Their relationship is pretty tense."

"Oh." Ronni finished assembling her crostini and brought it to her lips. "How about one of the other officers? She's so freaking gorgeous. Who has naturally platinum hair and eyes that shade of violet without colored contacts? If she wasn't my friend, I would hate her." Ronni shook her head. "I doubt any red-blooded male could turn her down."

"But is it fair to get some poor schmuck in trouble with the chief for blabbing?" I really didn't care that much about a guy who let his little head rule over his big one, but I hated to see Poppy do something that would widen the chasm between her and her father.

"Do you have another suggestion?" Ronni narrowed her eyes and slid the tray of biscotti, amaretti, pizzelle, and cannoli out of my reach.

"We need a tidbit of info the cops don't know to swap for whatever they do know." I pulled the plate of desserts back toward me.

"But how do we get that?" Ronni wailed. "Make something up?"

"Only as a last resort." I dug my favorite fountain pen, a Retro 51 Tornado Lincoln, and an old envelope out of my purse. "Let's go over what happened yesterday again."

"Okay." Ronni gazed at the ceiling. "Kizzy and Lee got here around four thirty. Lee was driving. I had just gotten them settled in their respective suites when Fallon arrived in her own car. I was a little shocked at how much she resembled a younger Kizzy, and when I mentioned it, Fallon said that was one of the reasons she'd been hired, so she could stand in for Kizzy on the packaging."

"Interesting."

"Yeah. I always wondered how Kizzy never aged on the promo material." Ronni snickered. "Anyway, I showed Fallon to her room, she dropped off her luggage, and then I helped her carry in several boxes containing stuff for the competition, which we stowed in the pantry. Afterward we had a cup of coffee while she went over Kizzy's schedule and special requests."

"Did she have anything to eat or drink other than the coffee you both shared?" I asked as I nibbled on an almond macaroon.

"No." Ronni slowly shook her head. "And we both used the same container of cream." She bit her lip. "Fallon did use two packets of sugar, but they were sealed. I watched her tear them open."

"So any food she consumed was before she arrived, and she didn't mention feeling sick, right?" I selected a cannoli, ate the chocolate chips decorating it, then licked the powdered sugar from the top. "When you and Kizzy left for the restaurant, she was fine?"

"Yes." Ronni nodded emphatically. "In fact, I could

tell she was a little upset with having to wait for the delivery, because she complained about missing lunch and being hungry. I offered her a snack, but she said she was saving her daily calories for the Chinese food, specifically the crab rangoon."

"Then less than an hour later, she decided not to come to the Golden Dragon because she felt ill." I tapped my pen on my notebook. "Did Lee or Kizzy mention whether Fallon tended toward hypochondria?"

"No." Ronni got up and started to clear the table. "I heard Lee tell the EMT that Fallon had never been sick in all the time she'd known her, and Kizzy said something similar to Chief Kincaid."

"Hmm." I thought about the timeline, then asked, "Did the paramedics ask Lee if Fallon had eaten anything while she was waiting here with her?"

"They did, and Lee said Fallon hadn't had anything while she was present."

"Could you tell if Fallon had eaten anything after Lee left for the restaurant? Anything missing from the fridge or the cupboards?"

"Nothing I noticed." Ronni shrugged. "But I didn't take an inventory."

"Hell!" I slumped in my chair. "So much for gathering info to trade with the cops."

"Now that I think about it, there is one thing we might know that they don't." Ronni chewed on a fingernail. "I doubt Kizzy told them about the fight that she, Lee, and Fallon had before we left for the restaurant."

"Fight?" I perked up. "Spill."

"Unfortunately, I didn't hear much, but we were getting ready to leave for the Golden Dragon and Kizzy suddenly laid into Fallon for something—I didn't catch what her transgression had been—and when Lee stepped in, Kizzy started yelling at her, too." Ronni pursed her lips. "About that time Kizzy noticed that I was standing there, pulled them all into the parlor, and closed the doors."

"Crap!" I thought about the incident for a few seconds, then asked, "Could you tell if the argument was about the business or the competition or . . . ?"

"I can't remember why, but it struck me as something more personal." Ronni worried the skin around her thumbnail. "I could swear I heard the word *betrayal*. And it was only after this fight happened that Lee decided to stay behind with Fallon to wait for the delivery. Before that, only Fallon was going to wait here for it."

"Interesting." I stared at the ceiling. "If Kizzy had died, I'd wonder if Lee had poisoned her. I noticed at the restaurant that the cupcake queen seemed to treat Lee more like a servant than a business partner."

"I noticed that around here, too," Ronni agreed. "But Kizzy orders everyone around and Lee doesn't seem to mind."

"True." I was silent for a minute and then asked, "Did the police process Fallon's car?"

"I don't think so." Ronni pursed her lips. "They probably didn't realize that she'd driven here on her own, and maybe Kizzy didn't think to mention it. I sure didn't."

"Too bad we don't have the key or we could search it."

"Actually"—Ronni walked over to a rack made up of pink metal roses by the back door and selected a key from one of its many hooks—"we do. I asked for her spare in case I needed to move her car out of my way. With so many guests I figured we'd probably have to let people in and out of the parking area."

"Great." I stood. "Let's go take a look."

"Wait." Ronni moved over to the sink and reached into the cupboard underneath it. When she straightened, she was pulling on a pair of rubber gloves.

"Seriously?" I raised an eyebrow at the bright purple gloves.

"Here." She handed me a second pair. "If the cops decide Fallon's death was foul play and end up dusting her car for prints, we don't want them to find ours all over the interior."

"You have a point." I pulled on the neon orange gloves and followed Ronni outside.

Fallon drove a Fiat 500. It was a cute little vehicle with shiny white paint and hubcaps with an interlocking GG in the center. I had read about the Gucci edition of this car but never seen one before. The trademark red-and-green Gucci strip ran along the side, and if that weren't enough to identify the design edition, the logo and name were everywhere.

As Ronni unlocked the driver's-side door and slid inside, she said, "Fallon was so proud of this car. She said she'd just bought it and it was the first new one she'd ever possessed."

"That's so sad." I got into the tiny backseat.

"Fallon said she'd been saving up for the Fiat ever since she went to work for Kizzy five years ago," Ronni commented as she went through the glove box. "She told me that she grew up in foster homes and everything she'd ever owned was secondhand."

"How awful that she finally got the car of her dreams and didn't have time to enjoy it." My heart hurt for the poor girl. "Someone her age, dying so young, is always sad, but Fallon's death seems even more so for some reason. Maybe because she had turned her life around and was finally on a good path."

"You're right," Ronni agreed. "I feel that way, too."

I felt between the cushions and along the floor. There was nothing. The car still looked as if it had just driven out of the showroom. "Anything?" I asked Ronni.

"Not even a gum wrapper," she answered.

After checking the trunk, which contained only a first aid kit and jumper cables, Ronni and I dejectedly returned to the kitchen. It looked as though our only hope was that the police would decide that Fallon had died from natural causes and that Chief Kincaid would make that conclusion public before the cupcake tourists were scared out of town.

CHAPTER 7

I waited while Ronni packed up some sandwiches and cookies for me to bring to my father and Hannah, then thanked her and headed out to my Z4. Before getting inside, I examined the paint one more time to make sure that delivery guy hadn't scratched it.

As I used the bottom of my polo shirt to rub off a smudge near the handle, an idea flitted through my mind. With the hope that Fallon died from natural causes becoming harder and harder to sustain, I thought more about the possible cause of her death. If it wasn't something she ate that made her sick, what about something she touched? Something no one else had handled. Like something that arrived after everyone else left for the restaurant.

After placing the bag of food for Dad and Hannah in the passenger seat, I turned on my heel and jogged back up the sidewalk to the B & B. I rang the bell, and as soon as Ronni answered the door, I asked, "Whatever happened to the package that Fallon was waiting for last night?"

"I have no idea." Ronni's expression became thoughtful. "Once we got home from the Golden Dragon, and

Lee discovered that Fallon was seriously ill, I doubt anyone ever even thought about the delivery." Ronni wrinkled her brow. "You know, now that you mention it, Fallon said they weren't expecting anything, and Kizzy and Lee were both puzzled as to what was being sent."

"You didn't notice an extra box or padded envelope sitting around?" I asked.

"There was nothing in the public rooms or with the cupcake stuff in the pantry." Ronni shrugged. "But I wouldn't know if there was anything in the guests' rooms." She glanced at her watch. "We can ask Kizzy and Lee when we see them later at dinner."

"Let's remember to do that." I turned to go. "See you at six."

After leaving the B & B, I drove to the dime store and delivered the sandwiches and cookies to Dad and Hannah. The shop was busy and I took over at the register to give Dad a breather. Then once he returned, I manned the soda fountain so Hannah could have a rest. We had a nice steady stream of customers, and when we closed up at four, an hour earlier than our usual time, my cash drawer was stuffed with money, checks, and credit card receipts.

Arriving home to change clothes, I found the place empty. I thought my father would be there, but he must have had after-work plans. I had no idea where he was or what those plans might be, as he and I hadn't gotten back to the place in our relationship where we kept each other informed about our activities.

Not that I thought we should return to that status. We were both adults and didn't need to check in with each other. Still, I wondered where he was and if he was okay, since he didn't leave the property much except to go to work.

As always, he'd driven his own car to the store. While my mother had taken the family Lexus when she hightailed it out of town a few days after my father was convicted, my grandmother had made sure her son's Grand Cherokee was ready for his return. I'd never realized that Gran hadn't sold the fourteen-year-old Jeep, but when Dad came home and started driving the SUV, she'd informed me that she'd kept it tuned up and running, parked in an old barn sitting on the edge of our property.

I knew that my grandmother had already gone to St. Saggy's to set up for the dinner. She and her friend Frieda were members of the church's Martha Society, a volunteer group that prepared the meals for the funerals and fund-raisers of the parish. Gran and the other ladies had been making side dishes and desserts for several days, but they would fry up the chicken just before the diners sat down to eat.

Tonight's dinner was limited to the cupcake competition participants and their guests, committee members and their plus ones, and the media. I wasn't sure just how many to expect, but there would be at least fifty, maybe more. Dad had declined the offer to be my date for the St. Saggy's event, saying that he wasn't comfortable with attending community functions yet. Now I wondered if he'd had other plans all along. And if so, why he hadn't just told me that.

Realizing that my father's social life was really none of my business, I hurried into my bedroom and stripped out of my work clothes. After a quick shower, I put on white cotton slacks, a navy striped top, and red strappy sandals. Examining my reflection in the mirror, I twisted my damp hair on top of my head, then applied concealer and ruby lipstick. I knew my outfit was a little on the "Hello, sailor" side, but tomorrow was the

Fourth of July, so when better to break out the red, white, and blue?

Having justified my fashion choice, at least to myself, I hopped into my car and headed back into town. Ten minutes later, I arrived at the church parking lot. Most of the spaces were taken, but I noticed the ones near what had once been a six-foot-tall fiberglass figure of Jesus were vacant.

The statue had stood in front of St. Saggy's for as long as I could remember, but several months ago, it had been struck by lightning. Like a pile of charcoal briquettes squirted with too much starter fluid, the sculpture had burst into flames. After the fire died down, all that was left was a blackened steel skeleton, a pile of ashes, and a brass memorial plaque that read IN MEMORY OF MY BELOVED HUSBAND, BLAISE FIAMMETTA. The irony of the dedication was not lost on me. I knew that in Italian, the word *fiamma* meant flame, so basically the stature had been erected to honor a man named Blaze Flame.

Gran had told me that the burned effigy was affecting attendance at Sunday Mass and Father Flagg was frantically trying to raise money to replace Jesus. Unfortunately, the cost was prohibitive and few people were contributing to his pet project. He had been lobbying for the proceeds of tonight's dinner to be deposited in the statue fund, but I didn't know if the church's finance committee had agreed.

I had to admit, I understood why no one wanted to park near the twisted hunk of metal, but there were no other available spots. So averting my gaze from the disturbing image, I pulled the Z4 into an empty slot, got out of the car, and hurried past the unsettling steel carcass.

The fellowship hall, a faded green aluminum pole building, was on the far side of the lot. It was divided into a trio of gathering rooms, with a long kitchen accessible to all three. The bare-bones structure was used for catechism classes, weddings, showers, and funeral luncheons, as well as the always-profitable bingo night.

Pushing through the glass door, I noticed a poster pinned to the bulletin board on my right. It read LADIES, DON'T FORGET THE RUMMAGE SALE. IT'S A CHANCE TO GET RID OF ALL THOSE USELESS THINGS IN YOUR LIFE. BRING YOUR HUSBANDS.

I was still snickering over the flyer when Poppy met me a few steps down the hall. She had on a slinky black chiffon tank with a pink scallop-hemmed skirt that barely covered her hoo-ha. As always, she was ethereally beautiful, but I wondered at her skimpy clothing choice, considering that we were in a church hall. However, as soon as she spoke, I understood her decision.

"My sources tell me that Dad is planning on making an announcement here tonight." Poppy twisted her mouth. "Just because I'm involved in the Cupcake Weekend, he has to try to ruin it."

Her voice had risen to a level that would soon attract attention, so I took her arm and tugged her into the nearby restroom. Thankfully, it was empty, and I turned the lock on the outer door so we wouldn't be disturbed. It was time for some tough love.

"Everything the chief does is not about you." I stared at Poppy until her cheeks reddened. "I know the world of hurt you're in because of your problems with him." I held up my hand when she started to speak. "Maybe not the precise latitude and longitude, but I'm familiar with the coordinates. Even so, you need to get over your daddy issues."

"Sure. Now that your father has been exonerated, you think mine is innocent, too." Poppy pouted. "You have no idea how evil my dad is."

"You're right. I don't." I crossed my arms. "Because you've never told me what happened between you two. I know you and your father have never agreed with each other on most fundamental issues, but something pretty serious had to have caused you to actually stop speaking to him."

"I don't want to talk about that." Poppy mimicked my pose, crossing her arms, leaning against the sink, and frowning. "It doesn't have anything to do with what he's up to right now."

"Fine." I shook my head. "But seriously, girlfriend. Would your father really risk upsetting an event that's benefiting the whole town just to get back at you?" I sighed. "You have to admit, he would never use his position as chief that way. He loves the police department too much to risk giving it that kind of black eye."

"Maybe," Poppy admitted. "And truly, the last thing I want to do is hurt him." She grimaced, then winked. "But if he doesn't behave, it's still on my list."

"I understand." I had a few people on my own list that were one insult or nasty innuendo away from a punch in the face.

"So, what do you think the chief's going to say?" Poppy asked.

"My guess is that he's going to announce the cause of Fallon's death." I bit my lip. "There's been a lot of gossip going around about what happened to her. Maybe this is his way of putting a stop to the rumors."

"Yeah." Poppy nodded. "I've heard people speculating that it was everything from food poisoning to a deadly virus." She paused. "But what if it was something like that rather than natural causes? Either contagion or contaminated chow would freak out the tourists."

"True."

"Do you have a strategy if it's bad news?" Poppy asked. "I mean, you always have a plan, right?"

"Not exactly a fully formed plan." It appeared Poppy had stepped away from the edge of her emotional cliff, and was no longer about to publicly attack her father, so I unlocked the bathroom door and held it open for her. "But I do want to speak to the chief before he makes his big announcement. Is he here yet?"

"Of course he is." Poppy tugged the neckline of her tank a bit lower and the waist of her skirt a bit higher. "He arrived at precisely five fifty-nine and is now holding court at the head table."

"He's sitting with Kizzy, Lee, and the judges?" I trailed Poppy down the corridor as she marched to the largest of the church hall's three rooms, then pointed to the long table at the front.

"Right next to the cupcake queen herself." Poppy frowned. "And from what I saw before you got here, Ms. Kizzy was flirting with him."

"I take it your mom isn't with the chief?" I asked, although I could plainly see Mrs. Kincaid wasn't seated next to her husband.

"No." Poppy shook her head. "Dad's in uniform, which means this is official business." She jerked a thumb to the end of the head table. "Take a gander at the mayor. He's super ticked off that Kizzy is ignoring him in favor of my father."

I glanced at Eggers. His face was twisted in a pout. Chief Kincaid and our esteemed mayor had a long-standing rivalry. When Eggers wrested control of the city council from the chief, they had begun voting down police department budget increases. Not one to be easily thwarted, Chief Kincaid applied for federal funds. And when the chief's applications began to bring in money, he'd remodeled the station, held professional development classes for his personnel, and purchased up-to-date gear. Then he won the Powerball Lottery of grants and was able to buy his very own crime scene unit and mobile lab, as well as get his staff trained in their uses.

His Honor had been beyond incensed that the chief had managed to get what he wanted without financing from the town treasury. I hid a smile. Geoffrey Eggers played the game of one-upmanship as if it were an Olympic sport, and now that the chief had muscled in on the mayor's territory—sitting next to the visiting celebrity—I suspected that there might be fireworks rather than a gold medal at tonight's dinner.

Poppy nudged me. "Look at His Honor. He wants to get into Kizzy's panties so bad he can hardly stand it."

"Like that would ever happen." I was a hundred percent sure that when the cupcake tycoon hooked up with a guy, he was a lot richer and more important than a small-town politician. "The mayor is drooling up the wrong tree."

"Yep." Poppy sniggered. "Kizzy already has one asshole in her underwear; she doesn't need a second one."

It took me a second to get Poppy's allusion, but when I did, I let out a loud bark of laughter. My BFF was sometimes a little vulgar, but she was always funny.

"If you want to talk to my father before he makes his announcement, you'd better nab him now." Poppy gestured to the rest of the tables. "It looks as if almost everyone is here, so the Marthas will probably start serving dinner soon."

"You're right." I hurried over to the chief and said, "Could I speak to you for a moment?" When he nodded, I added, "In private."

Chief Kincaid excused himself, silently stood, and followed me out into the corridor.

Once I was sure we were alone, I asked, "Do you know why Fallon died yet?"

"We know what *didn't* cause her death, but unhappily, not what did."

"What wasn't it?" I asked, then added, "I might have an idea."

"There wasn't anything harmful in her stomach contents," the chief answered. "And the autopsy and review of her medical records showed no disease or hidden condition that could explain her symptoms."

"So maybe my theory is viable," I murmured half to myself, then asked, "Are there poisons that can be transmitted through the skin?"

"Several." Chief Kincaid hooked his thumbs in his pockets. "Or something like dimethyl sulfoxide can be used to transfer the poison. It's readily available for purchase to treat muscle injuries or arthritis and is a colorless liquid that dissolves both polar and nonpolar compounds. DMSO easily penetrates the skin." He looked at me until I nodded my understanding, then added, "For many people, it causes a garlic-like taste in the mouth."

"Earlier on the night that she died, Fallon told Kizzy that she had a bad taste in her mouth," I informed the chief. "I'd forgotten that part of her conversation. Did Kizzy or Lee mention that?"

"No." Chief Kincaid took a pen and small notebook from his breast pocket. "They just said she'd had a headache and was dizzy."

"They probably either forgot it like I did or didn't think something like a bad taste in the mouth could be important," I assured him.

"I take it by these questions that you think Fallon

was a victim of contact poison." The chief glanced at his watch and frowned, clearly getting antsy about the passing time. "What besides that bad taste in her mouth steers you in that direction?"

"Well . . ." I paused to run the scenario through my mind one more time. I definitely didn't want to share some crackpot theory with Chief Kincaid and have him regard me as a total lunatic.

"Ticktock, Devereaux." The chief tapped the face of his Timex.

"Okay." I took a deep breath. "But bear with me and let me tell you the whole story before you decide that I've watched one too many episodes of *Murder, She Wrote*." I started with Fallon's absence at the restaurant because she was waiting for a package and led the chief through my thought process, then asked, "What do you think?"

"I think someone should have told me all this earlier today." Chief Kincaid jotted a couple more notes, then made a phone call to his crime scene team.

When he ended the call, I asked, "So, how long will it take the medical examiner to figure out if she was poisoned and by what substance?"

"Without being able to narrow down what toxin to test for, it could take a while to figure it out." Chief Kincaid's mouth thinned. "Nearly anything can be lethal in the right amounts. Everyone who watches those fool *CSI* shows thinks that we can put the victim's blood in a fancy machine and get an instant result. But poison disperses in the body and changes into other elements. Looking for poison, without specifically knowing which toxic substance the victim was administered, is like looking for an image in a mirror after the person has stepped away from the glass."

"Oh." I slumped. I thought I'd given the police a

solid lead, but instead, I'd given them no more than a whiff of smoke to follow.

"Buck up, Dev." Chief Kincaid patted my shoulder. "This is still more than we had before."

"Thanks." I straightened. "Does that mean you'll let me know what happens?"

"I'll think about it." Chief Kincaid smiled. "But now, since you said that Ronni didn't know what had happened to the package that was supposed to be delivered, I need to speak to Ms. Cutler and Ms. Kimbrough."

"Do you want me to go and ask them to step into the hallway?" I was hoping the chief would let me stay when he talked to Kizzy and Lee.

"Yes." Chief Kincaid nodded absently as he phoned another officer and directed him to find the service that had made the delivery to the B & B Thursday night, then said to me, "Once you tell Ms. Cutler and her partner to come out here, make sure no one follows them." He inclined his head toward me. "And that includes you."

Damn! So much for the police sharing information with me. On the bright side, maybe they'd solve the case and I wouldn't need to get involved.

CHAPTER 8

Chief Kincaid's declaration that Fallon's death was not due to food poisoning or anything contagious went a long way in calming the Cupcake Weekenders' fears. If anyone but me noticed that he hadn't ruled out murder, thankfully they didn't mention it.

Soon after making his announcement, the chief received a call that I suspected was about Fallon's case and hurried away. Having traded my one tidbit of info, I would need to come up with some fresh piece of evidence if I wanted Chief Kincaid to tell me about any new discoveries. I sure wished that I had a spy at the police station. Maybe it was time to make friends with one of the cops. It would have to be one of the female officers since I didn't think either Noah or Jake would be too happy with me cozying up to one of the men.

The mouthwatering aroma of fried chicken snapped me out of my reverie, and after poking my head into the kitchen to say hi to Gran and her friends, I slipped into the chair that Poppy had saved for me next to her. While Kizzy, Lee, Mayor Eggers, Winnie, the Dessert Channel host, and the judges had reserved seating up front, the rest of us were on our own and it was survival of the hungriest.

The Marthas had set up six tables of eight, and as I placed my napkin in my lap, Poppy began the round of introductions. "Everyone, this is Devereaux Sinclair. She owns Devereaux's Dime Store and Gift Baskets, the location where the final judging will take place."

"Hi." I nodded. "The store also has official Cupcake Weekend souvenir T-shirts and any odds and ends you might have forgotten to pack."

"Nice to meet you." The man across from me grinned. "I'm GB O'Rourke, one of the finalists." He winked. "The only rooster in the henhouse."

"Sounds like fun." I couldn't decide if GB looked more like a leprechaun or a palm tree. He was less than five feet tall and wore neon green pants that battled with his sunflower yellow sports jacket splashed with images of tropical leaves. His beard formed a red fringe around his chubby little face, and a pipe stem peeked from his breast pocket. All he lacked was a derby and a Celtic harp.

"I'm GB's wife, Millie." The plump woman next to him waved. "We're from Oswego, Illinois."

"Is that near Chicago?" I didn't really care, but it seemed polite to ask.

"About thirty minutes southwest of the city," a delicate woman on GB's other side answered. "My daughter lives in the next suburb over." She tucked a light brown curl behind her ear and said, "I'm Lauren Neumann from Des Moines." She blinked her soft green eyes and added, "Iowa. Oh, and I'm also one of the contestants."

We exchanged pleasantries, and then her husband introduced himself as Russell. We paused to pass around the carafes of dressing. Bowls of salad had already been on the table when we arrived. Once everyone had selected either ranch or Italian—our two choices—and the basket of bread had been circulated along with the butter dish, I glanced at the remaining young man and woman.

The guy was tall and thin with a neatly trimmed goatee and bulging blue eyes that seemed to throb. He was perched on the edge of his chair, almost as if he was about leap up at any moment. Although he was sitting, his hands and feet were in constant motion.

After swallowing a bite of lettuce, I smiled at the pair and said, "Sorry. I don't believe I caught either of your names."

"Dirk Harvey." The man mumbled around the piece of Parker House roll he'd just stuffed in his mouth. He jerked his thumb at the woman. "This is my sister, Q. We both work for the Dessert Channel."

"Q?" GB asked with a puzzled look. "Is that short for something? My initials stand for Gerald Bartholomew."

"Nope," the young woman answered, fingering the iron bar between her eyebrows. "Just Q. Like on the *Star Trek* shows, *The Next Generation*, *Deep Space Nine*, and *Voyager*." When we all looked confused, she sighed and explained, "He's from the Q Continuum."

"Really?" Realizing that her responses weren't going to get any more enlightening, I answered for the rest of the group, "How remarkable."

"Yes." Q nodded, and the four steel studs over each of her eyebrows winked in the fluorescent light. "He was by far the most fascinating of the noncrew characters. He was omnipotent, you know."

"Wow. That would be useful." It was time to change the subject before Q launched into the whole story line, so I asked, "What is it you and your brother do for the network?"

"Dirk's the cameraman and I do makeup, hair, and styling," Q answered.

"Nice." I was running out of adjectives but couldn't think of any other responses. I mean, seriously. *This woman* was the show's stylist. She looked as if she had a curtain rod running across her forehead. All she needed was a sconce on either temple to make the image complete. Forcing myself to come up with something positive to say, I added, "Both your jobs sound wonderful."

Thank goodness Kizzy chose that moment to stand and clap her hands for silence, because I was completely out of small talk. Once she had everyone's attention, Kizzy said, "Welcome, contestants, judges, and everyone who has assisted me in bringing this wonderful event to my beloved hometown." After a round of applause, she continued. "When I came up with my flagship cupcake recipe, I never dared to dream my company would become such a huge success. I knew that the recipe was awesome, and that I would need to work hard to bring my vision to fruition. Now, on the brink of introducing a second line of cupcakes and doubling my business, all I can say is that I'm proud to be a Shadow Bender."

There was some polite applause, and then as soon as Kizzy sat down, the Marthas started bringing out the entrée. Dishes of fried chicken, scalloped corn, and mashed potatoes were slipped in front of us and we all focused on the food. It might not be the gourmet fare seen on cooking shows, but it was all kinds of yum and I eagerly picked up my fork.

As we ate our way through the main course, talk turned to the various hometowns, casserole recipes, and the contestants' children—all of whom were beautiful and brilliant.

While the others chatted, I turned to Poppy and asked, "How are things going between you and Tryg?" Tryg Pryce was Poppy's boyfriend du jour. He was an Illinois attorney whom she'd met a few months ago when he came to Shadow Bend to defend our friend Boone against a murder charge. Tryg had lasted longer than most and I suspected it was because he lived in Chicago. Unlike me, Poppy felt distance was a good thing in a relationship.

"I don't know." Poppy shrugged. "He can be a real jerk sometimes. He's arrogant and I think he's seeing other women when I'm not there."

"You seem to date a lot of men like that," I said. "Maybe that's a mistake."

"True." Poppy sighed, then giggled. "But some mistakes are too much fun to only make once."

I rolled my eyes, knowing she was serious. "How about going out with some nice guys instead? Maybe someone who's a little bit more monogamous even if he is a little less wealthy."

"Nah." Poppy shook her head. "If there's one thing I've learned, it's that regardless of how good a relationship is in the beginning, that warm, fuzzy feeling fades, and there had better be a lot of money to take its place."

Considering my own messed-up love life, I let the subject drop. Soon afterward the head Martha announced that the dessert table was in the rear of the room and we could help ourselves. The out-of-towners proceeded to do so in a leisurely fashion, but the Shadow Benders made a mad dash. We all knew the good stuff would disappear fast and all that would be left would be Mrs. Cormac's store-bought angel food cake with icing straight from a can of frosting.

I nabbed the last piece of Gran's marshmallow chocolate chip pie, and gave Poppy a thumbs-up when she outmaneuvered Mayor Eggers and snatched the final brownie from the batch Vera Thom had baked. Vera was famous in Shadow Bend for the best brownies in town and they were always highly sought-after at these kinds of dinners. Happy with my own prize, I took the long way back to my seat so I could get an idea of how the event was going. No one was discussing Fallon's death, which I took to be a good sign.

From Kizzy's introductions in the village square that afternoon, I recognized all the contestants and deduced that the people seated next to them were their plus ones. The other unidentified diners, I assumed, were the folks on the Dessert Channel crew.

Of course, I knew all the committee members and most of their guests, and I smiled and nodded my way through the maze of tables until my gaze collided with Gwen Bourne's scowl. What in the hell was she doing here? Gwen wasn't on any of the committees—Ronni didn't like her, and since she was organizing the Cupcake Weekend, she had taken pains not to invite Gwen to help. Which meant that Gwen had to be someone's date. But who had succumbed to the socialite's fake charm and phony smiles?

I looked to her left and right to see which guy was the unlucky fellow. Knowing her penchant for successful men, I figured it had to be Vaughn Yager. He and I had been high school pals, but the boy he'd been back then was an entirely different person from the man he was today.

Nerdy, and the son of the custodian, he'd been tormented throughout his adolescence. But after using his amazing mathematical skills, as well as a genius for tactics and strategy, to make a fortune playing professional poker in Las Vegas and Atlantic City, he'd become Shadow Bend's wealthiest entrepreneur.

It didn't hurt that he now had muscles, a straightened nose, and a jutting chin—the latter two features owing to the wonders of plastic surgery. Transformed into the handsome prince, he'd returned to town, where he purchased a nearly bankrupt factory that he built into a thriving business. All of this made him one of our community's most eligible bachelors. I loved the quirk of fate that had turned the bullies of his high school years into the sycophants who now were his entourage.

I flashed Vaughn a grin, both because we had been buddies at the bottom of the teenage hierarchy and because it would drive Gwen nuts.

He beamed back at me, tilted his head toward his date, and stage-whispered, "Me with a homecoming queen, who would have thunk it?"

Hoping Gwen wouldn't use and abuse my starstruck friend, I smiled at him and moved on. Just before reaching my chair, I glanced at the head table. Geoffrey Eggers was leaning close to Kizzy and whispering in her ear. Kizzy's demeanor was easy to read since she wasn't trying to hide that she was bored out of her skull. But Lee's expression was tougher to figure out. Was it concern that her partner would be rude to the mayor or something else?

Could it be jealousy? It had to be hard always to play second fiddle to Kizzy. While Lee was attractive in a quiet sort of way, her business partner was stunning. Tonight, while Lee had on a nice pair of khaki slacks with a white blouse and cream jacket, Kizzy's full-skirted green and white polka-dot dress was cinched in the waist with a velvet ribbon. Her trademark blond French twist was perfect, as was her polished pink fingernails.

As I neared the coffee urn, I saw GB O'Rourke and his wife, Millie, filling their cups. Their backs were to me and I heard Millie say to her husband, "If that witch suggests one more time that your recipe isn't the real McCoy, we're going to need to take care of her."

I paused. Was the "her" Millie referred to another contestant?

"Ms. Cutler says she knows she's seen my cupcake somewhere before." GB's voice was tense. "I made up that recipe, but she warned me that she's got one of her employees searching the Internet, and if she finds proof it isn't an original creation, she'll kick me out of the contest. What if someone else thought of the same recipe before me and she finds it?"

"That can't happen," Millie snapped. "Even if you're completely innocent, your congregation wouldn't forget an accusation like that."

Evidently, GB was a minister. I tucked the piece of data away, making a note to myself to avoid the preacher and his wife in the future. It always seemed to me that people who wanted to share their religious views with me never wanted to have me share mine with them. When I noticed Millie staring at me, I nodded and quickly continued on to my table.

Taking my seat, I whispered to Poppy, "Did you see that Gwen's here?"

"It was hard to miss her." Poppy giggled. "She made a big deal about moving her aunt's lame angel food cake to the front of the dessert table."

"She could have put that dried-up piece of crap on an illuminated pedestal and offered to pay people to eat it, and it still would be the last item of bakery left." I rolled my eyes. "Mrs. C always buys her pastry contributions from the day-old shelf, and everyone around here knows it. Her only hope of getting someone to take a slice is that one of the out-of-towners forgot his or her glasses and can't see how shriveled up it is."

"Yep. People in these parts take their food seriously." Poppy took a bite of her brownie. She moaned at the chocolaty goodness, then said, "And it's the ultimate humiliation to have your contribution to the potluck dinner be the platter that's still full."

"Too true." With the edge of my fork, I cut into Gran's chocolate chip marshmallow pie. "I doubt city folks would understand, but in a small town, it's a matter of pride to be thought of as a good cook." I brought the delectable morsel to my lips. "I've seen sweet old ladies who normally wouldn't harm a fly ready to slit their neighbor's throat with a cake knife when they suspected that their secret family recipe had been stolen or replicated."

We finished our desserts in companionable silence; then as Poppy scoured her dish for crumbs, she said, "I just realized that I haven't seen Harlee today. I know she didn't answer her phone when Ronni tried to contact her about Fallon and she didn't come to the door when you went by last night, but was she at the village square this afternoon for the Cupcake Weekend kickoff? I didn't notice her up on the bandstand with Winnie and the other committee heads."

"I don't think so. But we weren't up there, either." I craned my neck and scanned the church hall. "It doesn't look as if Harlee's here." My chest tightened. "You don't think anything has happened to her, do you?"

"Surely Ronni's been in touch with her," Poppy said, frowning. "She's called and texted me a bazillion times today to make sure Gossip Central is all set for the after-hours party tonight."

"Yeah. Ronni's on top of things and she certainly would have said something if Harlee was AWOL." I scanned the room one more time but still didn't see

Harlee anywhere. "There's a full house for the fashion show. We sold the last pair of tickets for the show by three o'clock."

"Mystery solved." Poppy's brow smoothed. "Harlee probably was too busy getting everything ready for the show to come here for dinner. I was amazed that she managed to talk the school board into letting us use the high school auditorium."

"That was quite a coup." I sat back and sipped my coffee. "The board doesn't usually allow groups to rent out the school facilities."

"The hefty donation that Kizzy Cutler's Cupcakes made probably was more persuasive than anything Harlee said at the meeting." Poppy smirked. "I heard that even the superintendent was impressed."

"I wonder why Boone isn't here." I didn't have to look around. If Boone St. Onge had been at the dinner, he would have been sitting with Poppy and me. The three of us had been best friends since childhood. "He was invited, wasn't he?" Boone was one of only three attorneys in Shadow Bend and had done all the legal work for the contest weekend, so he should have been given a ticket for the dinner.

"It's his folks' fortieth anniversary. The three of them were going to Kansas City for dinner and a show," Poppy explained.

"Seriously?" I asked. "Mr. and Mrs. St. Onge celebrate their anniversary?" Except for a brief time when Boone was falsely accused of murder, his folks hadn't spoken to each other since he was five. They were still married and still lived together in the same house, but they only communicated through notes. The invention of e-mail and texting had saved both Boone's sanity and a couple of dozen forests.

"What can I say?" Poppy shrugged, not much for incongruity. "They must figure if they're still married, they've earned an anniversary celebration, even if Boone has to go along as their private interpreter."

"I suppose." Now that everyone was accounted for, I glanced at my watch. It was seven thirty-five. "We should start to head over to the high school. The fashion show starts in less than half an hour."

"Speaking of missing in action," Poppy said, picking up her purse and standing, "have you heard anything from either of your hot hunks lately?"

"No." I shook my head. "But Noah just left this morning and it's hard for Jake to call."

"So you subscribe to the theory that if you love someone, you should let him go?"

"Unfortunately, I didn't seem to have a choice in the matter." I shrugged. "At least if they return to me, they're mine."

"Or"—Poppy grinned—"if they come back to you, maybe no one else wanted them."

"How comforting."

Poppy strolled toward Ronni, who was standing with Kizzy and Lee at the front of the church hall. "But it might be time to find a guy who isn't too busy to be around for you."

"My thoughts exactly." I followed Poppy. "If a relationship is going to grow into something long-lasting, the two people involved need to share the same geography more often than not. Although some absences are more understandable than others."

"Possibly." Poppy stopped and turned to look at me, her expression serious. "But everyone makes choices, and just because those choices are noble ones doesn't mean that you have to accept them."

Before I could respond to Poppy, Ronni announced to the crowd, "Those of you attending the fashion show should begin to make your way over to the high school now. Afterward, there will be a party at Gossip Central with music and munchies. Everybody's invited."

Poppy and I were standing right near the head table, and just then we overheard Lee call out.

"Oh, shoot!" she said, looking up from digging through her purse. "Can one of you give Kizzy a ride? I forgot something at the B and B."

"She can ride with me," Ronni offered. "If that's okay with you, Kizzy."

"That's fine with me," Kizzy answered, then turned to her business partner and asked, "What did you forget, Lee?

"My pills." Lee took off at a trot. "Thanks, Ronni! See you all there."

A few minutes later, the rest of us headed toward the exit. The mayor trailed us like a lost puppy until one of his constituents beckoned him over. As Kizzy reached the door, her cell beeped, indicating she had an incoming text. She was a few paces ahead of the rest of us and continued to move as she gazed down at her phone. I was watching her, wondering how she could walk without tripping, when she stepped onto the asphalt of the parking lot. At that exact moment, a car with its headlights turned off sped toward her.

We all froze, staring at Kizzy, who was apparently so engrossed in reading her message that she didn't seem to notice the three tons of steel hurtling toward her. Without thinking, I made a flying tackle. The cupcake tycoon and I soared through the air, landing hard on the blacktop. As the car roared past, I swear I could feel the bumper kiss my rear end.

CHAPTER 9

"Really, I'm fine," I repeated for the fiftieth time, brushing bits of gravel and dirt from the knees of my white slacks. "Is Kizzy all right?" I didn't remember seeing the cupcake queen after Poppy yanked me to my feet and led me over to the sidewalk.

"She seemed okay. She complained that you ruined her dress and messed up her hair, so once Ronni was sure you weren't hurt, she drove Kizzy back to the B and B to change." Poppy took my hands and gazed at the scrapes on my palms. "That woman makes me want to high-five her . . ." Poppy paused dramatically. "In the face . . ." Another dramatic pause. "With a baseball bat."

"Yeah." I snickered at the image. "Me, too."

"Why in the hell did you throw yourself in front of a speeding car for that self-centered witch?"

"I didn't think about her character, just that she was about to become roadkill." I looked myself over. It seemed as if I had escaped serious injury, although I couldn't say the same for my pants.

A concerned group from the dinner had gathered, including Winnie, who said, "We never used to have crazy drivers like that in Shadow Bend. Everybody is in such a doggone hurry these days."

"Anyone who drives like hell is bound to get there someday," I commented, then looked around and asked, "Did the car that almost creamed us stop?"

"Nope." Poppy scowled. "If anything, the driver put the pedal to the metal and tore out of the parking lot as fast as he could."

"Oh, my Lord." Lauren Neumann, our dinner companion from Des Moines, joined the circle around me. "I was in the bathroom and a lady dashed in and said two women had almost gotten killed in the parking lot." Lauren rummaged through her purse, plucked out a packet of Wet Ones, and ripped it open. "Here, you'd better clean up your hands before you stain your nice outfit."

"Thanks." I accepted the moist towelette. Although my slacks were a total write-off, I didn't want to wreck my tunic as well, so I gingerly wiped the blood from my palms. "I'm sort of surprised anyone had time, or the presence of mind, to witness the accident, run to the restroom, and announce the incident to everyone."

"I thought that was odd, too," Lauren said, nodding solemnly as she tugged at the Peter Pan collar of her pale blue blouse.

As she returned to digging through her purse, I noticed that although Lauren wore a navy-and-green-plaid jumper that I had last seen in a catalogue selling Catholic school uniforms, there was a tiny vine of roses inked around her wrist. I would have missed the tattoo if her watchband hadn't been pushed up her arm when she plunged her hand deeper into her handbag. It made me wonder if there was more to this woman than her appearance would suggest.

Lauren produced a small tube of antiseptic ointment,

squirted some on my wounds, and said, "You would think that lady would have stayed around to help rather than make a beeline for the bathroom to announce what had happened."

"Or call the police." My heart was still racing. It felt as if I had downed a can of Rip Rock. I had tried that energy drink once when I was working ridiculously long hours in my job as a financial consultant, and the insane amount of caffeine in it had kept me up for two days straight, which I sort of liked. But since I could do without the migraine, dizziness, and tremor hangover, I'd never drunk the stuff again.

"You were lucky." Lauren gave me a couple of Band-Aids. "My daughter's friend is in a wheelchair because of an intoxicated driver like that."

"Who said the driver was smashed?" I gave a ragged little laugh. "There wasn't any alcohol served at the dinner."

"Did anyone get the license number of that car?" Poppy asked.

I looked around the circle, and everyone was glancing at his or her neighbor.

When no one answered, Poppy said, "Did anyone call the cops?"

Winnie waved her cell phone in the air and said, "I did. The dispatcher told me they would be here any minute. I wonder what's taking them so long. It's not as if Shadow Bend is a hotbed of crime."

As if Winnie's words had summoned it, the distant sound of a siren grew louder and louder. A second later, we all watched as a squad car pulled up next to the church hall and Chief Kincaid got out.

He glanced to where Poppy and I stood, then hurried over to his daughter and demanded, "Are you all right? I was told there was a hit-and-run."

"I'm fine, Dad." She seemed shocked by his concern. "Dev was the one who was nearly flattened by some stupid guy who thought the parking lot was a warm-up lap for the Indy 500 track."

"Explain." Chief Kincaid turned to me, flipping open his notepad.

"Someone nearly ran Kizzy Cutler over. Then, instead of seeing if she was okay, they drove away." I wanted to make it clear I hadn't been the one wandering around without watching where I was going.

"Hold on." Chief Kincaid uncapped his pen. "Start from the beginning."

After I told him everything I remembered about the incident, the chief turned to the people standing around us and asked, "Did any of you get the make, model, or license plate of the vehicle?"

They looked at each other, then at the chief, and finally someone said, "It was low to the ground. Maybe one of those sports cars. But it was too dark to see the color."

"Anyone recognize the driver?" Chief Kincaid demanded with a sigh.

More headshakes.

"No one saw anything." The muscle beneath the chief's left eye twitched.

"We weren't paying attention," I explained. "The car didn't have its headlights on, and then when I saw it speeding toward Kizzy, my focus was on getting her out of the way."

"How about the rest of you?" Chief Kincaid addressed the crowd.

"Most of them got here after the car was long gone," Poppy said.

"And you, did you see anything?" the chief asked his daughter.

"Sorry." Poppy's voice broke. "When Dev darted in

front of the car, my eyes were glued on her. I was worried that she was about to be flattened."

"Maybe Kizzy or Ronni saw something," I offered. "They went to the B and B so Kizzy could change, but they'll be at the high school auditorium for the fashion show after that." I checked my watch. "Actually, we all need to get over there ASAP."

"Stop by the station tomorrow to sign your statement." The chief sighed again. "You know the drill." Then he raised his voice and announced, "If anyone remembers anything, let me know."

"Should we have Kizzy and Ronni call you?" I asked, edging toward my car.

It had dawned on me that Gran hadn't been among the crowd. Then I remembered she and Frieda had been on the committee in charge of setting up for the dinner, so they were excused from cleaning afterward. They had probably left as soon as the food was served. *Shoot!* I needed to let Gran know I was okay before the grapevine got to her and she thought I was dead.

"No, thanks." Chief Kincaid shook his head. "I'm going over to the high school right now. I need to have a long talk with Ms. Cutler." There was an expression on his face that I couldn't interpret as he muttered to himself, "And it needs to be in person."

After the chief left, Poppy grabbed me in a hug and said, "Don't ever scare me like that again. I was sure you were about to be killed."

"Believe me, in the future, I'll think twice before rushing in to save someone."

"You'd better." Poppy squeezed me harder. "I don't want to have to break into your store and steal your laptop."

"Huh?" I eased out of Poppy's embrace. "Why would you need to do that?"

"Because when you die, a BFF's duty is to immediately clear your computer history." Poppy snickered. "You especially need that last favor with the kind of merchandise you research for your erotic baskets."

Chuckling at the way my friend's mind worked, I told Poppy that I'd meet her at the fashion show, then grabbed the pair of jeans that I kept in the trunk of my Z4 and raced back into the church hall. Once I was in the empty bathroom, I immediately called Gran. Luckily, no one had informed her about my near miss, and after telling her what had happened, I reassured her that I was fine.

Until Gran said she'd let my father know I was okay, it hadn't occurred to me that he might hear the rumors and be worried about me, too. I thanked her, told her not to wait up, then disconnected. I still wasn't used to my dad being around, and the adjustment was a lot harder than I was willing to admit.

Pushing aside my personal life, a talent for which I should have been given an Academy Award, I stepped out of my white slacks. Not only was the cotton stained with tar and blood, but the fabric was shredded beyond repair. I wadded them up, stuffed them in the trash, then examined my shins. The scrapes weren't too bad, and after washing off the dried gore, I shimmied into my jeans. Since I kept them in the trunk mainly in case I had to change a tire while I was dressed up, they weren't the nicest pair I owned. But they were a darn sight better than walking around in the ruined pants I'd just discarded. At least the faded denim was blood free.

It was nearly eight thirty by the time I turned into the high school parking lot. I had already missed half an hour of the fashion show, and once again, parking spots were at a premium. As I circled the lot, hoping for a miracle, or at least for someone needing to leave early, I admired the sprawling brick structure.

Shadow Bend's education system had come a long way from the original one-room schoolhouse that my great-grandparents had attended. An elementary and high school had been built in the forties. Then a few years ago, the board had moved the sixth, seventh, and eighth graders into the old high school and put up this new building. The locals wouldn't admit that it was because of the commuters relocating into the area from Kansas City that the schools could finally afford to expand. But it was their taxes, and the taxes of the businesses that sprang up because of them, that financed the construction.

Having attended the old high school, I'd only been inside the new one a few times, but the brightness and space were a welcome change from the gloomy, cramped institution where I had spent four years sitting in tiny, dark classrooms. I walked down the quiet, well-lit hall, noting the graffiti-free lockers and the fresh paint on the walls. This was nothing like what I remembered from my high school days.

When I neared the auditorium doors, I could hear Harlee's rich contralto describing the outfit currently being modeled. Plainly, Poppy had been right, and Harlee was fine. She had probably just been too busy organizing the show to answer her phone. I was relieved that the consignment shop owner was present and apparently okay. In the back of my mind, I had half believed that she'd disappeared.

As I scanned the audience for Poppy, I was amazed at how the theater had been transformed to accommodate a fashion show. A runway had been built from the stage midway down the center aisle. That alone must have cost a pretty penny. Evidently, Kizzy Cutler's Cupcakes had spared no expense for the rollout of their new line.

"What took you so long?" Poppy whispered as I slid into the seat she'd saved for me. "I was starting to get worried that you'd thrown yourself in front of another speeding vehicle or dived in the river to save a drowning dog."

"Maybe tomorrow," I joked, keeping my voice low. "I had to call Gran, which took a while. Then I needed to clean up and change."

"You missed some cute clothes." Poppy's attention was riveted to a pretty redhead wearing a short black-and-white sundress and currently walking the runway. "I wonder how much that is."

"It depends." I squinted at the model. "Are these outfits from Harlee's consignment shop or are they brand-new from the designers?"

"They're all from Forever Used," Poppy said, making a note in her program. "I had no idea that previously worn clothes could look like they were fresh from the racks of Nordstrom or Lord and Taylor."

"Uh-huh," I murmured noncommittally. I actually did know. When I'd quit my megasalary job, I put a lot of my barely worn or never-worn clothing in consignment shops. I'd raised enough cash from selling them to pay for the first batch of materials I'd needed for my basket business.

The next hour passed quickly as we oohed and aahed over the fashions. Then while a blonde wearing a powder blue Alexander McQueen draped-silk chiffon bustier gown stomped the runway, I heard a male voice behind me say, "The word on the street is that instead of the ten-thousand-dollar grand prize being given in cash, that Cutler bitch is going to do some kind of structured payment. We need that money now, not a few bucks at a time."

Casually turning my head so that I could see the speaker from the corner of my eye, I recognized Russell Neumann from our dinner table.

"Honey, you shouldn't get so upset." Lauren patted her husband's arm. "There's no guarantee that I'm going to win, and anyway, that's just a rumor."

"Oh, you're going to win all right." Russell's smile was smug and he lowered his voice and whispered, "Thomasina Giancarlo and I had a little chat during supper, and she understands that if she wants to stay in the good old U.S. of A., it's in her best interest for your cupcake to be deemed the best one."

"Russell," Lauren hissed, "you could get fired for using your position with immigration to blackmail someone."

"Not without proof." Russell held his finger to his lips. "I might actually get a promotion for discovering that someone as prominent as her is here illegally."

Before Lauren could respond, Harlee stepped onto the stage and announced, "If you are interested in purchasing any of the pieces you've seen here tonight, there's a form in the back of your program listing the size and I'll be at a table out front to collect the orders and the money. It will be on a first-come, first-serve basis."

Kizzy joined Harlee, and after she thanked everyone for coming, she reminded them about the after-hours party at Gossip Central hosted by Kizzy Cutler's Cupcakes and wished everyone a good evening. Basking in the applause, she threw the audience a kiss and walked offstage.

"Well, that was an interesting performance," I murmured. I hadn't seen Kizzy in the audience and had wondered if the chief had taken her to the police station for questioning. If he had, she was already back, and she had changed into another gorgeous vintage dress—this one a strapless red-and-white floral silk with a red grosgrain sash—and her French twist was once again perfect. "Hard to believe that she was nearly killed a couple of hours ago. She either has nerves of steel or is a really good actress."

"My vote is all of the above." Poppy pushed into the exiting throng and hurried to follow her. "You don't have a hugely successful business like hers without both of those traits."

Poppy wanted to place an order for one of the outfits she'd seen, so we wormed our way through the crowd and made a beeline for Harlee's table.

There was already a long line and Poppy thrust her form and credit card at me and said, "Here. I have to get to Gossip Central to welcome the first arrivals." She waved. "See you in a few."

While I waited to place Poppy's order, I thought about why Chief Kincaid might be so interested in talking to Kizzy, beyond the obvious reason that she had nearly been run down by a hit-and-run driver. Could he suspect that the incident was deliberate and not an accident? Now that I'd had the thought, I realized how much sense it made. Could it be that whatever had happened to Fallon was intended for Kizzy? Was someone trying to kill the cupcake queen?

CHAPTER 10

When I got to the front of the line, I handed Poppy's order form and charge card to Harlee and said, "The fashion show was wonderful. It must have been a lot of work to bring it all together."

"It wasn't too bad." Harlee checked to see if the dress Poppy wanted was still available. Nodding to me that the outfit hadn't been purchased yet, Harlee ran Poppy's Visa though the reader on her smartphone and gave it back to me. "I have a lot of experience coordinating large numbers of people and materials."

"That's right." I smiled. "You recently retired from the armed forces. What branch did you serve in?"

"Army," Harlee answered, then looked over my shoulder and said to the person behind me, "Which piece were you interested in?"

Not one to miss an obvious dismissal, I picked up the receipt, wrapped it around Poppy's credit card, tucked the packet into my purse, and moved aside. But instead of leaving, I said, "We haven't seen much of you the past couple of days. I hope you're coming to the after-hours bash at Gossip Central."

"Probably not," Harlee answered as she continued

to process the next customer's order. "I'm not much for that kind of party."

"You should stop by for a few minutes anyway," I urged. "Have one drink and relax after a job well done. People have commented about your absence. You may have been gone from Shadow Bend a long time, but I bet you remember how important it is to show your face."

"I need to make sure everything here is ready for the teardown crew tomorrow," Harlee hedged. "And I'd like to get a head start on assembling the orders from tonight. I promised the buyers that they could pick up their clothes by Sunday afternoon."

"That's all well and good, but from one businesswoman to another, community relations trump almost anything else you can do to promote your shop." I wasn't sure why I was so interested in Harlee's coming to the party, but the more she resisted, the more I was intent on her attending. "An hour's socializing is well worth your time. Believe me, you don't want people to start wondering if you think you're too good to hang out with them."

"You seem to really know your way around the potholes of small-town living," Harlee commented as she took care of another customer.

"I should." I grimaced. "I've taken the wrong route enough times to qualify for a free AAA membership."

"You're probably right," Harlee conceded. "I'll stop by as soon as I finish here." She gestured to the remaining women in line. "See you in an hour or so." Smiling, she added, "Save me a seat."

Gossip Central's lot was packed. The parking situation tonight was beginning to remind me of when I worked in downtown Kansas City, and I wasn't enjoying the trip down memory lane. I finally called Poppy, who sent someone out to open the door to her garage so I could leave my car inside next to her Hummer. She had put up the metal storage building at the same time she added her apartment and offices onto the barn's original structure.

Once I climbed out of my Z4, the server who'd unlocked the garage door for me let me in through the delivery entrance. She hurried back to work, but I detoured into Poppy's office to put her receipt-wrapped Visa under the fake flowers in the high-heel-shaped vase on the desk. After texting Poppy to tell her that her credit card was in our usual hiding spot, I wound my way through a long hallway and pushed open a pair of metal swinging doors into the club's central area. The noise hit me like a tsunami, and I paused, letting my ears adjust to the sound, before stepping into the room.

Poppy was behind the bar, mixing up drinks and serving customers, and I waved at her as I worked my way forward to the middle of the room. The place was bursting at the seams, and it took me a good ten minutes to get from the entrance to the center of the dance floor. Locating Ronni, Winnie, Kizzy, and Lee took even longer.

The quartet had claimed one of the smaller lounges Poppy converted from the original stalls. Its theme was nineteen fifties and early sixties beauty salon. Seating was the old-fashioned, chrome-domed hair-dryer chairs, which seemed apropos for someone like Kizzy, who dressed to match those decades. The tables were Art Deco manicure stations, and the posters on the wall featured ads for Gayla bobby pins, Max Factor lipstick, and Jewel invisible nylon hair nets.

After greeting everyone, I claimed the only empty seat, and said, "That's quite a crowd out there. Every single parking spot is taken."

"The Cupcake Weekend is even more successful than we had hoped." Ronni grinned. "My B and B is full, the Cattlemen's Motel has their no-vacancy sign lit up, and I've heard some of the people in town have even rented out rooms."

"Terrific!" I was thrilled that Shadow Bend was getting such an infusion of cash. "My store has been packed all day, too."

"I'm not at all surprised." Kizzy tilted her head back and drained the remaining liquid from her martini glass. "Kizzy Cutler's Cupcakes have become an American icon. Everyone is anxious to be a part of the new line and be able to say they were present when the winning flavor was selected."

"Of course." Ronni nodded. "I knew this promo would do well, just not this well."

"Then you underestimated the appeal of my cupcakes," Kizzy said, dismissing Ronni.

"Before we go on, don't you have something to say to Devereaux?" Lee asked her partner.

Kizzy remained silent until Lee tapped her arm; then she bared her teeth in a false smile and said, "Ah, yes. Thank you for pushing me out of the way of that car." Before I could respond, she added, "Although a simple shouted warning would have been sufficient and prevented the destruction of one of my favorite dresses."

"You're welcome and I'm sorry." I wasn't sure what the proper reply was, so I decided to use them both. "I guess I leaped before I thought."

"Yes." Kizzy nodded. "You did." She held out her empty glass and said to no one in particular, "I'd like another, but drier this time with Bombay Sapphire gin and two olives."

"I'll get it." Lee rose to her feet. "Anyone else want a refill?"

Ronni and Winnie both ordered frozen margaritas, so I volunteered to help Lee carry the drinks. As we made our way out of the lounge and across the dance floor, I excused myself to use the restroom, telling Lee I'd meet her at the bar.

There was a line snaking out of the ladies' room, and I briefly considered using the men's bathroom, which appeared to be empty, but stopped when I spotted Q and her brother a few feet away. They were having an intense conversation, so I drifted over and ducked behind a partition. I wasn't certain why I had decided to eavesdrop on them, but if I had learned one thing as a financial consultant, it was that knowledge was power. With Fallon's poisoning, the hit-and-run that almost wiped out the cupcake queen, Russell Neumann's blackmail scheme, and Reverend GB's possible recipe plagiarism, there was no doubt in my mind that something odd was going on. And I was pretty darn sure I needed to keep on top of it.

Q was crying so hard that I had to lean forward to make out what she was saying between her sobs. Finally, she wiped at her tears and said, "Kizzy claimed that I had ruined her hair and that she looked ridiculous. She threatened to get me fired if you don't arrange to reshoot her segment, so I had to try to stop her."

"Why are you just telling me this now?" Dirk demanded. "We did that piece with her Thursday afternoon. Is that the reason for your emergency visit to your shrink?"

"Yeah," Q admitted. "But after I talked to my therapist, I thought I could handle Kizzy's demands myself."

"Why were you doing Kizzy Cutler's hair in the first place?" Dirk asked. "You aren't supposed to work on anyone that isn't in front of the camera."

"She made me," Q whined. "She said that since she was taping an interview for the program, I had to do her hair and makeup." Q hiccupped. "Kizzy said it was in her contract with the network."

"Shit!" Dirk exploded. "I pulled a lot of strings to get you this job. What in the hell did you do to that bitch's hair to upset her?"

"Nothing," Q said. "I mean, something, but it looked good even though I had never done a French twist before. Who in this day and age wears that style?"

"Hell if I know." Dirk was quiet, then said, "There's no way Merry is going to be willing to redo that interview. She's one of the most hard-assed of the channel's hosts." He sighed. "And I doubt there's any way I could edit a new interview into the existing one."

"You can't let them fire me, Dirk," Q sobbed. "If I don't have this job, Mom and Dad will make me go back into the nuthouse."

"There's just no way to fix the spot, baby sis. There are too many shots with both Merry and Kizzy in the same frame." Dirk's voice hardened. "Which means we may have to come up with a plan B."

"One of your plan Bs is what got me sent to the loony bin in the first place," Q wailed, then changed her tone and teased, "On the other hand, before that incident, I did enjoy a good plan B."

I blinked and eased away from the duo. Now, that sounded scary. How had Q tried to stop Kizzy? Could it have been with a speeding car? I needed to tell Chief Kincaid about this conversation tomorrow when I stopped by the cop shop to sign my statement.

While I had been eavesdropping on Q and Dirk, the line for the bathroom had dwindled, and fifteen minutes later, I joined Lee at the bar. She was still waiting her turn to be served, but it was too noisy to talk, so I used the time to look around. It was nice to see so many people having a good time. I waved to a few of our tablemates from dinner and noticed that Dirk was filming the event for the Dessert Channel. I wondered if the television exposure would bring in more customers to Poppy's club and hoped that the dime store would get some TV footage, too.

Lee had gotten Kizzy's martini and the margaritas for Winnie and Ronni, but since I was still waiting for my order, she asked for a tray and headed back to the lounge. I had requested a bottle of wine and two glasses, figuring that at some point Poppy would take a break and join us, and that she'd need a drink.

I had just stepped away from the bar when I spotted Harlee and shouted, "Over here!"

She signaled that she'd heard me, and I waited for her to make her way to where I was standing. Once she joined me, I led her through the crowd toward the Beauty Parlor.

"If I'd known it was going to be this much of a madhouse, I wouldn't have let you talk me into coming," Harlee said as we stepped into the relative quiet of the lounge.

"Really?" Kizzy stood and faced Harlee. "I remember when you and I both used to love a loud party." She raised a brow. "The crazier the better."

"People change." Harlee's voice was even, but her posture was rigid.

"Possibly." Kizzy shrugged. "But, in my experience, not very often." She sank back down and gestured to the chair next to her. "Have a seat.

I watched as Harlee reluctantly sat next to the cupcake tycoon. Harlee had mentioned going to school with Kizzy, but Kizzy's comments made it sound as if they had been close friends.

"You and I have so much to catch up on." Kizzy took Harlee's hand. "Lee will get you a drink while we talk about old times."

I glanced at Lee. If they were business partners, why did she allow Kizzy to order her around? In her interactions with other people, Lee hadn't struck me as spineless or easily intimidated.

"I'd love a glass of wine." Harlee quickly removed her fingers from Kizzy's grasp and reached for her purse. "Preferably Chilean cabernet sauvignon, but any red wine will do."

"The bar's swamped right now, but I have a bottle of Australian Shiraz and an extra glass." I held out the wine for her inspection. "Lee and I just spent nearly half an hour trying to get served."

"Sounds fine to me." Harlee took the glass offered her and held it out for me to pour. "Thanks, Dev." She took a sip. "I needed that."

"Now, what have you been up to since high school?" Kizzy leaned forward, an enigmatic expression on her face. "I was shocked to see your name on the Cupcake Weekend committee. I had no idea you had moved back to Shadow Bend. And why open a consignment shop of all things?"

"After you left town, I joined the army." Harlee's tone was cool, but little waves rippled across the wine in her glass, indicating that her hand was shaking. "I guess you and I both changed our mind about what we wanted to be when we grew up."

"Yes. I realized that college wasn't for me." Kizzy sat back. "I wanted to run my own business. It took me a while to convince a backer that people would pay big bucks for designer cupcakes, but once I found the right person and he tasted my amazing recipes"—Kizzy smiled triumphantly—"the rest, as they say, is history."

"Yes." Harlee took another gulp of wine. "History." She stared into her glass. "It's strange how often history gets rewritten."

"Sometimes the best thing we can do is forget the past and move on." Kizzy put her fingers on Harlee's knee and squeezed. "For everyone."

"You asked why a consignment shop," Harlee said. "It's because I like to see items that have perhaps had an unhappy past get a chance for a fresh start with a new owner that will treasure them."

There was a definite undertone present in the exchange between Harlee and Kizzy. I sensed that there was another, more significant meaning to all of their words. Clearly, the high school pals had had a falling-out. I wondered what had happened to make them go their separate ways and lose touch for such a long time.

Ronni and Winnie distracted me with a question about tomorrow's schedule, and I turned my attention to them. The three of us huddled together, discussing the logistics of transporting the finalists' first-round cupcakes to my second floor. We decided to use pairs of couriers so that no one could be accused of tampering with the finished products before the judges evaluated them.

When Winnie went off on a tangent about how we should trust everybody to act in an honorable manner rather than fear the worst, I glanced over at the other women. Kizzy and Harlee were speaking in low voices, and Lee was watching them both, a wary expression on her face.

Having finished with the details for Saturday's plan, I got up and sat next to Harlee. Kizzy had gone to the restroom—one task she couldn't ask Lee to do for her—and Lee was on her cell phone. Harlee had finished her

Shiraz and accepted another when I waved the wine bottle at her.

As she finished the refill in one gulp, I asked, "Drowning your sorrows?"

"Nope." Harlee held out her empty glass for more. "Just taking the little buggers for a little dip in the pool."

"I'm guessing that Kizzy is why you've been avoiding the various activities since she arrived in town," I said as I poured.

"Yep. I was home when you came by my place last night, I just didn't answer the door, and I ignored all of Ronni's messages." Harlee swirled the wine in her glass. "Considering how we parted twenty years ago, it seemed the easiest way to handle the situation. But your point about needing to show my face to ensure goodwill for my business was well taken." She sipped. "Kizzy will leave on Sunday, but I plan to be in Shadow Bend for the rest of my life."

"I take it, back in the day, you two were close friends?" I asked.

"We were besties." Harlee's eyes were sad. "Inseparable. We thought we'd go to the same college, marry our high school boyfriends, and live next door to each other." She sighed. "We had that fatal combination of hubris and a sense of immortality. We believed we could do no wrong and that nothing we did would affect us."

"Typical teenagers," I commented, then asked, "So, what happened between you two?" Yes, I knew I was prying, but she had aroused my curiosity. Had Kizzy let the teenage Harlee down the way Noah had me during our high school years? Not having been in school at the same time they were, I had no idea what had happened between them.

"It's not important now. Too much water has passed under that particular bridge for it to matter anymore." Harlee reached for her purse and dug out her wallet. "How much do I owe you for the wine?"

"It's on me." I waved her offer away. I was feeling flush with all the extra money from the Cupcake Weekend in my bank account and cash register. "You can buy the drinks the next time the Saturday Night Prayer Circle gets together."

"Thanks." Harlee stood up, then squinted at my hands and said, "Nice scrapes. Who's your exterior decorator?"

Evidently, Harlee hadn't heard about the hit-and-run, so I explained what had happened after the dinner.

Harlee shook her head. "Somehow, no matter what the situation, other people always get hurt and Kizzy always comes out unscathed." She sighed, then said, "I'm going to go and mingle, since that's why I came to the party to begin with. See you tomorrow."

A moment later, when Harlee and Kizzy passed each other in the lounge's doorway, I noticed that neither spoke. It was almost as if all of the good times they'd shared had been completely erased by whatever had happened that ended the friendship. What in the world had caused that kind of rift? I thought about losing either of my best friends and shuddered. Poppy and Boone were vital to my sanity.

Kizzy took Harlee's recently vacated seat, glanced at her watch, and asked, "How much longer do you think we need to stay?"

I checked the time and said, "Probably only another few minutes. I think most people will start to drift away soon after midnight. Remember, most small-town folks are early to bed and early to rise."

"Good." Kizzy leaned her head against the back of the chair. "It's been an exhausting day, and having that police chief tell me he thinks that Fallon was murdered and that I was the intended victim of the poison was the buttercream on the cupcake."

CHAPTER 11

When I arrived home after the party, the windows in my father's apartment over the garage were dark and only the night-light above the stove lit my way down the hall. As soon as I reached my room, I stripped off my clothes, washed my face, and fell into bed.

The next thing I knew, my alarm was buzzing and it was six the next morning. I'd been too tired the night before to think much about Kizzy's dramatic announcement, but now that I was rested, her words played over and over again in my mind as I showered, got dressed, and headed to the police station.

Although I had speculated that someone might be targeting the cupcake queen, it was an entirely different matter to hear that the cops agreed with me. And Kizzy's utter refusal to discuss the situation was beyond frustrating. She ignored my suggestion that a killer running loose in Shadow Bend could drive all the attendees out of town, and she didn't seem to understand my concern that the contest might be ruined.

Instead of answering my questions regarding exactly what Chief Kincaid had said to her, Kizzy had gotten to her feet, summoned Lee, and left Gossip Central. I wasn't used to being summarily dismissed like that, and it irked me to no end that I couldn't lash out at her. Next time, there was a good possibility that I wouldn't be able to control myself.

Unfortunately, the chief wasn't at the PD when I arrived, so I couldn't try to pry any info out of him or tell him about the discussion I had overheard between Dirk and Q. Instead, after I signed my statement regarding last night's hit-and-run, I was forced to write him a note outlining the siblings' conversation. I had briefly considered holding on to that tidbit in order to have some intel to trade for information the police had discovered, but my conscience wouldn't allow me to do that. What if Q was the one trying to kill Kizzy and her next attempt was successful?

Frustrated, I left the station and drove to work. As I entered the dime store, I mentally ran through the day's agenda. The store would close up at three, rather than four, which was its usual Saturday closing time. It would reopen in the evening to take advantage of the crowds that I anticipated would gather in the town square for the cookout starting at six and the fireworks show scheduled for nine thirty.

In our frantic planning for the Cupcake Weekend, we had nearly forgotten that Saturday was the Fourth of July. The mayor had hastily arranged for a pyrotechnic spectacular to be staged so that no one would accuse our community of being unpatriotic. In his estimation, the fact that the late-night event gave him a chance to make yet another speech was a bonus. Still, he hadn't insisted on singing the "Star-Spangled Banner" in his horrendously off-key tenor, so we were counting that narrow escape as one in the win column.

As I walked through my shop, putting on the lights

and readying the cash register for customers, I thought about how to persuade Chief Kincaid to share exactly why he thought Kizzy might be in danger. Did I have anything else to trade? I vaguely recalled something flitting through my mind right before I dropped off to sleep. What had it been?

Just as the idea was about to break to the surface of my consciousness, Dad and Hannah arrived. While I was giving them instructions for the day, the sleigh bells above the door jingled. I checked my watch. It was exactly nine o'clock and the first customers poured into the store. With people clamoring for my attention, all thoughts concerning Fallon, Kizzy, and the near accident fled my mind and I concentrated on helping folks spend their money.

The continued flow of shoppers was amazing, and even Gwen Bourne, who rarely patronized my store, came by to purchase one of life's little necessities. It was the only place in sixty miles that sold Espresso Addict dark chocolate bars, and Gwen had an eighty-gram-a-day habit.

I was distracted by the sight of Gwen flirting with my father at the candy case, and it took several seconds for me to notice that Kizzy had entered the shop. She wore her usual genial smile as she greeted her fans, but when she got to where I was standing behind the register, her lips pressed together in a displeased moue, which deepened the wrinkles that bracketed her mouth and the crease between her brows.

"Give me the key to your back entrance and the one to the second floor," Kizzy demanded, holding out her palm and tapping her foot.

"Why do you need the storeroom exit key?" I asked as I handed over the one to the second story. "I don't like to give that out."

"I have several cartons of material that I need to take upstairs and I assume you don't want me traipsing through your sales floor," she snapped.

"Are you by yourself?" I asked, surprised the cupcake tycoon was doing actual physical labor. "Where's Lee?"

"She's at the cooking school." Kizzy's lips pressed even tighter together. "My assistant would normally take care of putting the last touches out for the judging." The cupcake queen heaved a loud put-upon sigh. "But in Fallon's absence, I'm forced to see to the details myself since apparently no around here wants to earn any extra cash."

"How inconvenient for you," I commented, wanting to add that things were a hell of a lot worse for Fallon, but biting back the words just before they left my mouth. "Most available townspeople are already occupied with Cupcake Weekend activities, but I could ask my clerk if any of her friends would like a job."

"How about you lend me your clerk and you take one of her pals?" Kizzy suggested with a manipulative gleam in her eye. "I assume, since you seem to be a fairly sharp businesswoman, your employee's competent, or you wouldn't have hired her."

"I'm afraid that wouldn't work for me," I said firmly. "Let me go open that back door for you." I apologized to the customers waiting in line and promised that I would be right back, then flipped open the counter and gestured for Kizzy to follow me into the storage room. "This way."

"It would be easier if you just gave me the key," Kizzy complained.

"I don't mind." I unlocked the rear exit and said, "Please make sure you turn the dead bolt when you're finished unloading."

"Aren't you going to help me?" Kizzy asked, folding her arms.

"Sorry." I shook my head. "I'm certain you can manage just fine on your own. Last night, you mentioned missing your personal trainer, so think of this as a good workout."

"Your ridiculous little opinion has been noted." Kizzy's eyes swept my curves. "And I'm not the one who needs to get more exercise."

I drew in a sharp breath. Kizzy was getting damn close to my particular international enough mob, but instead of laying into her, I said, "You saw the line of shoppers waiting for me to ring up their sales. I need to get back out front."

"You wouldn't have that crowd if it weren't for my contest." Kizzy's pout was truly impressive. "Without help, I'm going to have to make three or four trips from the parking lot up to the display room."

"Sorry," I repeated, edging away from the petulant cupcake queen.

"Fine." Kizzy narrowed her eyes. "But I'm going to remember how uncooperative you've been and you might not be included in my next hometown promotion." She lifted her chin. "And I just might do this every year. That is, if I can get a little cooperation."

"Sorry," I repeated for the third time before hurrying back to the cash register. For about a second and a half, I questioned my decision, but then I mentally shook my head. I seriously doubted that Kizzy would have an annual cupcake contest in Shadow Bend, and even if she did, and she excluded me from the committee, the out-of-towners who attended would still patronize my shop.

Half an hour or so went by and the store was still crammed full of customers when I heard the faint ringing of the second-floor smoke detectors. For a moment, I froze and a voice inside my head wailed that my schedule was too full for a crisis today. Then my common sense kicked in and I yelled for everyone to get out of the building.

Leaving Hannah and my father to oversee the evacuation and call 911, I grabbed the fire extinguisher from behind the counter and raced over to the door leading to the stairwell. It was cool to the touch, so I yanked it open. When there were no clouds of billowing smoke to greet me, I took the steps two at a time, hoping against hope that the alarm was nothing more than a low backup battery.

Besides someone getting hurt or the store burning to the ground, my worst fear was of the fire sprinklers being triggered. Per the regulations for commercial establishments, the sprinklers had been installed every hundred and fifty square feet throughout the building, and they automatically came on if the temperature exceeded a certain point. Activation would cause an untold amount of water damage.

As I reached the top of the stairs, I called out, "Kizzy, are you up here?" There was no answer and I tried again. "Kizzy, are you here?" Again, there was silence.

Sniffing, I raced down the short hallway. The odor of smoke was coming from the office suite that had been left intact to use as a lounge for the judges. Skidding to a stop, I put my palm on the closed door's surface. The wood didn't feel hot, so I eased the door open. Kizzy lay on the floor, surrounded by a ring of burning papers.

Pulling the pin on the extinguisher, I aimed the nozzle at the circle of flames, squeezed the handle, and swept the fire from side to side. Ten seconds later, the fire appeared to be out, which was a good thing since I had used up all the foam and didn't have a second extinguisher with me.

Now that the smoke was clearing, I could see Kizzy lying facedown. It looked as if she had been hit over the head with the trophy lying next to her on the floor. The foot-tall Lucite pedestal topped with a crystal cupcake was spattered with gore, and the glass column was cracked near the metal base.

Kneeling by Kizzy's unconscious form, I grimaced. There was a lot of blood. Kizzy's French twist had come undone and her hair was matted with the sticky red stuff.

Oh. My. God! Was she dead? I resisted the urge to turn her over, having read that it was extremely dangerous to move an injured person. Instead, I checked for a pulse, then breathed a huge sigh of relief when I felt a strong beat against my fingertips.

I searched my pockets for my cell, until I remembered setting it down on the shelf under the register. As I debated whether I should leave Kizzy alone in order to go downstairs and telephone for an ambulance or wait for help to arrive in response to the alarm, I heard the fire truck's siren. A few seconds later, booted feet pounded up the stairs, and an instant after that, a firefighter in full turnout gear stomped into the office.

I pointed out the charred trash surrounding Kizzy, and after he made sure that the flames were totally extinguished, the firefighter called for an EMT. He then took my elbow and firmly escorted me out of the building. I joined my father and Hannah on the concrete bench in front of my dime store, and we all watched as various uniformed individuals hustled in and out of the glass door.

While we waited, I filled in my staff regarding the situation inside; then I borrowed Hannah's cell and called

Poppy. Thank goodness that I had her number memorized. After I explained the situation, Poppy promised to contact Ronni and Lee and have one of them telephone me on my clerk's phone. As I waited, I vowed never to be parted from my own cell again. If necessary, I would have it surgically Velcroed to my side.

The ambulance and Chief Kincaid had both arrived soon after I had been banished from my store. Both disappeared inside, the chief shooting me a frustrated glare. I wasn't sure why I was the object of his exasperation, but I was willing to bet that he would soon inform me of the reason. Meanwhile, I fielded questions from the folks who had gathered to watch the spectacle. While I was trying to downplay the incident to the crowd, both Ronni and Lee called and I lowered my voice, hunched my shoulders, and told each of them about Kizzy and the fire.

Speaking of Kizzy, I was surprised that the paramedics hadn't brought out the cupcake CEO yet, but then, time flies when you're in a panic. Still I had begun to fear that she had died when I heard her screech, "Put me down this instant. Do you have any idea who I am? I do not have time to go the hospital. I have a contest to run."

Luckily, Lee arrived just in time to hear Kizzy browbeating the poor EMTs. I noticed she was driving Fallon's car and wondered how she felt about having to borrow a dead woman's vehicle. Lee marched up to her business partner and said, "You most certainly are going to the hospital. Devereaux told me that you were struck on the head and unconscious when she found you. Not to mention possible smoke inhalation and loss of blood. You need to be checked out by a doctor."

She glanced at me and I waved but didn't join her. I was sitting only a few feet away and could hear the conversation perfectly. No need to get involved and give Kizzy more reasons to be upset with me. I only wished Lee hadn't named me as the snitch.

After some back-and-forth between the partners, Kizzy agreed to have a doctor take a look at her. No one was happy with the compromise. Kizzy sulked and the paramedics tried once again to persuade the injured woman to allow them to take her to the hospital.

While the EMTs completed a report reflecting that the patient refused treatment and/or transport, Lee called me over and said, "When Fallon was so ill, Ronni mentioned that there was a medical facility in town, but it wasn't open that night. Is it open today?"

"Yes." I pointed. "The Underwood Clinic is two blocks over. Just hang a right when you get past the town square and you can't miss it. It'll be the big brick building on your left."

Kizzy signed the document that the paramedics had prepared, then with the help of her partner eased into the car. Just before they drove away, Kizzy rolled down the window and beckoned to me.

When I approached, she said, "If we can't have the cupcake exhibition at your store, it is your responsibility to find somewhere else that's suitable and fund the change." I opened my mouth to protest, but she warned, "Otherwise, I expect a full refund of all the money already paid to you." I opened my mouth again and she advised, "Check your contract if you doubt my sincerity."

Lee exchanged a sympathetic glance with me, then put the Fiat in gear and pulled into the street. As I hurried into the dime store, I checked my watch. I had less than two hours to determine if we needed an alternative location for the first round of judging and, if we did, to find a place that could accommodate the event.

Having sent Hannah and my father home with instructions to return for the store's evening hours, I now stood alone in the middle of the sales floor. Firefighters had been hurrying past me for the last twenty minutes, and the last of the crew clomped out the front door without acknowledging me. Did that mean they were finished with my shop? I looked around. Everything seemed about the same as when the smoke detector went off and we cleared the place. Were they still inspecting the second-floor space?

"Yoo-hoo! Anyone around?" I called up the stairwell. "I need to talk to someone." I put my hand on the railing. "Are you all done up there?" I raised my voice. "May I speak to whoever is in charge?"

Nothing.

"Hello!" I started to slowly climb steps, then nearly fell backward when a massive figure loomed at the top of the landing.

Thank goodness, my common sense took over before I screamed like a five-year-old. Mentally smacking myself, I took a deep steadying breath. The guy was decked out in a bright yellow coat, trousers, and helmet. He was obviously one of the firefighters rather than the mad arsonist that my fevered imagination had immediately feared.

He raised his visor and said, "We meet again."

Wowie! Even all dirty and sweaty, or maybe because of that, this guy was a hunk. Trying to regain some of my cool, I asked, "Were you the first firefighter on the scene? The one who called the ambulance?"

"Yep." His frown was teasing. "Guess I didn't make that much of an impression on you."

"Sorry. You all sort of look the same in that getup of yours," I explained.

"Well, let me take off my turnout gear so you recognize me next time."

As he descended the stairs, I hastily backed up, then remembering my manners, asked, "Would you like a bottle of water?"

"That would be great. Thanks." He grinned. "Let me slip into something more comfortable and I'll tell you about your fire."

"Great," I echoed. It was ironic that such a hot guy put out fires for a living. My guess was that he lit a lot of women's flames and dousing those blazes involved a hose different from the one on his truck.

CHAPTER 12

While I waited for the firefighter to return, I went behind the soda fountain to pour myself a cup of coffee. Miraculously, no one had turned off the pot. I had just taken my first sip and nearly choked when, as if by magic, Chief Kincaid appeared in front of me. That man was quieter than my grandmother's cat, Banshee. And nearly as intimidating as the Siamese who enjoyed dive-bombing my head whenever I got close enough to his kitty condo for him to pounce.

The chief had questioned me earlier while I was sitting on the bench outside, but now he informed me that his crime scene techs were currently processing the second floor, and until they were finished, that area was off-limits. When pressed, he grudgingly admitted that the techs would *probably* be done by late afternoon, but he refused to name a specific time.

As he hurried away to track down Kizzy, I walked over to the front counter and retrieved my cell phone from the shelf underneath the register, where I had carelessly left it before the fire. As I was dialing Poppy's number, it suddenly dawned on me that the chief didn't know that the cupcake queen had nixed the

EMTs' original plan to transport her to the hospital. If I'd remembered, I could have told him she would be at Noah's clinic, but I'd been so rattled at his declaration that my upstairs was going to be unavailable for the next several hours, I'd forgotten.

Because Winnie's cooking school was too small to accommodate observers, the Dessert Channel had agreed to provide a live feed, and Kizzy's company had outfitted Gossip Central with several large plasma screens so the Cupcake Weekenders could watch as the finalists whipped up their entries. With most of the audience already at Poppy's bar, I suggested that we move the cupcake exhibition to her place. She agreed to set up the Hayloft for the presentation but stipulated that I had to get the displays over to her by two. Now all I had to do was figure out how to sweet-talk someone into releasing the stands to me in time.

I chewed my thumbnail. How was I going to do that? None of the police officers were particular friends of mine, and unfortunately, no one on the force owed me a favor. I needed another option, but my mind was a blank. Then, as if a sign from heaven that a hero was coming to my rescue, the sleigh bells above the store's entrance jingled. Maybe the cute firefighter walking toward me would be my knight in shining running shorts and white T-shirt.

Allowing myself a couple of long seconds to admire the powerful physique that his abbreviated outfit revealed, I almost drooled at his broad shoulders, well-developed arms, and muscular thighs. Then I reminded myself of the two handsome men already creating confusion in my life and forced myself to look away. But not before I took one more tiny peek at his massive chest.

Finally, getting my hormones under control, I asked,

"Would you like to sit here or would you prefer to talk in the back room at my desk?"

"Here's fine." He swung a leg over the stool and sat down. "Sorry about the clothes. They're the only ones I had in my unit."

"Not a problem," I assured him, then realized that I had seen the fire truck leave. "You didn't come over with the others?"

"No. I drove my own vehicle." The firefighter held out his hand. "I'm Chief Cooper McCall. But my friends call me Coop."

"I'm Devereaux Sinclair and my friends call me Dev," I said. "So you're the new fire chief. The one they hired when Augustus Leary retired."

"Right. I started a month ago." Coop took the water bottle I silently held out to him. "Since the department is mostly volunteers, the city council hired me to take over when he left. I've only been on the job a couple of weeks."

"Are you a native Shadow Bender?" I asked. I was pretty sure he wasn't since we were roughly the same age and I, like any other woman who set eyes on him, would have remembered him if we'd been in school together. "Or did you move here for the job?"

"I'm originally from a small town in Georgia, but I joined the marines right out of high school, which is where I got my fire protection training." He took a long swig of water, finishing half the bottle in one gulp, then said, "I've been working in Kansas City since I got out of the service."

"I worked in Kansas City for years before buying the dime store." I took a sip of coffee. "But I've always lived in Shadow Bend."

"That had to be an awful commute." A sprinkle of gold dust sparkled in Coop's warm brown eyes, and he added, "Part of the condition of my employment was living inside the Shadow Bend city limits, which evidently put off some of the job candidates. But I would have moved here anyway. An hour or more on the highway each way every day is not my idea of a good time."

"I doubt anyone enjoys it. At least no one without a helicopter or a Maserati." I toyed with the teaspoon, hating to end our pleasant conversation. Still, knowing that time was ticking by and I had a lot to do before the cupcake exhibition at three o'clock, I asked. "So, is my second floor structurally okay?"

"Yes. There was no evidence of any additional fires." Coop instantly became serious and the sharp planes that appeared in his face made me wondered if there was a touch of Native American blood in his pedigree. "The only damage is to the floor of the small office and you can just throw a rug over the scorch marks."

"Tell me about the fire." I breathed a sigh of relief at his news.

"Unless the injured woman was trying to roast marshmallows and then accidentally hit herself over the head with that trophy, it's pretty safe to say it was arson." Coop grinned, his sexy mouth and firm jaw sending a tingle of appreciation to my girl parts.

"Well, by my count this is the third attempt on Kizzy's life, so I'm going to go with rejecting the bonfire theory." I grinned back.

"No shit!" Coop's slight Southern drawl that had been delighting my ear grew more pronounced. "She did seem a touch contrary—someone who made you itch to take her out behind the barn and show her what for and how to—but what in the holy hell did she do to piss off a person that much?"

"That's exactly what someone needs to figure out

pretty damn soon." I rinsed out my empty coffee cup and put it on the rack to dry, then came out from behind the soda fountain counter. "Otherwise this whole Cupcake Weekend extravaganza is going to fall faster and flatter than a soufflé in a cold breeze."

"Yep." Coop nodded. "You all need to put a blanket on that horse so no one can see it's ugly."

"Right." I grinned, enjoying his way of talking.

"A day-tripper who thinks there might be a murderer running loose is bound to be about as calm as a hog on ice," Coop added.

It took me a second to translate, but then I snickered at the picture of Porky sliding across a frozen pond and said, "Precisely."

"Too bad, you all have no more chance than a kerosene cat in hell with gasoline drawers on of keeping an attempted murder quiet."

After another pause to interpret Coop's quaint colloquialisms, I agreed with his estimation, and then I asked, "So, is the fire department finished?" It was time to get back to the matter at hand—opening my business back up. "Chief Kincaid said he was sending his crime scene techs over to process my second floor, but I thought you guys were in charge of arson investigations."

"Kincaid is reluctantly sharing jurisdiction on this case." Coop stood and was suddenly so close to me I could feel the heat from his body.

"Oh." I nodded stupidly. When had Coop moved? "Chief Kincaid can be a bit of a control freak, but then, who am I to talk?"

"I find intense women mighty fetchin'." Coop's smile was suggestive. "They seem more passionate about everything they do."

"Really?" I wasn't sure I liked the suggestive tone of

his voice . . . but then again, I wasn't sure that I didn't. "I don't know if that's true. Most people find me somewhat aloof, even coldhearted."

"Maybe those folks don't look far enough beneath the surface." Coop pushed a loose curl behind my ear and raised an eyebrow.

"Perhaps." I stepped out of his reach. His strong callused fingers had sent a thrill through my body, and even though he radiated a vitality that drew me like a duck to bread crumbs, I knew I had to put a stop to the electricity flickering between us. "But on the other hand, there may not be anything underneath but more ice."

"It would be mighty fun to find out." Coop leaned an impressive shoulder against a shelving unit and crossed his arms. "Are you married?"

I shook my head.

"Engaged?"

"No."

"In a committed relationship with one guy?" His smile had grown wider with each question and answer, until now he was beaming.

"Uh . . ." I stuttered, searching for a way to describe my love life that didn't make me sound either a complete ditz or the worst kind of slut. "Sort of."

"How can the answer be sort of?" Coop straightened and narrowed his eyes. "If it's not a definite yes, then you aren't."

How to explain the situation with Noah and Jake? I pondered the problem, then said, "It's complicated. My whole existence is complicated." I sensed that I was blushing, something I rarely did, and it made me feel like a ten-year-old with her first crush. "Believe me; you don't want to get into the middle of my messy life."

"I'm partial to complicated." Coop peered at me intently. "Keeps things interesting." He shrugged. "After all, no one calls nine-one-one if they're having a good day. Most firefighters are adrenaline junkies, so we don't do well with predictable or simple. I find it's best not to let myself get bored."

Having no rejoinder to that, I decided it was time to change the subject. Turning my back to him, I pretended to be unaffected by his teasing tone, but I couldn't help myself from noticing the tingle of excitement his words had ignited. Why was it that opportunity only knocked once, but temptation repeatedly used a battering ram? I rearranged some merchandise until I had myself under control.

Finally, clearing my throat, I said, "Be that as it may"—*Shit!* I sounded like an uptight spinster—"there's a cupcake contest to deal with, and within the hour I have to get those two display units currently sitting in the large room upstairs over to Gossip Central or I'll be in big trouble." I walked away from where Coop stood. "Chief Kincaid said he won't release the second floor until late this afternoon, which leaves me with a problem that I need to concentrate on."

"Maybe I can help you with that," Coop said. "As I stated earlier, this is a joint investigation and Kincaid doesn't have the last word."

"That would be wonderful." Before I even turned around, I knew Coop was behind me. His scent tugged at some primitive female response deep inside me. "But I don't like being in anyone's debt."

"I'm sure I could think of something that would even the score." Coop's expression was innocent and he tapped his chin thoughtfully. "Do you sew? I need some patches put on my duty shirts."

"Sorry." My feeble attempt to construct an apron in

home ec class popped into my head and I winced. "I'm all thumbs with a needle and thread."

"Hmm." He moved a little closer. "How about baking? I sure do miss my mama's made-from-scratch brown sugar pound cake with rum glaze."

"I'm sure my grandmother could whip that up for you, but baking isn't my thing." I pondered what I could offer him that didn't include me getting naked and horizontal. Wait a minute! Where had that thought come from? I'd only met the guy a few hours ago.

"Then you'd be in your grandma's debt." Coop shook his head. "So, what are you good at? I'm sure you have a talent that I'd like."

"I doubt you need your books balanced or the perfect gift basket." I watched him closely. I did need his help, so I had to figure out something I could give him in exchange for riling up Chief Kincaid. "How about some investment advice?"

"Nope." Coop frowned. "If I want to gamble, I'll put my money on a sweet little filly in the fifth race at Hialeah."

"Then I'm stumped." My shoulders sagged. I really needed his help.

"You said you don't bake." Coop's eyes brightened. "Do you cook?"

"I make a mean lasagna dinner," I admitted. My other specialty was eggs Benedict, but that smacked of breakfast and I wasn't going there.

"Homemade marinara sauce?" Coop asked, his expression hopeful.

"Yes, sir." I sketched a mock salute. "Caesar salad and garlic bread, too."

"I've been hankering for a meal that didn't come out of the freezer or a cardboard box or from a local carryout joint." Coop licked his lips. "How about I get you those cupcake displays and you promise to come to my place and make me an Italian feast? Chianti's on me."

"I thought firehouses had good cooks." I raised a skeptical brow. "Aren't you getting homemade food at work?"

"When I'm on duty, yes," Coop admitted. "I'm talking about when I'm on my own." He crossed his arms. "So, do we have a deal or not?"

I wrenched my attention from my ridiculous preoccupation with his handsome face—he was too attractive by far—and I stuck out my hand. "Deal."

Instead of shaking, Coop leaned forward, planted a soft kiss on my cheek, then walked toward the stairs, saying over his shoulder, "I'll go get those cupcake stands. I think they'll fit in the back of my unit so I can run them over to Gossip Central for you."

"You don't have to do that. Getting them released from the crime scene is enough," I protested, but remembered that when I realized that we wouldn't be reopening the store until evening, I'd sent Hannah and Dad home. By the time I reached my father and asked him to come back with his Grand Cherokee, it might be too late. Which meant I had no other way of getting the displays over to Poppy's place. "But it's really sweet of you to offer."

"No problem." Coop turned and his hot chocolate gaze met mine. "I look forward to collecting my payment."

My heart turned over in response and I realized I was smiling. I wiped the idiotic grin from my face and said, "Let me know when you want your lasagna dinner and Sinclair Catering Service will be there."

"How about Monday night?" He winked. "All the cupcake people will be gone and we can relax."

"I never relax," I cautioned him, then watched his sexy rear end as he took the stairs two at a time.

Shaking my head, I dug out my cell to call Poppy and tell her the displays were on their way. He was so damn good-looking and his powerful presence really resonated with something inside me. What combination of Karma and chemistry had put me in this position? For years, I hadn't felt a spark with any of the men I dated, and now I was attracted to not one, not two, but three guys. I had been either very, very good in a past life or extremely bad. Sadly, I suspected that it was the latter, as I couldn't see myself wearing wings and a halo in any incarnation.

CHAPTER 13

Whistling Survivor's "Eye of the Tiger," Coop started his Ford Expedition. He purely loved competition, and doing battle for a girl's affections didn't scare him one little bit. In fact, it revved his motor. As did feisty gals with generous curves and red amber hair that reminded him of the heart of a fire. He could still see the bumfuzzled expression in Dev's pretty blue-green eyes as she tried to deny the attraction that had sizzled between them.

Looking into his rearview mirror as he backed into the road, Coop caught sight of the huge neon pink Ferris wheel and bright yellow roller coaster wedged in the cargo area of his SUV and felt a twinge of guilt. His mama would have tanned his backside for misleading Devereaux into believing that he was going against the police chief and sneaking those cupcake stands out of a crime scene, when in reality he'd just asked the techs to dust the displays for prints ASAP and then taken them as soon as they finished.

It hadn't been exactly chivalrous to bend the truth, and letting Dev think she owed him a favor wasn't any too gallant, either. But how else was he going to get her to agree to see him again? It was clear that she was already involved with some romantic situation that was addling her brain and wasn't too keen on adding another guy to the mix.

Coop hated to disappoint his mama, but Miss Laura Jane McCall might just cheer him on if it meant him finding a good woman, settling down, and producing grandbabies. Having settled the matter of his slight detour from the path of true righteousness with his conscience, he sat back and enjoyed the ride out to Gossip Central.

Patting the Expedition's leather-covered steering wheel, Coop grinned. He'd been mighty pleased his first day as chief when the city council presented him with the keys to a brand-spanking-new command unit. The bright red Ford was tricked out with light bars, sirens, long- and short-range radio antennas, bumper guards, communications systems, souped-up engine, and all sorts of other cool equipment.

He'd wondered how a small town like Shadow Bend could afford such an awesome vehicle. But then one of his men had given him the scoop regarding the feud between the mayor and the police chief. The guy had explained that because of the vendetta, the lion's share of the money that would normally have had to be split with the police was allocated for the fire department.

Coop felt kind of sorry for Kincaid, but the situation sure worked for him. And as a young first-time chief, he needed all the advantages he could get. He liked Shadow Bend. It was a nice community that reminded him of home. Small towns fit his personality better than big cities, and now that he'd met Dev, he intended to stick around for a long, long time. Maybe the rest of his life.

It was one fifty-eight when he turned into Gossip Central's crowded parking lot. Dev had emphasized that the deadline for delivery was two o'clock, so he pulled the Expedition up to the back entrance and honked. As he was wrestling the five-foot-tall Ferris wheel from the back of the SUV, the door swung open and his jaw dropped. Outside of the movies or magazines, he'd never seen such a gorgeous woman.

As she walked toward him, her long white-blond curls seemed to float in the breeze. When she got closer, he saw that her eyes looked exactly like the violets that his granny grew in a pot on the shelf over her kitchen sink. This gal looked like a fairy princess. Well, except for the pissed-off expression on her beautiful face. But even that couldn't make her any less stunning.

Wow! He was definitely staying in Shadow Bend forever. The ladies here were incredible. He crossed his fingers that the men weren't as impressive. Without being vain, Coop knew that he was passably good-looking and there were always firehouse groupies who wanted to sleep with firefighters. On the other hand, there were a lot of women who weren't thrilled with the idea of dating a guy who ran into burning buildings for a living. A man who could never guarantee that he'd be around for a holiday. He sure hoped that his occupation wouldn't be a negative for the gals in his new hometown.

Flashing his dimples, Coop held out his hand and said, "I'm Coop McCall. Dev sent me with the cupcake displays. Are you Poppy?"

"That I am." Poppy place her fingers in his outstretched palm and nodded toward the words stenciled on the side of the Ford. "And you must be our new fire chief. It's nice to meet you."

"Yes, ma'am." Coop noticed that Poppy barely

squeezed his hand, while Dev's grip had been firm. He imagined that wasn't the only difference between these two women. "Where would you like the stands?"

"They go in the Hayloft." Poppy's gaze was speculative. "I'll get one of my guys to carry them up there. Why don't you come in and have a beer?" She winked. "You can tell me how Dev persuaded the fire chief to run errands for her. She's not usually so . . ."

"So?" Coop asked, scowling. He'd understood Dev to say that Poppy was one of her best friends. Was the striking club owner implying that Dev wasn't attractive enough to get men to help her?

After a moment of thought, Poppy finished her sentence. "So ready to accept favors." She smoothed her palms over her tiny waist and slim hips. "Dev tends to be unwilling to depend on the kindness of strangers. I, on the other hand, am more than happy to let men do things for me." She winked. "In fact, I encourage it."

"Yeah." Coop nodded. "Dev did strike me as the independent type."

"Very perceptive." Poppy tilted her head. "Are you coming in?"

"Sure." Coop was off duty, but since he was driving an official vehicle, he said, "But, if you have it, I'll take a Dew rather than a brew."

"Sure." Poppy marched through the outer door, pointed to an office off the hallway, and said, "Have a seat in there. The contest cupcakes should be arriving any minute, and I can listen for the delivery better back here." She waved as she walked away. "I'll get your pop and tell the boys to take the displays to the Hayloft."

Coop settled into a folding chair and watched the club owner walk away. She was wearing some sort of stretchy black jumpsuit that looked as if it were spray-painted to her butt. He appreciated the plunging neckline but wasn't sure about the elbow-length leather gloves with metal studs or the pointy-toed high-heeled ankle boots. Both those items seemed as though they could inflict some serious pain, and no way, no how was he into that kind of kinky stuff.

When Poppy returned, Coop was examining a picture of Dev, Poppy, and some guy. She handed him a can of Mountain Dew, then sank gracefully into her desk chair and said, "So, tell me what happened at the dime store."

Coop outlined the facts, finishing with, "Dev tells me this is the third crack on that cupcake gal's life. What else happened to her?"

"There was a hit-and-run last night, but Dev pushed Kizzy out of the way." Poppy tented her fingers. "As for the other try, Dev and I haven't had a chance to talk about it, but my guess is that Dev must think that Fallon's death was murder, and the killer was after Kizzy, not her assistant."

"The police must agree since Kincaid is all over the situation," Cooper mused, then asked, "Is the chief any relation to you?"

"He's my dad," Poppy admitted, then changed the subject. "What about the fire? Any clues as to who was after our cupcake tycoon?"

"If it were a true arsonist, there would be a signature, but this guy couldn't even figure out how to disconnect the smoke alarm, so I doubt he's an honest-to-goodness pyro." Coop pressed his lips together. "Especially since the fire was probably set to cover up the attempted murder, or maybe finish the job." He frowned. "The police crime lab is going to send me the results of their analysis and maybe something will turn up, but I wouldn't hold my breath on that possibility."

"That's too bad." Poppy grimaced. "A lot of folks, Dev included, are counting on the profits of this weekend to keep their businesses in the black."

Before Coop could reply, a pretty woman with shiny brown hair burst into the room and demanded, "What's this about the dime store burning down and Kizzy almost dead? Do we have to call off the contest?"

Once Poppy and Coop had explained the situation and the attractive brunette had been introduced as Ronni Ksiazak, B & B owner, Coop took his leave. As he drove back into town, two thoughts were chasing each other in his head. One, Shadow Bend sure had a lot of fine-looking women. And two, how could he help the three he'd just met find a killer?

CHAPTER 14

Once Coop left, taking his distractingly handsome face with him, I could once again focus on what was important—my business. After a few calls from various reporters, I ignored the ringing of the store's phone. But as I finished cleaning up, my cell started buzzing with IDs I didn't recognize. How had the media gotten that number?

I turned my cell phone to mute, put a sign in the window indicating the cupcake exhibition had been relocated to Gossip Central, and locked the entrance. The two crime scene investigators had finished with the stairway and assured me that they would secure the dime store when they were through processing the second story, so I went upstairs to give the back exit key to the techs.

As I handed it over, I remembered Kizzy's request to use that door and dutifully reported my conversation with the cupcake tycoon, ending with, "Which might mean that even though I instructed Ms. Cutler not to leave the exit unlocked, she very well could have done so, and the assailant could have come in that way." I tapped my chin, considering the recent events. "Especially if he or she had been following Ms. Cutler and looking for an opportunity to do her harm."

The female tech seemed to be in charge, and as she pocketed the key, she said, "I'll go down with you right now and dust that area." She pursed her lips. "If I remember correctly, we have your prints on file, but we'll have to get Ms. Cutler's. Anyone else use that door?"

"Not recently." I ran through the past few days in my mind. "My staff usually comes through the front entrance and I haven't had any deliveries since Wednesday." I paused, then added, "My cleaning lady was here last night and she would have wiped down the knob with an antibacterial cleanser, as well as the metal around it."

"Well, that's a break we don't usually get." The tech beamed. "I'll get Ms. Cutler's prints and we should be good to go."

"Any idea when I can reopen the store?" Since the tech and I were apparently now pals, I figured it didn't hurt to ask for a more specific time than the chief had been willing to divulge.

"We should be done in another hour, two at the most, so say four thirty." The tech shrugged apologetically. "But there will be fingerprint powder all over and it can be a little hard to remove."

"I know." I rolled my eyes, then asked, "But you're only going to be dusting the upstairs and the back exit, correct?"

"Yes." The tech glanced around. "In a public place like a store, there's not much use processing an area unless we know for certain the suspect is likely to have done more than pass through it."

"So the first floor, the dime store itself, will be untouched?" I wanted to make sure I understood what I'd be facing.

"Right." The tech raised her brow. "As I just said, public areas have too much trace to sort out what is evidence and what isn't."

I thanked the tech—for what, I wasn't sure—then left her to her work. After putting the cash drawer in the safe, I grabbed my purse from the desk, edged around the woman who had opened the back door and was busy dusting the knob, and walked to my car. Sliding behind the wheel, I pulled out my cell and Binged trauma scene remediation services. I found a company based in Kansas City that specialized in fingerprint powder removal, punched in their number, and a few minutes later had a promise that someone would be at my store by five o'clock.

The cupcake crowd would be occupied over at Gossip Central from three until six for the exhibition and the tasting of the finalists' first round of treats. I knew I should at least show my face at the event before going home, but I was determined not to stay long. If I just popped in and out, I'd still have a couple of free hours to spend with Gran. Having resolved the matter to my satisfaction, I put my car in gear and headed over to Poppy's club.

I was getting used to the packed parking lots and the crowds, and the money they were spending at the local businesses made it worth the hassle. After double-parking behind Ronni's car, and ignoring yet another call from the media regarding the fire, I entered Gossip Central. I spent a few minutes greeting people, then headed up to the Hayloft to see the cupcakes.

As I made my way into the center of the room, I was transfixed by the gorgeous display of yumminess in front of me. The contestants had outdone themselves. From the blue velvet cupcakes frosted with almond icing and decorated with tiny candy pearls that resembled bubbles to the pale orange honey ginger delicacies, I was amazed by the competitors' creativity. Each little temptation had a three-by-four-inch card providing the cupcake's name and creator.

After admiring all the entries, I turned my attention to the two flavors that appealed to me the most. The Caribbean breeze cupcake was a coconut and rum concoction with a cute little fondant palm tree planted in the whipped cream icing. The sugar cookie cupcakes had teeny-tiny star-shaped sugar cookies nestled in the swirled buttercream frosting. I itched to nab one of the delectable treats, but there were too many witnesses for me to get away with the crime.

Instead, I stepped away from the cupcakes and worked my way toward the exit. Twenty minutes of socializing seemed sufficient, so I said my farewells, hopped into my car, and drove home. It had been a while since I'd spent any real time with Gran, and the whole point of my quitting my job in the city and buying the dime store was to be around more often.

Having Dad out of prison and living close by in the garage apartment had lessened my apprehensions about leaving my grandmother alone, but I still felt it was my responsibility to make sure she was okay. After all, when Dad had been sent to prison and Mom had dumped me on Birdie's front step, Gran had taken care of *me*, so I wanted to be the one to take care of her now.

It took me a while to battle the drivers cruising around Gossip Central's lot looking for parking spaces and get back out onto the road, but I finally turned the Z4 into our long driveway. We lived on the edge of town on the ten remaining acres of the property my ancestors had settled in the eighteen sixties. Premature deaths, a few generations of only children, and lots of relatives moving away meant that Dad, Gran, and I were the last Sinclairs in Shadow Bend.

When my grandfather died fifteen years ago, and my father declined to become a farmer, Gran had begun selling off the land surrounding the old homestead to pay taxes and support herself. Inch by inch, my heritage had vanished before I was old enough to realize what it meant, so now I cherished the acreage we had left.

I slowed to gaze at my favorite spot, the duck pond. When Dad had been released from the penitentiary, we had his welcome-home party there. Next along my way was our small orchard. The William's Pride apples wouldn't be ready for a few more weeks, but once they were, Gran would bake one of her famous pies and make the rest into the best apple butter north of the Mason-Dixon Line. As I drove the final quarter mile through the white fir and blue spruce lining either side of the lane, I felt myself relax. Gran and this place were my refuge. Only here could I let down my guard and feel at peace.

I found my father and grandmother in the kitchen. Before Dad's return, I would have sworn that Birdie was more of a Jack Daniel's type of gal, but having him home seemed to have calmed her and they'd grown into the habit of having afternoon tea together.

Another change from what I was accustomed to was that Gran now used the delicate china cups and saucers adorned with violets and wisps of curling ivy that she'd previously saved for special occasions. After kissing them both on the cheek, I took down one of the cups and turned up the heat under the copper teakettle, then filled the acorn-shaped infuser with my favorite Prince of Wales tea leaves.

As I prepared my tea, I said to Gran, "I'm surprised you aren't at Gossip Central, looking at the cupcakes."

"At my age, there are fewer and fewer things that I'm willing to stand in line for." Gran shrugged. "It's not as if I've never seen a fancy dessert before. I've probably baked more cupcakes than all those contestants combined."

"True," I agreed, then added, "And I'm sure yours taste much better."

"Darn tooting they do." Gran nodded, then asked, "Everything okay at the store? Kern told me all about the smoke . . . uh . . . smoke . . ." She trailed off, her face getting red.

"Detector," I supplied. Her doctor had said it was best to supply the word she couldn't recall, rather than let her become stressed.

"Right." She shook her finger at me. "And don't you look so worried. Lord a' mercy. Just because I misplaced something or can't come up with a word once in a while doesn't mean I'm senile. Now that my baby boy is back here where he should be, I can concentrate again."

Gran's memory issues had improved dramatically with Dad's return, but she still had trouble coming up with the exact word she wanted. And she wasn't happy that I insisted she keep taking her medication and continue seeing the gerontologist.

"The police are dusting the upstairs for prints, and even though the first-round exhibition had to be moved to Poppy's club, we can reopen on schedule." I sat at the old wooden table and waited for the water to boil. "The fire chief was able to get the cupcake displays out of the exhibit room for me, and he drove them over to Gossip Central."

"That was nice of him," Kern commented. "I guess since he's new in town, he wants to make a good impression on the business community."

"That must be it," I agreed quickly. "It's hard to be the new guy on the block, especially since everyone liked the previous chief."

I certainly wasn't telling my grandmother and father what I suspected Coop's real motives were in helping me. Neither of them needed to know about my love life. Dad and I were trying to adjust to our new relationship. To him, I was still the sixteen-year-old that I'd been when he went away. And as for me, I wasn't used to having a father around. Gran had encouraged my independence; Dad not so much.

"Kern tells me that cupcake woman was there when the fire started," Birdie said. "Holy crap on a cracker! She seems to be having a real bad run of luck since coming back to Shadow Bend." Gran folded her arms across her chest and frowned. "I doubt she'll want to do this contest again."

"You're probably right." I hesitated, then realized that both Gran and Dad would soon hear that the police suspected someone was trying to kill Kizzy, and said, "Actually, the cops don't think it's bad luck. They believe that she might be the target of a murderer."

"Sweet baby Jesus!" Birdie got up and snatched the whistling teakettle from the stove. As she poured the boiling water over the infuser in my cup, she asked, "So the car in the church parking lot almost hitting Kizzy last night after the dinner and the poor little gal's death the night before, none of that was . . . uh . . ."

"A coincidence?" I waited for Gran to nod, then shook my head. "Nope. At least, that's the police's current theory and I agree."

"I wonder if they know about Kizzy's big fight with Annalee Paulson," Gran mused.

"The cupcake queen fought with the TV star judge?"

I asked, wanting to make sure that I was clear on what Gran was saying. "When was that? At the dinner?"

"Don't be silly. They didn't fight here in Shadow Bend." Gran flicked me an irritated glance. "On television. Kizzy was a guest on Annalee's program last fall."

"What happened?" Evidently, the cupcake tycoon had made more enemies than a bacon-eating cat sitting in a tree surrounded by a yard full of dogs. Not that I was surprised. Having experienced her "gratitude" when I'd saved her life, I had firsthand knowledge that Kizzy wasn't the easiest person to be around.

"Well, you know that *Sugar and Spice* is a live show?" Gran asked.

Even though I had no idea, I nodded since agreeing would speed up Gran's explanation. The last thing I wanted was to have her go off on a tangent and forget what she'd been about to tell me.

"Kizzy and Annalee were doing a segment on the show where Kizzy was demonstrating how to bake her original cupcake—the one that made her famous," Gran explained. "And as they chitchatted, Annalee remarked at how amazing the whole cupcake fad was and how lucky Kizzy was to have started her company at just the right time to cash in on the craze."

"That sounds like an innocent enough comment." Dad tipped his head.

"Exactly what I thought," Gran agreed. "But Kizzy's face turned as red as one of my blue-ribbon-winning tomatoes and she said it wasn't luck—it was her fantastic business plan. She also claimed that she had started the cupcake trend and all the other companies stole her brainchild."

"Ego much?" I snickered. Kizzy was certainly self-confident.

"Annalee snapped back that Kizzy's business was far

from the first to offer upscale cupcakes." Gran smirked. "Then she reeled off the names of half a dozen companies that were doing it before Kizzy Cutler's Cupcakes started."

"And?" I asked.

"Kizzy threw her spoon in the mixing bowl," Gran continued. "The batter splattered all over Annalee's chest and into her hair."

"Oh. Oh." I had no idea what the television star's temperament was like, but I'd bet no matter how nice she was, being covered in raw cupcake in front of an audience would bring out her inner bitch.

"Then Kizzy laughed and said something about the batter improving Annalee's appearance." Gran crossed her arms. "So Annalee dumped the bowl of frosting on Kizzy's head. They went to commercial, and when the show came back on, Kizzy was gone and Annalee was demonstrating how to bake a pie," Gran ended her story. "But they must have made up since Kizzy invited her to be a judge."

"I suppose," I agreed, then tuned out Gran and Dad's discussion as to which of the two women was justified and which had acted badly. As they debated the issue, I looked around. There was nothing HGTV worthy in this room, but everything reminded me of Gran and the home she had given me as an abandoned teenager. It was here at this table, drinking from these cups, that she'd broken all the bad news since we'd lived together. I sighed. Maybe now with Dad back we could have some good news instead.

But apparently not today.

My father and Gran had run the topic of whether Kizzy or Annalee was at fault into the ground and now Dad fiddled with his spoon, then without looking at me said, "There was a letter from your mother in the mail."

"Oh?" I tried to think of something else to say, but every response that flitted through my mind was snarky, and from the expression on Dad's face, sarcasm wasn't what he was hoping for from me.

"Evidently, there are a few people in Shadow Bend that she still keeps in touch with, and one of them told her I was out of prison."

"Really?" I was surprised to hear that my mother was in contact with anyone from town. Gran and I only heard from her once or twice a year—mostly at Christmas, but occasionally she'd remember my birthday—and that was only a scrawled signature on a preprinted greeting card. "I wonder who her informative little friends are."

"Hell's bells! It's probably someone as shallow as Yvette." Birdie flipped her long gray braid over her shoulder and got to her feet. "Or someone who wants to stir up trouble for you or Kern."

"Maybe." I shrugged. "But what trouble could my mother cause us?"

My mother was on husband number four, or maybe five. I'd lost track. The only way I ever figured out she had divorced and remarried again was when her last name changed on the return address label on the cards she sent. I paused, trying to remember her latest surname, but drew a blank. It had been something vaguely familiar, not that I spent a lot of time thinking about it.

"Mom." Kern blew out a breath. "Yvette isn't the villain you make her out to be."

"Of course not, dear." Birdie patted her son's hand, then rolled her eyes at me. "No one could expect her to stand by you when you were falsely accused or stick around and raise her daughter."

"Mother," Kern sighed again, his shoulders slumping. "Not everyone is as strong as you are." He shook his head. "Yvette's just . . ." He shrugged and threw up his hands. "Just more easily broken."

"That's—" I closed my mouth. I hadn't exactly been my father's staunchest supporter, either. What could I say? My only excuse was that I had been a teenager when it all happened and incredibly immature. Plus, no one had bothered to tell me the whole story.

"What was in the letter?" Birdie's pale blue eyes sparked with resentment.

My father flinched and I smiled inwardly. "Yes, Dad, what did Mom write?" I was glad that for once Gran's pissed-off Pekinese look wasn't directed at me.

"Nothing much," Kern mumbled. "She wished me well and hoped that I could forgive her for running away." Red stained his fair complexion and he added half under his breath, "And, uh, she might drop by for a visit next time she's traveling in the Midwest."

"Next time?" I asked. She hadn't come to see me once since taking off. "She's been in this area before, but never came by here?"

"That's what the note said." Kern stood, clearly wanting to end the conversation about his ex-wife's actions. "You know, every time God closes one door, he opens another one."

"Too bad it's usually hell going down the hallway between them," I muttered.

"I'm going to take a nap. I'll see you at the store at six." He reached for a cookie, stuffed it into his mouth, and hurried out of the back door.

"Well, that was interesting," I commented. Gran was quiet, so I got up and rummaged in the fridge. My empty stomach reminded me that I hadn't had lunch. "Do you think Mom really will show up here?"

"Who knows? That woman doesn't know shit from Shinola, so whatever she does will cause a problem."

Gran pushed me out of the way and reached for a Tupperware container. "How about a chicken salad sandwich and coleslaw?"

"Great." I cleared the teacups from the table and put them in the sink.

"Have you heard from Jake lately?" Gran's tone was casual, but I could feel her stare. "It's been a while since Tony's talked to him."

Tony Del Vecchio was Jake's great-uncle and Gran's high school sweetheart. Because he was a couple years older than Birdie and she wouldn't marry him until she finished school, he enlisted in the marines after he graduated. Then, near the end of the Korean War, Tony was reported MIA, and Gran married someone else.

Gran had never shared her reasons for marrying so soon after Tony went missing, and I hadn't had the heart to pry the information from her even if I could. I was just happy that she and Tony had rekindled their friendship and were seeing each other again after all those years.

Previously, although our properties shared a border and Tony had purchased all the land we had sold off, Gran and Tony had avoided each other. Even after both their spouses died, they hadn't reconnected. It was only when Gran needed to ask for help from Tony's nephew, the U.S. Marshal, that they had gotten back together again.

"Not since last Tuesday," I answered Gran's question about Jake.

"I hope he's okay." Gran's brow wrinkled. "I bet that ex-wife isn't really in any danger at all. She probably made all this up."

"I doubt she could fool the entire U.S. Marshal Service." I took a bite of the sandwich Gran slid in front of me, nearly moaning with the mayonnaise goodness of her homemade chicken salad.

"They could all be in cahoots with her."

"And why would they be?" I asked before forking coleslaw into my mouth.

"Because they don't want Jake to quit being a marshal." Gran turned on the faucet.

"So they allowed a serial killer to escape and staged a kidnapping?" I knew I shouldn't have told Gran that just before Meg had been kidnapped, Jake had resigned his job and intended to manage Tony's cattle ranch. "That's a little far-fetched."

"It's amazing what people will do to someone whose past they've shared." Gran squirted dish soap into the sink and plunged her hands into the water.

"Still . . ." I trailed off. I had been about to argue Gran's premise, but then it dawned on me. Maybe it was someone who shared a past relationship with Kizzy who was trying to kill her. Actually, that made sense. The attempts on her life had all started when she returned to Shadow Bend. I chewed thoughtfully. Who from Kizzy's history in the town still held a grudge after all these years?

CHAPTER 15

When Gran finished the dishes, she decided that she would take a nap, too, and retired to her bedroom. With Dad and Birdie resting, I decided to give Chief Kincaid a call. I wanted to see what he thought about my idea that Kizzy's past had come back to bite her in the butt now that she had returned to town. And I hoped that he would tell me what area of investigation the police were pursuing.

The dispatcher put me on hold, and as I waited for the chief to pick up, I ate the rest of my lunch. I had time to wash my plate and pop the top on a can of Diet Coke before he came on the line.

"Chief Kincaid," he announced with an exasperated sigh.

"Dev Sinclair here," I informed him. He sounded as if he was in a bad mood, but I resisted the urge to hang up. Channeling my inner financial consultant, I put a smile in my voice and said smoothly, "I've been thinking about the attempts on Kizzy Cutler's life."

"You and everyone else," Chief Kincaid muttered.

"I was wondering if you had considered the possibility that someone from Kizzy's past has a grudge against her because of an act she committed before moving away from Shadow Bend."

"Naturally," Chief Kincaid snapped. "We aren't the Barney Fifes some people assume we are just because we work in a small town."

Ouch! "I never meant to imply your department was anything but competent." Who had been getting on the chief's last nerve? He and I usually had a cordial relationship, but apparently this time I'd caught him at a bad moment. "However, it occurred to me that since I've been around Kizzy quite a bit and have seen her in situations the police might not be privy to, I might be able to give you some suggestions as to who to question."

"Of course you do." The chief's tone was sarcastic. "Such as?"

"Well—"

"Hold on a second," Chief Kincaid ordered, then said to someone who had apparently barged into his office, "Get the hell out of here. What part of 'no comment' don't you reporters understand?"

Damn! Now I understood the chief's irritation. I knew that someone had leaked the attempted murders to the press because in the last couple of hours, I had been bombarded with calls regarding the fire, but I hadn't realized how that attention would affect the police department. I'd been able to fob off the journalists by pleading ignorance or just not answering the phone, but that wasn't an option for Chief Kincaid.

While I sympathized with his position and I understood that media interest about the attempted murder wasn't good news for the cops, it was worse for the businesses that had invested in the Cupcake Weekend. If the attendees decided they didn't want to risk being in a town with a killer running loose, this evening's and tomorrow's events would flop. And if the events bombed, all the money the committee members had spent to purchase extra merchandise and hire additional personnel would be flushed down the toilet.

As the chief continued to yell at the reporter who had invaded his office, then laid into the dispatcher for allowing the journalist to get past her desk, I thought about the risk to my bottom line. The more I fretted about going into the red, the angrier I got. By the time the chief got back to me and I recounted the conversation between Harlee and Kizzy, I was just about as angry as he was.

It didn't help my frame of mind that Chief Kincaid curtly thanked me for the information, then, dismissing my theory, said, "The conversation you quoted sounds to me like Harlee's attitude was that whatever happened between her and Kizzy was too long ago to matter anymore. You said she seemed sad, not vindictive."

"Perhaps she was both distressed and bitter," I suggested, barely able to keep the snarl out of my voice. When the chief didn't respond, I let the matter drop and asked, "Did you have any luck finding out what was in the package that was delivered the night Fallon died?"

"No," Chief Kincaid snapped. "No one at the B and B could identify any item that wasn't there before they left for dinner."

"How odd." I thought back to the phone call from Fallon that we had all overheard at the Golden Dragon. "Fallon definitely said the delivery person had finally arrived, but because of the funny taste in her mouth and headache she wasn't coming to dinner."

"That's correct," Chief Kincaid confirmed. "We've talked to everyone there and they've corroborated your account."

"Was the delivery company able to give you any

idea what they had transported?" I asked. "Surely they had a record of who sent it."

"None of the companies that cover Shadow Bend had any deliveries scheduled for the B and B on Thursday." Chief Kincaid paused. Then, before I could think of another question, he added, "And, yes, my officers have been canvassing the neighborhood of the B and B, trying to find anyone who might have seen the vehicle or driver at the guesthouse during the time the victim was there alone."

"Too bad that all the homes along that stretch are so large and on such big lots," I commented. "It would be hard for anyone to see next door to them. Your only real hope would be the people across the street in that big Gothic revival house."

"According to Veronica Ksiazak," the chief sighed, "the folks who bought that place left town to avoid the Cupcake Weekend crowds."

"Well, double damn it to hell!" I was getting more and more frustrated. "Any chance they didn't get out of Dodge until Friday morning?"

"We won't know until they get back." Chief Kincaid sounded as dejected as I felt. "Since they're relatively new in town, we can't find anyone who has a cell number for them, so we have no way of reaching them. Unlike in those stupid crime shows on television, the phone company doesn't really just turn over people's numbers to us without a court order. And considering this is a holiday weekend, there's no way I can find a judge before Monday willing to issue one."

"That's too bad," I commiserated, then decided to try one more time to get him to take my theory seriously. "I still think that this has something to do with Kizzy's past, and even if Harlee isn't holding a grudge, she might know someone who is."

"When I can free up an officer, I'll check that idea out." Chief Kincaid's tone made it clear that in his opinion our little chat was over. "We've asked Ms. Cutler if there is anyone from her years in Shadow Bend that might wish her harm, and she has assured us that she was very popular. She says that everyone loved her."

Certain that he was about to hang up, I hurried to mention Russell Neumann's problem with how the prize money might be awarded, Kizzy's hints that Reverend GB's recipe might not be original, and Q's hairstyle issue with the cupcake queen. I summarized all the conversations that I'd overheard, ending with, "Also, the blogger and the television star both had a feud going with Kizzy."

"Which apparently was resolved since she invited them to judge the contest and they accepted," Chief Kincaid said, refuting my conclusion.

"How about the two contestants?" I asked. "The one's husband is upset that the cash might not be given in a lump sum, and the other is ticked off because Kizzy thinks he stole his recipe."

"Neither of which would require instant action," the chief countered. "Maybe once the contest is won and the money really isn't paid out as was promised or if the contestant is kicked out for plagiarism, but neither party has any reason to act against Kizzy yet."

"How about the camera guy and his sister?" I asked. "Their problem with Kizzy seems fairly urgent."

"I'll certainly keep in mind all you've told me," the chief said when I paused for breath. Then before I could say anything more, he added, "But we already have a suspect who we'll be taking into custody as soon as we finish gathering a few pieces of additional evidence."

"Who?" I demanded, wondering why he hadn't just told me that to begin with.

"No comment," Chief Kincaid said, and immediately hung up.

"Damn!" Why was I not reassured? I could understand that the chief wouldn't want to advertise whom they were about to nab, but he didn't sound as if he truly believed they were on the verge of wrapping up the case. If anything, he'd sounded as though he was lying through his teeth. They might have a suspect, but I'd bet my Chloé Paddington leather satchel that they were far from making an arrest.

As I contemplated that conclusion, I stewed over the fact that the bad guy had chosen to set a fire in my store. If it weren't for that, I'd be inclined to let the cops do their job. It was clear Chief Kincaid didn't want my help. But trying to burn down my shop had been a serious miscalculation on the killer's part. He or she could have had just the cops to deal with, but then the murderer threatened my family's livelihood. And I definitely wasn't going to take that lying down.

I'd figured out whodunit three times before, and I could do it again. I certainly wouldn't get in the police's way, but being present for so much of the cupcake contest events meant that I had a better chance of discovering what was really happening in Kizzy's world than the cops did. So if I solved the case before Chief Kincaid, oh, well. He'd just have to accept it.

I briefly considered getting a pad of paper and a pen to outline my investigative strategy, but quickly realized that I had nothing to write down. My only lead was Harlee and I was fairly sure that I wouldn't forget my intention to question her.

Checking the kitchen clock, I saw that I had forty-five minutes until I needed to meet the trauma scene remediation company at the dime store, so I decided to swing by Forever Used and see if I could persuade Harlee to talk about Kizzy's past.

I didn't want to have to waste time parking and then moving my car, so I left the Z4 in the tiny lot behind my store and hiked over to Harlee's shop. She had leased the empty building located between Brewfully Yours and City Hall. It had previously been inhabited by a supermarket that had moved out to a strip mall on the edge of town to be closer to the new subdivisions, and the spot had been empty for a couple of years. All the merchants had been happy when we found out that it had been rented. Any business that would bring in more foot traffic to the square was good for all of us.

Forever Used occupied over seven hundred and fifty square feet of retail space, and as I entered the shop, I noticed that like I had with my store, Harlee had kept the vintage feeling of the structure. The wooden floors and original beadboard ceilings gave an impression of Old World elegance.

There were several customers browsing through the clothing racks, and a few more were wandering among the shelves. Scanning the shop, I saw that all four fitting rooms were full and Harlee and her clerk were both busy. Maybe this wasn't the best time to try and chat with the consignment store owner. Still, I was already there, so I decided to glance through the offerings and hope the place would clear out before I had to leave to open up my shop for the trauma scene remediation company.

There was a trio of large glass jewelry cases, and I peered into the one nearest the cash register, surprised at what was available. A set of four Chanel vintage goldtone bangles caught my eye, but when I saw they were priced at five hundred and ninety-five dollars, I quickly diverted my glance to the next piece. The David Yurman sterling-and-gold necklace was a thousand bucks, so I moved on to the second display case.

There, I fell in love with a pair of Stephen Dweck blue agate and quartz drop earrings, and even though they were a bargain at three hundred dollars, they were out of my price range. A few years ago, I wouldn't have thought twice about dropping that kind of cash on something that caught my fancy, but both my circumstances and priorities had changed. When I was still working as a financial consultant, I often told my friends that I liked to keep my money where I could see it—dangling from my ears or hanging off my back. Now, while I could still view my dough, it was in the form of merchandise lining the racks of my store.

The crowd inside Forever Used had thinned, but Harlee continued to be occupied with helping one of the remaining customers, so I drifted over to the shelves of designer purses. Handbags had always been one of my weaknesses, especially those that came in any shade of pink, and I found an absolutely fabulous Carlos Falchi Fatto a Mano strawberry metallic snake-print clutch. Next to the clutch was an even cuter Gianni Versace rose crocodile-embossed leather shoulder bag. I loved the Medusa head and chain strap, but even previously owned, both purses were ridiculously expensive, and I reluctantly walked away from them.

Harlee was ringing up the last shopper's purchases as her clerk lovingly wrapped each item in cream tissue paper and reverently placed them in a black-and-white shopping bag with FOREVER USED written in silver script across the front, so I stepped over to one of the clothing racks. Lucky for my wallet, most of the clothes were way too small for me. Sizes 2, 4, and 6 were well represented, and there were quite a few 8s, but the double digits were sparse and anything over a 10 was nearly nonexistent.

I was turning away when I spotted a Gucci dark brown leather jacket that might fit me. It had three silver-and-tortoise-trimmed Gucci engraved buttons down the front, faux flap pockets, and a silver-tone Gucci crest on one pocket. Before I could drool on the luscious jacket, I heard Harlee thank the woman at the register.

I moved toward Harlee as she said good-bye to her clerk and added, "See you tomorrow at ten."

When the teenager left, I strolled over to the counter and said to Harlee, "Hi." I waved my hand at the shop's interior. "Looks as if sales have been brisk. The dime store is doing well, too."

"Yeah. It's been incredible." Harlee glanced around, then scooted out from behind the register and hung the closed sign on the front window. "I have to admit I wasn't wildly enthusiastic about the whole Cupcake Weekend, but between the items I sold from the fashion show last night and the increased foot traffic and awareness of the shop, I'll be in the black for the first time since I opened my doors."

"Was the reason you weren't exactly eager for the event due to your past with Kizzy?" I figured I might as well get to the point since I couldn't figure out a good way to ease into the topic or to trick Harlee into telling me about the history between them.

"Partly," Harlee confessed. "But I also wasn't at all sure that a cupcake contest would attract the kinds of crowds Ronni promised."

"It is a little amazing that so many folks are interested," I agreed. "But I think it's as much an excuse to do something different, have a chance to taste some cupcakes, and not have to travel too far." I hooked my thumbs into the front pockets of my jeans. "From what I can tell, a lot of the visitors are day-trippers."

"Which is great since that means they might come back if they find our merchandise to be unique enough." Harlee's eyes gleamed, and for a second I could have sworn I saw dollar signs in the pupils. Then she frowned. "I heard about this morning's fire at the dime store. Where did it start? Was there much damage?"

"It started in the second-story office and luckily the only real damage was some singeing on the wooden floor." I watched her expression carefully as I explained, then asked, "Were you working here when it happened? Did you see the fire trucks go by your shop's window?"

"No." Harlee shook her head. "I was at the school, packing up the rest of the clothes from the fashion show, but when I got back to Forever Used, my clerk told me all about it." She grimaced. "And it's been a hot topic of conversation among my customers."

"I bet." I couldn't decide if I was relieved or disappointed that Harlee didn't have an alibi for the time of the fire. I liked her, but I really needed a suspect. "Have the Cupcake Weekenders sounded scared, like they might decide to leave right away or maybe not to come back for tomorrow's activities?"

"Some." Harlee took out her cash drawer and started to sort through the bills. "Especially the ones that have connected the dots between Fallon's death, the near-miss hit-and-run involving Kizzy, and the fire." Harlee looked at me. "Any insight on what the police are thinking about the coincidence of those events?"

"I assume they're considering that those three things are related, but my guess is that they have no idea where to go with that information," I lied easily. Total honesty had not been encouraged by my former boss. "The Shadow Bend cops don't have much experience solving any really complex cases, let alone something like this."

"That's a shame." Harlee started toward the back room. "Though I'm not surprised to hear you say that. The town never did have much crime and it doesn't seem to have changed much since I left twenty years ago."

"Speaking of that, you and Kizzy both went away right after high school graduation." It was evident that Harlee was ready to close for the day, so I knew that I only had a couple of minutes at the most to get to the bottom of what had gone wrong between her and Kizzy.

"Yes." Harlee's expression was neutral. "Lots of kids do that."

"But neither of you was planning on leaving until you went to college in the fall." I paused, and when she didn't deny what I'd said, I asked, "So, what happened? What changed both of your plans?"

"I'd had my doubts about college for quite a while," Harlee hedged.

"Really?" I raised my brow. "Both you and Kizzy seemed to have your futures mapped out. Wasn't Kizzy sure about college, either?"

"I can't speak for her." Harlee edged closer to the storage room entrance. "We didn't keep in touch, so I never knew what she did."

"I suppose twenty years ago without e-mail and cell phones being so prevalent, it was easier to lose track of people," I conceded. Harlee had her hand on the exit's doorknob, so I quickly said, "You know, I wondered if someone is trying to kill Kizzy for something she did in high school, but Chief Kincaid told me that Kizzy says she was very popular and everyone loved her back then." I tilted my head. "Being her best friend from then, is that how you remember it?"

"Think about it." Harlee pushed open the door. "How did everyone really feel about the most popular girl in your class? I doubt love was the emotion the majority of the less popular kids felt."

CHAPTER 16

The trauma scene remediation company's van pulled into the parking lot behind my store as I was unlocking the back door. After I showed them the areas that I needed cleaned and they got to work, I started the coffeepot behind the soda fountain brewing. While it dripped, I thought about my brief conversation with Harlee. She hadn't answered my question about why she and Kizzy had changed their post–high school plans so abruptly, but she had made a good point about the most popular girl in class usually being more feared than loved. A consideration I should have thought of myself.

Recalling my own adolescent experience, I was fully aware of how cruel teenagers could be. Before my father was convicted, I had been on the fringes of the in-crowd. Although too curvy to be a real part of the clique that ruled the school, I was tolerated because of my last name. The Sinclairs had been one of the five founding families of Shadow Bend, and even though we weren't as affluent as the other four had become, the fact that my ancestors were the original settlers of the town had been enough to protect me.

In addition to my family name, the inner circle had also overlooked my deficiencies because I was dating Noah, the most popular boy in our class. But once my dad went to prison and Noah broke up with me, my immunity was revoked and the clique turned on me like a tornado going after a mobile home. Their relentless bullying had been devastating.

Considering what I had witnessed of Kizzy's adult behavior and attitude, my guess was that her kind of narcissistic callousness didn't happen overnight. It made me wonder how Harlee fit into the scenario. As Kizzy's best friend, she would have had to be mean, too, or at least willing to turn a blind eye to her BFF's maliciousness.

That Harlee didn't appear that way now was puzzling. She seemed a little distant and guarded, but not spiteful or unkind. Could someone's basic personality change that much? Had her stint in the army reformed her? Or maybe getting away from Kizzy's influence and twenty years of maturing had allowed Harlee to be her own person.

Or had she completely fooled me? Harlee didn't have an alibi and had avoided answering my questions. During the last murder investigation, Jake had said that unless people had something to hide, they generally didn't mind answering questions. Maybe what Harlee was hiding was that she was the killer.

The cleaning crew finished their work by the time my father and Hannah arrived for the store's evening hours. We turned on the neon OPEN sign, put the standing sandwich board outside, and piped patriotic music out to the sidewalk.

At six o'clock, we unlocked the door, and the first people to push inside were reporters wanting to take pictures of the fire scene. They didn't like my nonresponses to their questions and they didn't believe me when I told them the damage had been so minor that there was nothing to see. Instead of wasting my time arguing, I pointed them to the stairs and told them to feel free to look for themselves. They swarmed up the steps, but less than fifteen minutes later, they stomped back down, grumbling about the lack of photo ops.

As happy as I was that the media had lost interest, I was equally thrilled when the folks attending the cook-out in the square started drifting into the store to browse. I manned the soda fountain, Hannah handled the candy case, and Dad took his favorite position behind the register, where he could charm all the lady shoppers. As I scooped ice cream and made sundaes, I chatted with the customers and eavesdropped on their conversations.

Most had heard about the fire and seen the news stories speculating that a killer was targeting Kizzy Cutler. There was a recurring theme of nervousness and concern for their safety, and I did what I could to reassure everyone that Chief Kincaid was confident that his officers would have the guilty party in custody soon. Crossing my fingers, I told them all that the police would probably arrest the suspect before the fireworks ended that evening.

Of course, I didn't believe that line of bull for a minute. I briefly considered making another phone call to the chief to share my new theory that someone was trying to kill Kizzy because she had been a mean girl in high school, but quickly rejected that idea. I was pretty darn sure that I'd never convince Eldridge Kincaid, a man who'd undoubtedly never been teased, how destructive bullying could be.

If the police weren't an option, that meant I needed to track down a list of those whom Kizzy might have tormented during high school. With Jake and Noah out of town, and Poppy busy with Gossip Central, I needed someone else to help me. Especially since I didn't have a clue as to how to find out about possible harassment that would have taken place over twenty years ago.

But my friend Boone might. He had a nose for gossip, and his genealogy hobby had made him a whiz at research. As an attorney, he wasn't trying to sell anything to the tourists, so he hadn't been as involved as Poppy and I in the whole Cupcake Weekend hubbub. But Boone loved a good mystery, and he would be more than eager to solve the case of the coldhearted cupcake queen.

As soon as the crowd thinned a little at the soda fountain, I sent Boone a text asking if he could come over to the store when we closed. His answer came in a few seconds later. He'd be there at eight fifty-nine, but he had to bring his cat along.

Since Tsar was adorable, I had no problem with him accompanying Boone, but wondered why he *had* to bring the Russian blue with him. Pushing aside my pet puzzlement, I went back to work. By eight forty, there were only a couple of shoppers left in the store, so I sent Hannah over to the square to enjoy the fireworks. She was anxious to join her friends and there was no pressing reason for her to stay the twenty minutes until we officially closed.

Dad left soon after Hannah to pick up Birdie, Frieda, and several of their pals. He'd agreed to chauffer the senior citizens to the festivities so they wouldn't have to worry about parking. He'd return after the pyrotechnics were over and drive them home.

As I waited for Boone to arrive, I tidied up the shelves, locked the cash drawer in the safe, and poured myself a cup a coffee. A few minutes later, when the sleigh bells jingled, I looked up, expecting to see Boone, but instead Lee Kimbrough hurried toward me. Her porcelain complexion had a grayish tinge and her rapid breathing made me wonder what new catastrophe had happened. Had the murderer succeeded in killing Kizzy?

"Dev, you have to help me." Lee's usual calm was completely shattered.

"With what?" I took her arm and guided her to the soda fountain. "Was Kizzy's injury worse than we thought? Or did something else happen to her?"

"No. She's fine. I just left her at the gazebo in the square, finishing up dinner." Lee collapsed on a stool. "The police think I poisoned Fallon and that I'm trying to murder Kizzy."

So Lee was the suspect that Chief Kincaid had referred to this afternoon. But since she wasn't in jail, his evidence must still be lacking.

"I take it the cops are mistaken?" I filled a glass with water and handed it to the distraught woman.

"Of course." Lee gulped down half the contents of the tumbler. "Why would I want either of them dead?"

"No idea." I sipped my coffee. "How do you know you're a suspect?"

"I got word from my accountant that the police obtained a warrant to exam my financial affairs." Lee finished the rest of the water.

"Did they discover anything they could use against you?" I asked.

"There was nothing for them to find. The business is doing spectacularly well and my personal finances are doing even better." Lee thumped her empty glass on the marble counter. "But several of my friends have texted me that they've been questioned regarding my relationship with Kizzy and Fallon."

"Which is?"

"Purely business on both counts." Lee raised a brow. "What else?"

"I have no idea." I met her gaze without blinking. "You tell me."

"Evidently, that small-minded police chief thinks that two single women can't be just partners." Lee sighed. "Kincaid's theory is that Kizzy and I are lovers and she started an affair with her assistant, so in a jealous rage, I killed Fallon and am now after Kizzy."

"Any part of that scenario a possibility?" I asked. "You do appear a bit subservient to Kizzy, which doesn't seem businesslike to me."

"No part of that scenario is remotely possible." Lee crossed her arms. "Just because I pick my battles with Kizzy doesn't mean I'm in love with her. Quite the opposite, actually. But she's the talent. Without her, there is no Kizzy Cutler's Cupcakes or all the lovely cash the company makes for me."

"Okay." I could certainly understand Lee's reasoning. As a financial consultant, I'd always been happy to cater to the egos of my clients. Whatever it took to make money, as long as it was legal, I had been all in. "So we've established why the cops suspect you, but not what kind of help you want from me."

"Rumor has it that you've solved more murder cases than the local police," Lee said. "I want you to find the real killer and clear my name."

"Well . . ." I thought about telling her that I couldn't possibly do what she asked, but then mentally shrugged. I was already investigating; why not admit it? Unless she was the murderer and this was some sort of trick to find out what I knew.

As if she'd read my mind, Lee pleaded, "Look, you don't have to tell me a thing. But if you figure this all out before the cops, I'll write you a check for five thousand dollars," she offered. "If you do it before the end of the Cupcake Weekend, I'll double that amount."

"Deal." I held out my hand and we shook. "In the meantime, I assume you've got a good criminal lawyer on speed dial?"

"Yes." Lee rose to her feet. "Ronni gave me the name of an attorney who stayed at her B and B when he defended a friend of yours. I've got Mr. Pryce on retainer."

"Smart move." I escorted Lee to the door. "I'll let you know if I figure anything out."

Boone arrived a few minutes after Lee's departure. After a quick hug, I locked the door, turned off all of the lights except for the one over my workbench, and carried two cups of coffee to the table. Boone had been wheeling a red cat carrier behind him, but now he parked the kitty transporter, pushed down the telescoping handle, and unzipped the mesh flap. Tsar poked out his nose, took a couple of sniffs, and trilled a greeting. Then having made sure that all eyes were on him, he exited the carrier and began to check out the boxes containing bits and pieces for my baskets.

With the elegant Russian blue occupied, Boone and I took a seat and I said, "Not that I mind, but why did you *have* to bring the cat?"

"Tsar's therapist says he was traumatized by my absence when I was away on the cruise a couple of months ago and it would be a grave mistake to leave him alone again until he emotionally heals," Boone said, a solemn expression on his handsome face, then added in a whisper, "He has abandonment issues."

"Oh." I struggled to keep a straight face. It was difficult to take the idea of kitty counseling seriously. "That's a shame."

"Doctor also recommends adopting a little brother

or sister for Tsar since he's missing Banshee." Boone grabbed a paper napkin from the table, reached down, and wiped a smudge from his Italian leather shoes.

"Really?" The Russian blue had formed an attachment to Gran's Siamese when he stayed with me while Boone was on vacation. The two cats' affection for each other still shocked me considering that Banshee hated everyone and everything except my grandmother. I had been pleased that the Siamese hadn't eaten Tsar as his midnight snack, but also flabbergasted that the kitties had become friends. "Are you getting another cat?"

"I'm looking into it," Boone said. "But he or she would have to be the perfect match for Tsar, both physically and personality-wise."

"Right." I bit back a giggle. Boone was a sophisticated man who wore designer suits and Serge Lutens Bornéo 1834 cologne; the picture of him as a feline matchmaker was almost too much for me.

"Don't laugh," Boone ordered. "It's Tsar's world. He just keeps me around to open his Fancy Feast cans."

"So I see." I reached down and scratched behind the pretty kitty's ears.

"What's up?" Boone asked me with a wide smile, his teeth strikingly white against his tanned face. He claimed that his skin was naturally bronzed from his Greek great-great-great-grandmother, but I knew about the tanning bed stashed in his back bedroom.

"How much have you heard about Fallon Littlefield's death and the attempts on Kizzy Cutler's life?" I asked, then took a sip from my freshly refilled coffee cup.

"Assume I have no knowledge and tell me everything from the beginning." The corners of Boone's hazel eyes crinkled. "I'm guessing the details are important or you wouldn't have asked me to come here and we'd be over in the square with everyone else watching the fireworks."

"Oh, my God!" I clapped my hand over my mouth. "I didn't even think about that. Did you have plans with someone for the evening?"

"Nothing important." Boone wrinkled his nose. "I was sort of glad to have an excuse to cancel. It was more business than pleasure."

"Anything you want to share?" I asked. Boone dated, but never discussed his love life, and he'd never been serious about anyone.

"Nope." Boone patted a strand of his tawny-gold hair back into place.

"Okay." Even though I was dying of curiosity, I respected his desire to keep his love life private. "So here's what's happened so far." I outlined what I knew about the two attempts on Kizzy's life and the death of her assistant.

"Interesting." Boone frowned, then used his thumb to smooth the line between his brows. "So the media was right about those three events being linked. I figured the reporters were jumping to conclusions."

"Not this time." My stomach rumbled and I wished that I had asked Boone to pick up dinner on his way. Generally, there were leftover bakery items at the soda fountain, but the crowds had completely cleaned out both my food stock and all my cupcake-emblazoned items. Good thing I had fresh supplies coming first thing tomorrow. It had cost extra for Sunday delivery, but I'd decided to take the risk and placed a large order to replenish my empty shelves.

"What are the police doing about the situation?" Boone asked.

"My impression is that they don't have any leads." I

recounted the conversations I'd had with Chief Kincaid and Harlee, ending with, "So my working theory is that someone from Kizzy's past here in town is the killer, but the question is, what happened that would make someone hold a grudge for over twenty years?"

"First, we need to find out who was in her class." Boone whipped out his cell, and his thumbs flew as he sent a text. "I'm reaching out to my friend Jeffrey, who was in high school during that time. I just asked if he had the yearbook for Kizzy's senior year."

Before I could tell Boone how brilliant he was, his friend texted back. Not only did he have the book, but Boone could pick it up tonight. Jeffrey had somewhere he had to be in twenty minutes, but if Boone didn't make it to the house in time, Jeffrey would leave the yearbook in a plastic bag hanging from his doorknob.

"Any other ideas about how to find out what happened back then?" I asked. "Do you think there'd be anything in the newspaper?"

"There might have been." Boone shrugged. "But the newspaper had a fire a few years ago, and since there were no digital files from back when Kizzy was in high school . . ."

"There's no way to search the old papers." I completed his sentence, adding, "And due to lack of funds, the city council closed down the Shadow Bend Library, so even if the library had them, there's no way now to find the old editions." I tapped my fingers on the tabletop. "It's doubtful that the library in the county seat would have archived issues of the *Shadow Bend Banner*, which makes the newspaper a dead end."

"So it seems." Boone toyed with his cup. "Although I agree with you that the killer is probably someone from Kizzy's past, I think we need to consider other possibilities. Let's start with the girl who died. Tell me why you're sure it was murder and why you think whatever happened to her was intended for her boss."

"First, Fallon strongly resembled a twenty-year-old Kizzy. Ronni mentioned to me that Kizzy hired the girl as much for that resemblance as her clerical skills. It seems that as Kizzy aged, Fallon's picture was used on the cupcake packaging and promo material, not Kizzy's. If someone remembered a young Kizzy, and the lighting was dim enough, they could easily mistake Fallon for her boss."

"And?" Boone waved his hand for me to go on.

"Second, the ME has ruled out natural causes, and Fallon's symptoms prior to her death are consistent with poisoning using DMSO, which is a substance that penetrates the skin." When Boone raised an eyebrow, I added, "DMSO often causes a garliclike flavor sensation, and Fallon reported having a bad taste in her mouth."

"And?" Boone waved his hand again.

"And three, Chief Kincaid said that none of the delivery services that cover Shadow Bend have any record of a package for anyone at the B and B's address that evening."

"Okay." Boone nodded. "I agree that it sounds as if Fallon was poisoned and it was intended for Kizzy, but the killer doesn't have to be from Kizzy's past. Someone who only knows Kizzy through her public persona might also mistake Fallon for her boss."

"Like one of the contestants." I finished off my coffee. I told Boone about the conversations I overheard between GB O'Rourke and his wife, and Lauren Neumann and her husband.

"Both good motives for murder," Boone said. "You know, it could even be someone who recognized that

Fallon wasn't Kizzy but couldn't think fast enough not to hand over the delivery."

"Like one of the judges or the cameraman and his sister." I explained what I knew about those feuds. "Which leaves us with a lot of people who had a motive to try to kill Kizzy."

"Exactly." Boone nodded. "We definitely need to look into them as suspects." He narrowed his eyes. "And let's not forget the business partner. From what you said she was never around when the attempts on Kizzy's life were made, so we need to see if she has alibis for any of those times."

"True," I conceded, then filled him in on Lee's status as the police's prime suspect and her request that I figure out who really committed the crimes. "So she offered me five thousand dollars to figure who really killed Fallon, ten if I do it before the end of the Cupcake Weekend. Of course, I'll split it with you."

"That's not necessary." Boone shook his head. "I'm happy to help you."

"Thanks, but I insist." Even though I needed the money and he didn't, fair was fair.

"Fine. You can donate my half to the animal shelter." He paused until I nodded in agreement, then asked, "Do you believe Lee's innocent?"

"Possibly." I shrugged. "Her explanation regarding her behavior with Kizzy was credible."

"Even if we eliminate the partner"—Boone took a slim gold pen and tiny leather-bound notepad from his shirt pocket—"Fallon could still be an intended victim, with Kizzy as victim number two."

"But why? From what I've heard, Fallon has no family and spent most of her time working. I'm fairly certain that any reason someone would try to kill her would have to do with Kizzy and/or the business." I hated to admit that the possibility of both women being targeted by a killer hadn't occurred to me. "Who would want both of them dead?"

"I have no idea." Boone frowned. "But we can't rule it out." He jotted something down. "We have a lot to investigate and not much time to do it before everyone leaves town, so since Kizzy is still an active target, we'll concentrate on her." He checked his watch. "Now I'd better get going so I can catch Jeffrey before he leaves. I want to ask him what he remembers about Ms. Kizzy."

I was hugging Boone good-bye when knocking on the front door startled us. After one final squeeze, I hurried to the entrance to see who was ignoring the closed sign. My irritation was replaced with a pleased tingle when I saw the fire chief grinning as he waved a pizza box and a six-pack of beer at me. He wore a pair of cutoff jeans with a crisp white T-shirt, and it was lucky that he'd brought food because he looked good enough to eat.

CHAPTER 17

I introduced Coop to Boone and watched my friend size up the new fire chief. I could almost hear the wheels turning behind Boone's handsome face as he shook hands with the hunky firefighter. The man had come bearing gifts and out of uniform, so it was clear he wasn't at my store in his official capacity. I knew Boone was wondering if Coop was offering Jake and Noah new competition for my affections.

Boone's smile worried me. He liked Jake, but he wasn't at all sure that the deputy marshal would stick around long enough to make me happy. And the antagonism between Noah and Boone had a long history. It had started when Noah ran against Boone in the sixth-grade election for class president. There had been a brief cessation of their animosity in high school while Noah and I were dating, but the minute Noah dumped me, Boone's aversion to Noah had resurfaced. For the next twelve years, the two men hadn't bothered to hide their scorn for each other.

Noah and Boone had agreed to a truce a few months ago when Boone was accused of murder and Noah had used his connections to help us find the real killer. But the armistice was tenuous at best, and it would take a lot more time for Boone to develop any true friendship with Noah. People who have never lived in small towns have no idea how serious and lifelong a feud can be, and I knew Boone and Noah's hostilities were far from permanently resolved.

Which was why I was worried when I saw the speculative gleam in Boone's eye and heard him chatting with Coop as if they'd been pals since kindergarten. Then when Boone laughed out loud and clapped the fire chief on the back after some remark that I had missed, I knew his matchmaking instinct was fully engaged.

This was so not good. I liked Coop. *Hell!* If I was going to be completely honest with myself, I had to admit that I was attracted to him. But two hot guys in my life were enough. I had never had the intestinal fortitude to indulge in a one-night stand. And the idea of playing the field with numerous men wasn't my style at all. So why had I opened the door and invited Coop inside?

Self-reproach chewed at my conscience like a squirrel eating his last acorn during a long, hard winter. It wasn't fair to either Jake or Noah to add a third man into the mix. They had grudgingly agreed to give me time to decide between the two of them, but not sample any eye candy that crossed my path. I had no viable excuse for allowing Coop even an inch into my life, let alone welcoming him and his pizza into my store.

I felt my heart sink when Boone winked at me, then said to Coop, "Wish I could stick around for some of that delicious-smelling pie, but I have an appointment that I can't miss." He shook the chief's hand, put Tsar in his carrier, grabbed the handle, and strolled to the door. With his hand on the knob, he added, "You two kids have a great time without me."

Once Boone was gone, Coop and I stared at each other for a long awkward moment. The silence throbbed with something I couldn't quite put my finger on. Finally, I gathered my scattered wits and said, "Thank you for delivering those two cupcake stands to Gossip Central. Poppy told me they arrived just in time."

"No problem." Coop made his way over to my worktable and put down the pizza box and six-pack. "Glad I could help you out."

"So, uh, I'm sort of surprised to see you here tonight." My mouth was watering from the delicious odor of oregano and basil wafting from my workbench. If I made him leave, could I keep the food?

"Yeah." Coop shoved his hands in his back pockets. "Well, I was walking by the dime store and I saw that your light was on, so I thought maybe you were working late and hadn't had time for supper."

"And you just happen to have a pizza on you?" I raised an eyebrow.

"Martello's made a mistake." Coop flipped open the lid. "I ordered a medium and they made up a large, so I thought I'd share."

"Why aren't you in the square watching the fireworks?" I stepped closer, trying not to drool at the heavenly aroma of melting cheese.

"Not my thing." Coop picked up a slice and held it to my lips. "I'd much rather spend the time getting to know you better."

His natural tenor deepened into a baritone, sending a zing of awareness shooting south of the border. "Mmm." I opened my mouth and took the bite he was offering, nearly swooning when the spicy flavor of the tomato sauce exploded on my taste buds. I savored the crunch of the thin, crispy crust and the umami of the mushrooms.

"And I thought you might want to know what the crime techs discovered about the fire." Coop fed me another morsel of paradise.

Unable to talk with my mouth full, I nodded. Then, acknowledging to myself that I was letting him stay, I fetched dishes, napkins, and utensils from the soda fountain. He smiled in victory and took a seat, but his expression fell when I dragged my chair to the opposite side of the table, as far from him as possible.

"If we sat closer together, I could keep feeding you." His tone was husky. "This here pizza is slap-your-mama good."

"Thanks." I ignored the seduction in his voice. "But feeding myself is a skill I mastered by age two. Besides, this way we can both eat." Pushing the box toward him, I added, "And you can tell me all about the crime tech's report without any distraction."

"Lord a' mercy!" Coop chuckled—a low sound that was too sexy by far for my peace of mind. "You admit that you find me befuddlin'."

"I meant that I might sidetrack you." I put a slice of pizza on my plate and cut off a piece with my knife. "Let's hear what you got."

"No one eats pizza with a fork." Coop rose from his chair, stretched his long, muscular torso across the tabletop, and plucked the offending utensil from my grasp. "Even Miss Edna Lou says it's okay to use your fingers."

"Fine." I agreed with him and Miss Edna Lou—whoever she was. I wasn't sure why I had suddenly decided to behave so differently. Maybe his Southern accent brought out the Scarlet O'Hara in me.

"Just relax." He grinned. "No need to be so formal with a good ol' country boy like me."

"Okay." I picked up my piece of pizza, but before

biting into it, I demanded, "Now tell me what the crime tech report said."

"All in good time." Cooped twisted open a bottle and handed me a Dos Equis. When our fingers touched, his eyes flashed with a hotness that zoomed straight to my core. "Mixing business and dinner gives me indigestion."

"Seriously?" I glared at him. "That's your best pickup line?"

"That's colder than a mother-in-law's kiss." Coop's expression was hurt, but it turned determined and he said, "Besides, I'm just warming up."

Uh-oh. I hadn't meant to challenge him. Backtracking, I held up my hands in surrender and said, "Sorry. I was only teasing."

"Me, too." He scooped a bottle for himself from the carton, opened it, and took a long swig. "Believe me, real men don't need pickup lines."

Since I agreed with him, I kept my mouth shut and did as he had suggested earlier—relaxed. We were having a casual bite to eat in my store, not a romantic supper in some candlelit restaurant. Just because he was handsome and charming and sweet didn't mean I was going to fall for him. I wasn't being disloyal to Noah or Jake. Coop was becoming a friend, nothing more.

The warmth of his gaze, the powerful play of the muscles in his arms, and his overwhelming presence didn't affect me in the least. At least that was what I told myself as we laughed and chatted our way through dinner.

When we finished, I got up and started to clear away the debris. While I gathered up the rubbish, I said, "So, about that arson report . . ."

"You're real tore up about all this, aren't you, darlin'?" Sighing, he followed me back to the soda fountain, picked up a towel, and cautioned, "It's only their preliminary finding, but it appears the accelerant was hair spray."

"Which means the attacker was probably a woman." I rinsed a soapy dish and handed it to him. "Some men may wear hair spray, but around here very few carry purses or have a bottle of Aqua Net in their pockets."

"Yep." Coop dried the plate and placed it on the clean stack on the shelf. "Plus, it's not a typical accelerant choice. A habitual arsonist generally uses gasoline, paint thinner, or kerosene."

"Do you think the fire was an afterthought?" I turned off the faucet.

"Either that or the attempted murderer doesn't know which end of a fork to scratch her head with." Coop leaned a hip against the counter. "She obviously had no idea how to disconnect your alarm system. Heck, she might not even have realized the store would have a hardwired smoke detector until it went off."

"Great." I folded my arms. "On the one hand, we've narrowed it down to women who hated Kizzy. On the other, the killer is a disorganized mess, which means it'll be harder to catch her with logic."

"Put yourself in her shoes." Coop stared at me, his inspection far too intense for my comfort. What was going through his mind? Finally, he said, "If you can't use reasoning, you'll have to use her impulsivity against her. How do you think the attempt on the cupcake lady went down?"

"Well." I gazed at the ceiling. "My guess is that Kizzy propped open the exit while she brought in the stuff for the afternoon's cupcake viewing and judging." I peeked at Coop and saw him nodding. "The killer had been watching Kizzy, saw her opportunity, and sneaked inside."

"That seems to be the same idea the police have," Coop said.

"Then the murderer tiptoes up the stairs, finds Kizzy with her back to the office door, scoops up the trophy, which is maybe sitting in a box on the floor between them, and bashes Kizzy over the head."

"So far, so good," Coop encouraged. "My source at the PD says that the trophy was wiped clean of prints, but there was a partial on the alarm and another on your back doorknob."

"Your informant wouldn't happen to look like a pneumatic Barbie, would she?" I asked, picturing the skanky dispatcher that had tried to latch onto Jake. She'd been willing to give information to him on the basis of his good looks, and Coop was pretty much Jake's equal in that department. "Or is Chief Kinkaid actually sharing?"

Ignoring my question, Coop ordered, "Don't get distracted with details. What do you think happened after Miss Kizzy was knocked out?"

"Probably, the killer wasn't sure if she was dead or not but didn't want to get sprayed with more blood by hitting her again." I chewed on my thumbnail. "There was a lot of blood when I found her."

"Yep. Head wounds usually bleed like a son of a gun," Coop agreed. "The killer could have worried about getting splattered or she could be a tad squeamish. It's one thing to bonk someone over the noggin once or poison them or run them over with a car, but it's a lot more up close and personal if you have to hit them over and over again." He paused, then added, "And for some reason, I'm picturing the killer as a woman who's about half-preacher."

It took me a second to figure out Coop's meaning; then I realized he was referring to a person who was publicly virtuous, but privately immoral. "True." I hadn't thought of the killer as being skittish, but Coop had a good point. "So instead of beating Kizzy with the trophy some more, the killer decides to finish her off by burning her to death."

"However, as I mentioned, said perp doesn't realize the store has an alarm system," Coop said. "That would mean she'd be surprised when the smoke detector goes off and she'd try to take it down."

"But it's hardwired into place, so she panics and rushes out of the store, forgetting to wipe her prints from the detector," I finished his thought.

"Exactly." Coop levered himself from the counter and moved nearer to me. "It's just a darn shame that Kincaid didn't put a tail on Ms. Cutler after the hit-and-run incident. Maybe the officer would have spotted the perp sneaking into the dime store's back room."

"I take it someone is watching Kizzy twenty-four/seven now?" I stood my ground, but as he closed in on me, my stomach fluttered.

"Oh. Yeah." Coop took my hand. "But I understand she took on about the officer's lack of discretion something fierce and has hired a private bodyguard to replace him."

"Of course she has, but I bet Chief Kincaid still has a tail on her." I led Coop to the store's entrance. "Kizzy strikes me as a person who is rarely satisfied with anything, but the chief is no pushover."

"Yeah. I can't see Kincaid trusting a civilian. He'd want one of his officers there as a backup." Coop attempted to pull me nearer, but I didn't budge. He frowned, then suggested, "Why don't we take a walk over to the village square and see if we can rustle up dessert from one of the vendors? I saw a couple selling taffy apples and cotton candy, and the church ladies will for sure have a bake sale table."

"You go ahead." I freed my fingers from his grasp. "I'm going to track down some of my suspects and see if any of them have alibis."

"That doesn't sound like as much fun, but count me in." Coop held open the front door, gave a little bow, and swept his arm out. "After you."

"Thanks, but no, thanks." I backed away. "I have something I need to do here first." When he started to speak, I added, "Alone."

"So you're kicking me out?" Coop asked, his expression suddenly sober.

"Yes, I am." I had never been one to sugarcoat the obvious.

"Fine." Coop's mouth tightened, but then he grinned. "But I'll see you Monday night for that lasagna supper you promised me."

He leaned forward, his lips touching mine in a teasing promise. The warmth of his breath stroked my face and it took me a second to move away from him. "Thanks for the pizza." I smiled, then assured him, "I'll be at your apartment at quarter to seven. See you then." I pushed him over the threshold and locked the door behind him.

Once he was gone, I sat back down at my worktable and began making a list of the people who had a reason to want Kizzy dead. By the time my phone started playing Ross Copperman's "Holding On and Letting Go," I had nine names on my sheet of paper—Millie and GB O'Rourke, Thomasina Giancarlo, Russell and Lauren Neumann, Q and Dirk Harvey, Annalee Paulson, and Harlee Ames.

My heart sped up as I fumbled my cell from my

pocket, and said, "Noah? Is everything okay? I thought you wouldn't be able to call."

Noah's face appeared on the screen of my phone. "Everything's fine."

"Are you in Haiti?" I asked. The wall behind him was an anonymous gray.

"Uh-huh." Noah nodded. "I had a little time until the evening rounds, and since I miss you like mad, I decided to call you rather than go to eat with the others."

"You shouldn't have done that." A ball of guilt settled in my stomach. What if he'd called while I was chowing down with Coop? He had forgone food to talk to me, and I'd given in to the lure of a spicy pizza and a spicier firefighter. "You need to keep up your strength."

"I'll grab something quick later, but I wanted to see your face." Noah touched the screen. "I thought I'd try out the video chat feature on my new iPhone. It's not as good as being with you in person, but at least I can look into your beautiful eyes while we talk."

"That's so sweet." I tucked a stray curl behind my ear, conscious that I hadn't bothered with makeup that morning or combed my hair all afternoon. Even in the rough conditions of a field hospital, Noah looked perfect, while my appearance had undoubtedly not improved with the events of the long day I'd had. "Tell me all about what you've done so far." I attempted to get his attention off my lack of grooming.

After giving me a rundown on what his team had accomplished so far, he asked, "How's the Cupcake Weekend going?"

I filled him in, and then, feeling as though I had no choice since someone—and by someone I meant my dear friend Boone—was bound to mention Coop to him when Noah returned from Haiti, I added, "The new fire chief is involved in the investigation because of the arson. He dropped by the store a little bit ago to bring me up to speed."

"Really?" Noah leaned forward. "Then he was only there for a few minutes, right?"

"Uh." I bit my lip. *Hell!* Boone would spill all the details, so I had to fess up. "Well, not exactly. The pizza place messed up his order and gave him a large instead of a medium, so he shared it with me." I quickly added, "You know, waste not, want not."

"Pizza's not very good without beer," Noah commented in a deceptively mild tone.

"Coop had a six-pack with him," I confessed. "He was on his way home to eat his dinner when he saw that the dime store's lights were still on, so he decided to drop in. None of this was planned."

"Of course not. Why would I think that this sounded like a date?" Noah's pearl gray eyes darkened. "Just because my nurses were all talking about how handsome McCall was before I left doesn't mean you'd go out with him, right?"

"Right." I choked out the word.

"The women at the clinic were excited that he wasn't some paunchy old man like the previous chief," Noah continued as if I hadn't spoken. "Have you met his wife?"

"Is he married?" I squeaked, before it dawned on me that if Coop had a wife, he wouldn't be inviting me over to cook dinner for him.

"Maybe not." Noah sighed, as if I had confirmed something in his mind, then made a big deal of checking his watch. "I've got to get over to the clinic to give out the evening meds." He blew me a kiss and said, "Miss me."

"Always," I promised. Before I could add anything, the screen went dark. I couldn't help comparing Noah with Jake, who rarely found time to call me while he was on assignment. As I turned out the light and went to get my purse from the back room, I mentally tallied the score between the two men in my life—Noah 1, Jake 0.

A tiny voice in my head asked me what Coop's score was, but I firmly told that voice to shut up. I also hushed my conscience when it asked why I hadn't told Noah that I was seeing the fire chief Monday night. After all, I was just repaying a debt, and I didn't want to distract Noah from his important work.

Absolving myself from the sin of omission, I grabbed my shoulder bag from the desk drawer and went to find the first suspect on my list.

CHAPTER 18

"Son of a bitch!" Noah roared as he slammed his fist into the metal filing cabinet next to his chair. He winced, both from the throbbing in his knuckles and the knowledge that he'd handled Dev all wrong. Ending the call so abruptly had been exactly the opposite of what he should have done after hearing about her little tête-à-tête with McCall, but he couldn't stand the intrigued look on her face when she said the guy's name.

Hanging up was his only option, because the lump lodged in his throat made it almost impossible to speak. Where was his famous cool demeanor? It seemed to disappear whenever he was anywhere near Dev. When she worried her lip between her teeth, all he'd wanted was to kiss away the marks she made in the moist pink skin.

Noah had been so happy when he discovered that he had cell reception. Then when everyone had headed out to dinner and he'd finally had some privacy, it seemed like the perfect time to video-chat with Dev. What would he have seen if he'd been able to call half an hour earlier? Or would she have been too occupied with the new fire chief even to bother to answer the phone?

Once again, Noah pictured McCall's face on the cabinet and drew back his fist for another whack at the guy, but he stopped himself in midswing. No matter how much he hated the man who had snagged Dev's interest, damaging his hand because of his bruised ego was not an option. It would be too selfish to give in to some childish impulse and not be able fully to perform his duties to his patients.

He paused, thinking that an injury might get him sent home early, which would give him a chance to stop whatever was starting between Dev and Fire Boy. No. Noah shook his head. He'd made a promise and he wasn't the kind of man who went back on his oath, even if keeping his word put his own happiness in jeopardy. But hell, wasn't competing with Deputy Dawg enough? What kind of sadistic universe threw Mr. July from the firefighters' calendar into the mix?

Maybe he was blowing the whole situation out of proportion. Noah ran his fingers through his hair. The fire chief would certainly be eager to solve his first case of arson in his new job. And the whole pizza dinner thing could have been the result of a messed-up order and chance. Dev did say that McCall had just dropped by the dime store.

Nope. No matter how much he tried to convince himself differently, Noah knew that Dev was attracted to the guy. When she talked about McCall, her cheeks had gotten as red as a schoolgirl's. And the Dev he knew and loved for so long never blushed.

Noah slumped back in his chair. So what was he going to do about this new development? Maybe he should give Del Vecchio a call. Certainly, Officer Friendly had as much to lose as he did if Dev fell for McCall, and he was only a few hours away from Shadow Bend.

Lacing his fingers behind his neck, Noah gazed at the ceiling, considering the pros and cons of involving his rival. On the pro side, Del Vecchio could and probably would mop the floor with the fire chief. On the con side, the marshal might look a little too much like a knight in shining armor riding in to battle the dragon for his lady fair.

Damn! That might be a worse move than hoping Dev's interest in McCall would fizzle and die once she got to know the man. So whom could he call on for help? Boone would be happy to see Dev interested in another guy. For entirely different reasons, neither Noah's mother nor Birdie Sinclair wanted to see Dev and Noah together. And Kern Sinclair's feelings about his daughter's relationship with Noah were still a mystery, which left Dev's father out. Who did that leave?

Poppy! Noah straightened. She was perfect. She thought Noah and Dev made a good match. And she had the added advantage of being a knockout. She could lure McCall's interest away from Dev. But was it kosher to ask Poppy to steal a guy from her best friend?

Noah stared at his phone. No. It was wrong on too many levels. Despite his gut saying that all was fair in love and war, he couldn't do it. He couldn't ask Poppy to betray her friend and he couldn't manipulate Dev in that way. It might rip his heart out if he lost her, but he wanted her to be with him because she loved him, not because he'd eliminated any other temptations from her life. That was why he'd agreed to go along with Dev dating him and Del Vecchio at the same time.

Dev was a feisty, passionate woman who fought for what she believed in. Noah didn't want to change her or take away any of her choices. He wasn't going to try to outmaneuver her, but he also wasn't going to let anyone, especially some Don Juan fireman, get between them, either. As soon as he got home, he'd redouble his efforts to win her love. He'd had it once and he was going to get it back again.

Sighing, Noah glanced at the clock. Patients were waiting for him and all he could think about was the color of Dev's panties. Were they lacy black ones that matched the bra he'd glimpsed the last time they were together? Or were they pink and sweet like the ones she'd worn in high school?

He pushed back his chair and got to his feet. Time to put Dev and her underwear out of his mind and do his job. But damn, he loved that woman. And soon she was going to realize that she loved him back.

CHAPTER 19

After making sure both the front and back doors of the dime store were locked, I tucked the key into my purse, settled the strap on my shoulder, and walked outside. As I crossed the street to the town square, a huge sphere of silver and gold burst overhead, illuminating the ebony sky. Craning my neck, I watched as a trail of sparks arched from the dome of stars. The result reminded me of a glittering weeping willow tree.

Evidently, the fireworks were beginning. I had thought they were scheduled for earlier, but apparently the planned starting time was when the party began, not the actual pyrotechnic display. No doubt, people had staked out their slice of lawn by six o'clock and since then had been enjoying the patriotic music provided by the Shadow Bend Band, as well as the food and drinks for sale from the Presbyterians. I should have realized that shooting off fireworks before it was totally dark would have been too stupid even for our mayor, whose intellectual blunders were legendary.

It was a challenge to navigate the narrow paths between the blankets and folding chairs covering nearly every inch of the grass. And as I tiptoed through the maze, I saw that the gazebo had been reserved for Kizzy, Lee, His Honor, and other key players in the Cupcake Weekend.

When Coop informed me that the accelerant used to set the fire on my second floor was hair spray, I had eliminated Vance Buddy from the first tier of my suspect list. Kizzy's lawsuit forcing his blog to be removed might have infuriated him, but his extremely close-cropped hairstyle certainly didn't need Final Net to keep it in place.

I had hoped to talk to the other two judges during the event, but they were behind an impenetrable fortress of town dignitaries, so I moved on to plan B. The contestants hadn't scored seats on the gazebo, which meant they'd be easier to corner.

Unfortunately, the lack of illumination was a problem. The pole lights that lined the footpaths were dimmed so that the fireworks would be more visible, and although many groups had candles or lanterns, just as many didn't. Fishing inside my shoulder bag, I located my keys and switched on the flashlight attached to the ring.

As I crept through the labyrinth of blankets and lawn chairs, I casually swept the occupants with my tiny Maglite. To say that not everyone was pleased to have a bright beam of light aimed at his or her face would be like stating that snowbirds disliked winter—pretty darn obvious. Gritting my teeth, I persevered, apologizing again and again, but determined to find my quarry.

Just as I was about to give up my search until after the fireworks ended, I stumbled—literally—into GB O'Rourke. Tonight, GB wore green-and-orange-plaid shorts and a neon yellow shirt. His chubby cheeks were the color of the two bright red candy apples he was carrying in his left hand. In his other hand, he balanced a tray containing four hot dogs and a plate of nachos and cheese. Clearly, there was no chance he or his wife would leave the picnic hungry.

After we both regained our balance, I said, "I'm so sorry. How clumsy of me. If you dropped anything, I'd be glad to buy you a replacement."

"Not at all. None of the goodies are MIA." GB smiled. "Besides, I should have been looking where I was going."

"That's so nice of you to say. Let me help you with that." I eased the cardboard tray from his grasp. "Where are you sitting?"

"Millie and I have a blanket right over there." GB pointed over my shoulder.

"Great," I enthused. "Lead the way. I'll be right behind you."

GB's spot was only a couple of feet from where we bumped into each other, and his wife waved as we approached. While we put the food down, he explained to her about our little collision, then said to me, "Would you like to join us?"

"That would be nice, but just for a few minutes." I sat cross-legged, facing the couple. "Don't let me stop you from eating."

"Help yourself. There's plenty here to share." Millie tsked. "GB's eyes are bigger than his stomach." She glanced at her husband's potbelly, then winked. "Hard as that might be to believe."

"Thanks, but I already ate." I wiggled, trying to find a comfortable spot. "Are you two enjoying yourselves in our little town?"

"Very much." Mille smiled. "I hope your store is going to be open tomorrow morning. I've been meaning to stop by, but it seems like our every moment is scheduled with competition events."

"It's open until late afternoon," I assured her. "After that, I figure everyone will be at the award ceremony dinner."

"I'll stop by right after church." Mille picked up a nacho chip.

"Terrific." I pretended to think, then said, "Oh, yeah. I heard that back in Oswego, GB is a minister. Which faith is your congregation?"

"We're nondenominational." GB bit into a hot dog, then spoke around it. "When we travel, we choose the church that has the most welcoming building or the cleverest sign and worship there."

"That's very open-minded of you both." It sounded a little weird to me, but who was I to judge? I'd been a lapsed Catholic for so long I couldn't remember the last Mass that I'd attended. And if I ever went to confession again, all I could say was that the priest better not have anything else planned for that afternoon.

"Tomorrow we're trying the Presbyterians. The parishioners doing the cookout tonight were so friendly we decided to go to their service."

"Great." I smiled, then asked, "How did the first round of baking go for you today?"

"Excellent." GB licked mustard from his fingers. "I think I have a real shot to win."

"That's wonderful." I was running out of admiring adjectives and needed to steer the conversation toward his supposedly plagiarized cupcake. "How does that work? Do you bring your own secret ingredients or did you have to provide a list to the contest organizers?"

GB and Millie exchanged glances; then she patted the huge purse sitting at her side. "They have all of the standard fixings, but I've got GB's secret ingredient right here, and unless he wins, no one will ever find out what makes his cupcakes so scrumptious."

"That seems fair." I eyed her handbag. It was definitely big enough to hold a bottle of hair spray. Heck. It was large enough to hold the giant economy-size can. "But if the competition officials don't see your recipe, how can they be sure it's original? That you just didn't copy something from the Internet?"

"Why would you ask that?" Millie narrowed her eyes until they looked like raisins studding the buttermilk biscuits of her round cheeks.

"No reason." I pasted an innocent expression on my face. "Just curious."

"The contract we all had to sign says if Kizzy Cutler's Cupcakes discovers the winning recipe wasn't created by the contestant, the prize is forfeited," GB explained. "They have thirty days to investigate after the winner is announced."

"Ah." I nodded. "Now I understand." Time to change the subject since I couldn't figure out what else to ask about the cupcake. "Is it hard to produce your normal quality of cupcake in an unfamiliar kitchen?"

"It was a little tricky." GB brought a cheese-covered nacho to his mouth. "But the run-through we were allowed on Friday really helped."

"That's good." This was my opportunity to check Millie's alibi. I didn't need to know where she was for all three incidents. If she had an alibi for one, I was willing to put her on the bottom of my suspect list. "So, did you all come into town the night before so you'd be fresh and ready for Friday's practice round?"

"Unfortunately, we couldn't." Millie tsked. "By the time we got the word that GB was a finalist, we already had the children's choir recital scheduled for Thursday evening, and we couldn't miss that."

"That's a shame. But at least you said it didn't handicap him." *Hmm.* If they were telling the truth, Millie couldn't have been the one who delivered the poisoned package to Fallon. How could I ask for proof?

I was distracted when an eruption of large multicolored stars rocketed across the sky, and then with a loud crackling sound the fireworks broke apart into hundreds of smaller stars. The three of us oohed and aahed over the crisscrossing effect.

As I watched a teenager aim her phone at the display, an idea popped into my head and I said, "I love children's choirs. Did you record their program?"

Millie gave me a suspicious glance—I guess I didn't look like the type of person who enjoyed kids singing—but she dug through her purse, took out her cell, and pushed a few buttons. Once she had the video, she handed the device to me and shaky footage of six- and seven-year-olds crooning "God Bless America" filled the small screen.

"Wow." I forced admiration into my voice. "Those little ones are amazing."

"They are darling, aren't they?" Millie gushed, leaning over my shoulder.

As the camera panned the stage, a hand-lettered sign appeared. Printed in red was:

Christian Assembly of God
Children's Choir
Thursday, July 2, at 7:00 PM

It appeared that Millie and GB had an alibi for the night of the poisoning. Which meant I could remove them from prime suspect status. I watched the video for a few more seconds, then made my excuses and left GB and Millie crunching into their candy apples.

It was time to move my interrogation efforts to couple number two on my suspect list. I glanced at the sky.

It appeared that the fireworks show was ending, because the bursts were getting closer and closer together. I needed to locate Russell and Lauren Neumann before the finale. When the event broke up, everyone would disperse, and once the Neumanns headed back to their motel room, I wouldn't be able to talk to them until tomorrow.

Lauren and Russell hadn't struck me as people comfortable with sitting on the ground, so I concentrated on the lawn chair crowd. It was a little easier to scan them than the folks on the blankets, since there were fewer chairs and their occupants' faces were less difficult to see. I edged toward the gazebo, thinking that Russell had seemed like someone who would want to sit as close as possible to the big shots in order to have the best possible chance to schmooze with the VIPs and the judges.

My hunch paid off, and I found the Neumanns seated in the first row behind the reserved area. Russell's chair resembled a blue canvas throne. There was a table attached to the arm and even a footrest. Lauren sat by his side in a smaller version of the same elaborate chair, although hers was pale pink.

I caught Lauren's eye and she smiled. I waved, and as I drew closer, she said, "Dev, I hope you didn't have any ill effects from last night's close call." She smoothed an imaginary wrinkle in her sunny yellow dress. "Everyone said that you and Ms. Cutler hit the ground awfully hard."

"Thank you for asking, but I'm fine. The only fatalities were my dignity and white pants."

I had forgotten Lauren was one of the first people on the scene after Kizzy's near-roadkill experience. She couldn't have been behind the wheel of the vehicle that attempted to mow down Kizzy and gotten to us so fast.

But I hadn't seen Russell there, so he could have driven the car and Lauren could be the arsonist. It suddenly occurred to me that the couples might well be working in tandem. Good thing both the O'Rourkes had an alibi.

"Are you meeting friends or would you like to join us?" Lauren leaped up from her chair, whipped out a stool, and unfolded it. "The Presbyterian ladies outdid themselves. We have some of their delicious roast beef sandwiches left over, if you're hungry."

"Thanks, but I'm stuffed." I edged my ample backside gingerly onto the camp stool and breathed a sigh of relief when it supported my weight. "But I'd love to sit and chat until the fireworks are over."

"Goody." Lauren clapped her hands. "How are sales going at your store?"

"Very well, but my fingers are crossed that tomorrow will be the real showstopper." I smiled at her enthusiasm—and her bright red tights—then asked, "How did the baking go for you today?"

"You're sitting with the winner." Russell spoke for the first time. "Her cupcakes were the first to disappear this afternoon when the people who had snagged the golden tickets were allowed to taste and the judges loved them." He frowned, then asked, "By the way, why was the whole shebang switched from your store to the bar?"

I explained about the fire but omitted Kizzy's attack. I knew the media had written about it, but I wasn't sure what details had been released to the public and I didn't want to get either the cupcake queen or the police chief ticked off at me. I ended with, "I'm surprised you didn't hear about it. It was on the news."

"We haven't seen a paper or listened to television or radio since we got here," Russell said. "Why bother? It's all manipulated by the feds or the liberal fringe."

I wasn't surprised with Russell's view of the media. Heck, I half believed the same thing. Except I thought along with the government both the liberals *and* the conservatives controlled various news outlets.

"When did the fire start?" Lauren asked, fingering the tiny ladybug buttons that marched down the front of her dress. "I was at the cooking school prepping and baking from nine a.m. until a little before two."

"Of course." *Hell!* I had forgotten the contestants would have been occupied, not to mention filmed during that critical period. "But, Russell, weren't you downtown to see the fire engines?"

"Nah." Russell adjusted the crease in his khaki shorts. "I stayed with Lauren at the cooking school the whole time she was there." He glared. "I was on watch to make sure no one sabotaged Lauren's cupcakes."

"Do you really think something like that would happen here?" I asked, barely restraining myself from adding, paranoid much?

"You can't be too careful." Russell crossed his arms. "That's why I had our attorney look over the agreement Lauren had to sign."

"Oh?" I leaned forward, encouraging him to elaborate. This was exactly the stuff I wanted to hear.

"Yeah." Russell bared his teeth in what I guessed was supposed to be a smile. "There was a rumor floating around that the ten-thousand-dollar prize money was going to be some kind of structure payment bullshit instead of one big check, so I scanned the agreement and e-mailed it to our lawyer to check out."

"And?"

"And if that Cutler broad was planning on shafting us that way, she's in for a little surprise. The contract calls for a single payment." Russell's chest puffed out. "No one pulls one over on Russell Neumann."

"It's nice to see a man who's confident in his wife's ability, but judging is subjective, so how can you be sure Lauren will win?" I was curious about his scheme to blackmail the Italian judge into fixing the contest.

"Let's just say that the writing is on the wall." Russell leaned back, then muttered, "Or at least on the paperwork in my pocket."

CHAPTER 20

My interest in the Neumanns was waning, so I made my excuses and left them watching the last of the fireworks. Although it was possible that Russell might have slipped away from the baking, I doubted he would have left his wife's cupcakes unprotected. That, and the fact that his lawyer's assurance of a single payment for the prize meant he no longer had a motive to want to hurt Kizzy, made me decide to take the couple off my primary suspects list.

I hadn't decided what to do about the potential contest fraud or Thomasina Giancarlo's possible status as an illegal alien. If I didn't figure out something by the time Boone brought the yearbook over to the store tomorrow, I'd ask him for his advice as a lawyer on both matters.

Thomasina might have more reason to want Russell dead than Kizzy, but I still wanted to talk to her. Just not tonight. I was exhausted. It was close to eleven p.m. when I made my way through the mob exiting the town square and reached my car where I had left it behind my store. Poppy was holding another after-hours event at her club for the party animals, but I'd been on the go since my alarm buzzed at six a.m. and wasn't up to a party.

One or both of the judges whom I needed to question might show up at the event, but I couldn't make myself go to it. The idea of sitting around a noisy bar, socializing with hyped-up tourists, was about as appealing as a liver-flavored cupcake with anchovy frosting on top. All I wanted was some peace and quiet—and twelve hours of sleep. I was almost guaranteed the former, but the latter was just a dream until the contest was over.

I drove by Gossip Central, and was pleased to see that the parking lot was packed. It wasn't surprising that Poppy's party had a big turnout. Not only was it a holiday Saturday night, but her club was the hottest spot around in a forty-mile radius and evidently the news that someone was trying to kill Kizzy hadn't scared off any of the Cupcake Weekenders. The crowd at the fireworks and now at Gossip Central was proof that I'd been wrong to worry. It seemed that the threat of a murderer running around the competition didn't bother anyone except me.

Smiling at the prospect of how much money the dime store would rake in tomorrow, I headed home. It would be another early morning and busy day and I needed to be rested and ready to sell, sell, sell. Oh, and figuring out who was after Kizzy might take a little energy, too.

Sunday's wake-up call came way too soon. The delivery of fresh supplies was scheduled for six a.m., so I grabbed a quick shower and shimmied into jeans and a lime green Devereaux's Dime Store polo. After twisting my wet hair into a loose bun on top of my head, I drove into town, inhaling a Kashi blackberry graham cereal bar as I steered the Z4 down the deserted road.

Gran hated it when I didn't let her cook me a hot

breakfast, but there was no reason for both of us to be up at the butt crack of dawn. I'd make it up to her once the Cupcake Weekend was over and my life got back to normal. Monday morning, she could make me her famous puffy French toast with warm maple syrup and a side of crispy bacon. My mouth watering at the thought of Gran's cooking, I parked the BMW behind my store and went inside to wait for the bakery van and delivery truck to arrive.

It took me until nine to get the new merchandise unpacked and on the shelves, and I realized that I should have asked Dad and Hannah to come in early to help. Instead, they arrived as I unlocked the front entrance. Sales were brisk until just before noon, when the crowd thinned to go to lunch.

I had considered expanding the soda fountain's menu to offer sandwiches and chips, but with only three stools, I didn't have enough room to feed many people. I could have done a brown bag special that diners could have eaten in the town square, but Little's Tea Room traditionally provided box lunches and I didn't want to step on any toes or make enemies.

Although I regretted the loss of revenue, I was happy for the break. Hannah and Dad took turns eating their midday meals, and an hour later, when they both were back on duty, the place was full of customers again. I stole a few minutes and ducked into the back room to text Boone. I had expected him to come by the store earlier with the yearbook and I was concerned that he hadn't shown up yet. There was no message from him on my cell and it wasn't like him to go radio silent on me.

His reply chimed as I was gulping down a carton of Greek yogurt. He'd been delayed by an emergency with a client who was going through a messy divorce and custody battle, but he would be over as soon as he finished handling the woman's meltdown.

Disappointed that I'd have to wait to see the yearbook, I tucked my phone back into my pocket and returned to the sales floor. The final bake-off—again being broadcast on the large plasma screens at Poppy's club—was scheduled from nine until one. The Ferris wheel and roller-coaster displays had been returned from Gossip Central's Hayloft to my second floor this morning, and the entrants' finished products would be transported to the dime store between one and two. Once they were all in place, there would be an hour for everyone to view the exhibit; then the judges would taste and confer.

The winner would be announced at the conclusion of the dinner being hosted by the Methodist church ladies at approximately seven p.m. After that, the Cupcake Weekend, except for cleaning up and counting the cash, was officially over. Considering the stack of greenbacks in my safe, calculating the profits might take quite some time, but it was time I was more than willing to devote to the process.

Whistling, I returned to work. The first batch of cupcakes arrived a few seconds after I stepped back behind the register, and their appearance was followed closely by the three judges. I wasn't sure if they would be around for the entire viewing time and I needed to question them about their alibis, so since we were busy, but not swamped, I asked my father to keep an eye on things.

After telling Hannah to text me if they needed me on the sales floor, I headed for the stairs. I wasn't sure how I was going to get Annalee Paulson or Thomasina Giancarlo alone. But for once luck was with me and I found Thomasina on the landing with a confused expression on her face.

When she spotted me, she asked, "Do you know if there's a restroom I can use?"

"Yes." I introduced myself as the owner of the dime store, then said, "Follow me." The building had two sets of bathrooms, one off the main sales floor for the public and one located in the storage room for employees. As I led her to the latter, I said, "I haven't heard how the cupcakes are judged. Do you each get one vote?"

"The three of us taste all the entries. Then we give every cupcake a score from one to ten for originality, taste, and appearance," Thomasina explained with a charming accent. "In each round, thirty would be the best possible score any entry could receive and three the worst."

"So it would be difficult for any one judge to influence the outcome." I held open the back room entrance, motioned her inside, and closed the door. "In order to fix the contest, all of the judges would have to be in on the collusion."

"Collusion?" she echoed; then her face cleared and she said, "Ah, you mean we would have to all agree to make someone the winner."

"Right." I pointed out the restroom, and as she hurried past me, I added, "Like, if one of the contestants were going to blackmail their way to the prize, it would only work if they had something on all three judges." I paused and thought about the math. "Or at least they'd have to be able to influence two of you."

Thomasina stopped and turned to look at me, her eyes narrowed. "I am here legally." She crossed her arms. "Mr. Neumann is a foolish man. He doesn't realize that I am married and my husband is a United States citizen. I have all the proper paperwork." She smiled thinly. "Another piece of information that Mr.

Neumann doesn't possess is that Giancarlo is my mother's maiden name, so he wasn't looking in the correct place for me."

"And you didn't enlighten him because where's the fun in that?" I raised a brow. "Are you going to turn him in to the authorities?"

"No. If his wife does not triumph and he tries to seek revenge, I will let his actions do him in." She stepped into the restroom and before closing the door said, "I am not a chair bird."

Huh? I stared after her, trying to translate. It took me a second, but I finally decoded her meaning. Thomasina meant a stool pigeon. Smiling, I realized that I wouldn't have to be a chair bird, either. The Italian judge was legal and the contest wasn't fixed. There was no need for me to get involved in either matter.

Figuring that Thomasina could find her way back upstairs without my help, and having no real need to see if she had an alibi since I knew of no motive for her to want Kizzy dead, I returned to the second floor. I had a feeling getting information from Annalee might not be as easy as the process had been with Thomasina.

I found Annalee and Vance Buddy sitting in the space that had been reserved for the judges. The old office furniture had been removed and the room was now furnished with a couch, a couple of armchairs, and an occasional table. Against the far wall a lunch buffet with bottled water, soda, and coffee had been set up for them.

Knocking, I slipped in without waiting for a response, then said, "Hi, I'm Devereaux Sinclair, the owner of the dime store. I hope you all are comfortable."

"Yes, we are, thanks." Vance beamed, his teeth gleaming against his mocha skin. "Your delightful town has really rolled out the welcome mat for us."

"I'm glad to hear that." I smiled back. "Ms. Giancarlo was looking for the restroom and I thought perhaps you two might need to freshen up also but not want to use the public facilities. If so, please feel free to use the one inside my storage room." I hoped one or the other would get up, but neither budged. "Otherwise is there anything I can get for you?"

"Actually, since we seem to have a little time"—Vance rose to his feet and stretched—"I'd like to make some calls, but I forgot the charger for my cell. Is there a landline I could use?"

"Certainly." I nodded, happy to get rid of him. "If you go down the steps and make a right, you'll see the entrance to the back room. There's a phone on the desk that you're more than welcome to use." I added, "Just put the 'do not disturb' sign on the door if you want privacy."

"Oh, I don't need one of those." Vance chuckled. "But maybe a sign that says 'already disturbed, enter at your own risk' would be good." He winked at me and left.

Once he was gone, I took a seat in the chair opposite Annalee and tried to figure out how to ask her about her whereabouts when Fallon was poisoned and/or the two attempts on Kizzy's life were made. I wasn't sure how much time I had before Thomasina returned or how long Vance's calls would take, so I needed to come up with something soon.

My mind was still racing when Annalee said, "Heavens to Betsy! Will you look at all the food they have for us?" She bounced off the sofa and strolled over to the refreshment table, examining the various sandwiches and munchies. "Did you do all this?"

"No." I shook my head. "The contest organizers arranged everything."

"Not Kizzy, I'm sure." Annalee picked up a bottle of water, looked at the label, and put it back in the bucket of ice. "I wonder who's running her errands now that poor Fallon isn't around."

"Fallon's death must have been quite a shock to everyone." This was my opening and I didn't want to blow it. "Her being so young and all."

"We were all stunned." Annalee selected a plate. "But now that the police think she was murdered, the whole situation is even more bizarre."

"Yes, it is," I agreed. "Especially since Fallon might not have been the intended victim of the poisoning."

"Exactly." Annalee turned from her perusal of the food and looked at me. Tapping her finger to her chin, she asked, "What do you think is behind all the drama our little contest has stirred up?"

"Well . . ." I wasn't sure how to respond. It seemed awfully cold to refer to a young woman's murder as *drama*. "Anytime you have an influx of new personalities, there's a good chance there'll be some problems. I know when Shadow Bend agreed to host the competition, we sure weren't expecting someone to try to assassinate Ms. Cutler."

"That was a bit of a surprise." Annalee fluffed her short blond hair. "Although, considering how quickly Kizzy flies off the handle, it stands to reason that she's made quite a few enemies."

"She does seem a little short tempered," I agreed. "In fact, my grandmother is a huge fan of your show, and she told me about the episode when Ms. Cutler was your guest." I glanced at Annalee, whose mouth had tightened, and added, "When she splattered you with raw batter."

"Precisely." Annalee's pale blue eyes were frosty. "Kizzy's behavior was inexcusable." The TV chef sighed. "It's only because Lee and I are such good friends that I agreed to judge this contest."

"So you and Ms. Cutler haven't exactly kissed and made up?" I asked.

"She publicly apologized and I accepted." Annalee's expression was hard to read.

"Ms. Cutler doesn't strike me as someone who apologizes very often," I commented. "So that must have felt like a real triumph for you."

"Yes. Yes, it did." Annalee smiled widely, then said, "And that episode with the food fight went viral, which really shot our ratings through the stratosphere for a while." Her smile faded and she shook her head. "But I'll never have Kizzy on my program again."

"I sure wouldn't," I agreed. It sounded as if although Annalee didn't like Kizzy, she really didn't have a good motive to kill her. Still, just to be on the safe side, I wanted to know if the TV chef had an alibi. "It must be tough to get away for even a little while since your show is live five days a week."

"*Sugar and Spice* is on summer hiatus." Annalee returned her attention to the refreshment table. "If it wasn't, I couldn't have been a judge."

"Did you come in from Kansas City Thursday night?" I could ask Ronni when the TV chef arrived, but this was my lead-in for other questions.

"No. I couldn't leave town until the next morning." Annalee finished choosing her lunch. "I had agreed to provide the desserts for the Pink Ribbon Fireworks Ball, so I actually didn't arrive until Friday at noon."

"Just before the big contest kickoff in the town square?" I confirmed.

"Right." Annalee brought her plate back to where she was sitting, then returned to the refreshment table and selected a can of Dr Pepper. "That's why the opening ceremony started a little late. It took me longer to drive here than I was expecting. My GPS said an hour, but it was closer to ninety minutes with traffic and everything."

"I used to commute, and even under ideal conditions the trip was never under an hour and a quarter." I glanced at the door. Thomasina and Vance would be coming back anytime now. "I bet the desserts you made for the ball were gorgeous. Did you take pictures?" Hey, pretending interest had worked with the kids' recital; why not give it another try?

"Just a few." Annalee dug her cell from her purse and handed me the device. "But the newspaper covered the event, so there should be more on their Web site."

A dozen or so photos of Annalee with elaborate chocolate and sugar confections later, I was convinced that the TV chef had an alibi. I would check the newspaper's Web site to confirm the date and time, but it looked as if another suspect could be scratched from my list.

If Q and her brother were in the clear, I was going back to my original theory that the murderer was from Kizzy's past, rather than her present.

CHAPTER 21

By the time I finished admiring Annalee's dessert pictures and excused myself, Vance and Thomasina had returned and the three judges settled down to enjoy their lunch break before the cupcake tasting began. After checking the store and assuring myself that Hannah and Dad didn't need my help, I slipped into the back room to pull up the *Kansas City Star*'s Web site on my laptop. I could have done it on my phone, but Boone had informed me that squinting at the small screen to read a lengthy article would give me wrinkles. Since the idea of injecting the bubonic plague or botulism or whatever the heck disease Botox contained into my forehead made me queasy, I vowed to follow his advice.

The *Star*'s site confirmed Annalee's alibi. There was a feature about the Pink Ribbon Fireworks Ball and several photos of celebrities. A shot of the television chef dressed to the nines with her arm around the guest of honor in front of an elaborate chocolate and sugar tower confirmed her Thursday evening whereabouts.

The article said that the ball had begun at seven p.m., so even if the picture of Annalee was taken right after the event started, the absolute soonest she could have arrived in Shadow Bend would've been eight thirty. According to my calculations, Fallon had accepted the delivery about seven fifteen.

Satisfied that Annalee was in the clear, I returned to the sales floor. Although people were streaming through the dime store's entrance, few were stopping to browse. They all hurried to the stairs and headed for the second floor. Vouchers were being given to the first seventy-five folks to arrive, and once the viewing was over and the judges had done their tasting, all the ticket holders would be allowed to choose one cupcake to eat.

The entire event was being filmed by the Dessert Channel's crew with commentary and interviews provided by the host, Merry Woodworth. Dirk Harvey, along with a second cameraman, was already upstairs working the event. He and the rest of the television crew had shown up with the first wave of attendees, but there had been no sign of Q.

As I stood behind the candy counter and filled a gold-foil box with our special of the day, blueberries and cream truffles, I watched the door. I could only hope that Dirk's sister would be on hand, since I had no idea how else to find her. Surely, Merry would want her makeup and hair freshened during such a long event. If Q didn't show, I wasn't sure how I'd locate her, and I needed to figure out if she had an alibi for Fallon's murder.

I also kept an eye out for Boone. His latest text had informed me his client's meltdown had been handled and he promised that he'd be over with the yearbook right after Tsar's psychoanalysis session. Surprising as it was that kitty counseling was available at all, that the therapist worked on Sundays was astounding.

It was close to two thirty, and I had about given up

on Q when she, the ten contestants, and their significant others walked through the entrance. Following that group were Lee, Kizzy, and a man who by the look of his bulging muscles, military-style buzz cut, and the gun strapped to his hip had to be the bodyguard that Coop had mentioned. Evidently, Rambo wasn't available, so Kizzy had had to settle for this guy.

I smiled. Jake would be so happy to see that the Cupcake Weekend now had security. My smile faded. I hadn't had a call from him since we were interrupted by the Doll Maker summoning him to the latest rendezvous. What if Jake had been shot? Or what if that monster had kidnapped him, too?

My chest tightened; then I forced myself to breathe. Surely, I would have heard if anything had happened to Jake. If only because his uncle Tony would be notified.

With the cupcake exhibition in full swing, the dime store was down to fewer than a dozen customers, so I told Hannah to text me if a horde of shoppers descended; then I ran up the stairs. I waved at the three judges who were sitting at a bistro table near the door; then as I mingled with the crowd, I kept my eye on Q and Dirk. My plan, such as it was, included following one or both of them if they ever left the room.

When I finally made it to the platform where the cupcakes were displayed, I gasped. If anything, these creations were even more stunning than the first round. I recognized GB O'Rourke's Bananas Foster entries from the slice of caramelized banana inserted into the thick cream cheese frosting, and my mouth watered.

Next, I spotted Lauren Neumann's Caramel Espresso submissions. They were iced with Swiss meringue buttercream that was drizzled with caramel syrup and topped with chocolate-covered coffee beans. My stomach growled, and I was suddenly sorry I hadn't nabbed one of the golden tickets that would allow me to taste the amazing confections beckoning to me from the display stands.

The sight of all the sugary goodness had distracted me, but I looked away just in time to see Q slip from the room. With one last longing glance at the gooey treats, I hurried after the young woman. I needed to find out how Q had tried to stop Kizzy from getting her fired and what her brother's plan B had been. I was also interested in how Dirk's previous scheme had landed Q in a mental health facility. The fact that that info wasn't really any of my business unless it was relevant to the murder attempts didn't make me any less curious.

Q's minnowlike build allowed her to glide effortlessly through the throng of people going in the opposite direction. I, on the other hand, felt like a fat salmon trying to swim upstream. It was a good thing that she was again dressed as if she were trying out for the sequel to *The Rocky Horror Picture Show.* Although her Cyberdog T-shirt, Living Dead Souls jacket, and tutu skirt were mostly black, her horned headband was bright pink, which made her easy to spot as she slithered toward the exit.

When one of her Noctex skeleton garters popped and she stumbled, I nearly caught up to her. Evidently, keeping your balance on the seven-inch Demonia platform boots was as hard as it looked. Once she was outside the exhibition space, she paused and I hung back just out of sight to see where she was headed. The short hallway only had two options—the judges' lounge or the stairs. She glanced behind her, peered into the lounge, then darted inside. I was just about to follow her when Kizzy and her bodyguard walked past me and joined Q. I scratched my head. In none of the scenarios that had run through my fevered imagination did Q and Kizzy have a meeting.

Now the question was, how was I going to hear their discussion? Sadly, I didn't have wings, so hovering outside the office's second-story window was out. Did pressing a glass to the wall really work? Probably not, and besides, how would I explain my actions to the tourists going in and out of the cupcake exhibit?

Wait! The heating vent. The lounge was directly above the stockroom. During the remodeling, the builder had told me that the office's ductwork ran down the wall of the storeroom. He'd informed me of this when he was explaining that the construction had to be done a certain way. At the time, I hadn't been too interested since I wasn't footing the bill, but now I hoped this was the solution for my eavesdropping dilemma. Fingers crossed, I ran down the steps, into the back room, and over to the vent.

Pressing my ear to the opening, I heard Kizzy's voice. "If your brother isn't going to redo the interview, we have nothing to talk about."

Apparently, I had missed the part of the conversation where Q had delivered the bad news.

"And if that's the case," Kizzy continued, "why did you insist on meeting up? You could have just texted me Dirk's refusal."

"I don't think blackmailing me is something you want a permanent record of." Q's tone was smug. "In fact, if I were you, I'd ask Muscle Guy here to wait in the hall unless you want me to call him as a witness to your extortion attempt."

"I'll take my chances," Kizzy snapped. "You only want him gone so you can have another try at killing me."

"That wasn't me!" Q squealed. "I'm a vegan. I'd never harm a living soul."

Q was a vegan? I could have sworn she ate the chicken at the St. Saggy dinner. Had she thought it was tofu? And I distinctly remembered her chowing down on a piece of chocolate pie. Did she not realize that there was butter in the crust and milk in the filling?

"How about your fiancé?" Kizzy's voice interrupted my musings. "You certainly harmed him."

"How do you know about that?" Q shrieked. "That was an accident. I just wanted to punk him. He was always playing practical jokes on me and I could never get him back, so Dirk came up with the idea for me to mess with Abe's beloved Harley."

"Loosening the front wheel of his motorcycle is hardly a prank," Kizzy said.

"He shouldn't have been going so fast," Q cried. "And it was supposed to just wobble—not come off."

"And now he's a paraplegic." Kizzy's voice was growing faint and I figured she was walking toward the door. "But that's beside the point. Someone with your history of psychiatric hospital stays should not be working on a television show. There's too much stress. Then you make mistakes like you did with my hair."

"Dirk can't redo the interview because Merry refuses," Q sobbed. "You should be mad at her, not us. He'd do it if she would."

"That's not my problem," Kizzy said. "Since you are unable to meet my terms, I'm sending a formal letter of complaint to the producer and stating that I expect you to be fired." She paused, then in a falsely sympathetic tone added, "You're just too unstable to be trusted with something important like a star's appearance, my dear."

"I'm not." Q's voice was desperate. "When you were so upset Thursday afternoon, I immediately made an emergency appointment with my therapist for seven p.m. and Dirk drove me to Kansas City that evening. I talked to my shrink for three hours and she said that I was fine."

"So you were in KC from seven to ten?" Kizzy's voice grew stronger. Plainly, she had decided not to leave the lounge quite yet. "Can you prove that?"

"Yes," Q answered. There was a pause, and then she said, "Here's the parking ticket from the garage. Since Dirk was nice enough to drive me, I paid for it and kept the receipt for my tax guy. And here's my psychologist's card. She can tell you I'm fine. I'll give her permission to talk to you about me."

I grinned. Who would have guessed that Q would employ an accountant, worry about her taxes, or be so meticulous with her records?

"It looks like you aren't the one trying to kill me after all," Kizzy mused. "Unless you somehow figure out how to alter the time stamp—and frankly, my dear, I don't think you're smart enough to do that—you were in Kansas City from six forty-five to a little past nine fifty-eight on July second. I guess this lets your brother off the hook as well. Since this is his parking ticket, he couldn't get his car out of the garage without it registering. Which means he'd have to deliver you to your shrink, rent another vehicle, drive to Shadow Bend, deliver the package to Fallon, and be back in KC to pick you up before ten. That would be quite a trick." The cupcake tycoon hesitated, then said, "Okay. Provided your therapist can assure me you aren't dangerous, I'll let the hair incident slide, if—"

"Thank you! I—"

"Let me finish," Kizzy interrupted. "If you learn how to do a proper French twist and agree to do my hair and makeup for free for all my public appearances for the next year, then I won't write the letter of complaint."

"As long as I know enough ahead of time to trade gigs with another network stylist, I can do that," Q vowed. "But how will I get to your events?"

"I'll provide transportation to anything that's more than a three-hour drive."

"Thank you so much for the opportunity." Q sounded subdued. "I appreciate it."

"You have a good sense of style," Kizzy drawled. "Except, of course, in your own wardrobe choices. But I have to admit, your makeup techniques are amazing. You took at least ten years off my face."

"It's the under-eye concealer," Q gushed. "I mix it myself."

The conversation turned to makeup techniques, and after a few minutes of listening to which sponge or brush was best for what effect, I lost interest. Having ascertained that Q and Kizzy had come to a detente, and that both Q and her brother had an alibi, I felt free to leave my eavesdropping post in the storeroom.

I had run out of suspects from Kizzy's current life, and I was more convinced than ever that her would-be murderer was someone from her past. Now I just needed Boone to show up with that damn yearbook.

CHAPTER 22

There was a break between the end of the exhibition at four, and the award dinner, which started at five thirty. Hoping that as people left the display room upstairs they would stop to do some eleventh-hour souvenir shopping, I planned to keep the dime store open until the last minute, then head over to the Methodist church for the supper.

Happily, I had guessed correctly. After the judges did their final tasting and withdrew to vote for the winner, the shop was inundated with customers. As I scooped ice cream, boxed candy, and kept the shelves of cupcake-themed items fully stocked, I thought about Kizzy's sudden change of heart toward Q.

I would have sworn she'd never allow the French twist incident to slide. She seemed like the type to hold a grudge so tightly it would have to bite her before she'd let it go. Although, if Q really could perform antiaging miracles with her makeup applications, Kizzy was no doubt getting the better end of that bargain.

When the deluge of shoppers thinned to a trickle, I glanced at my watch and frowned. I was starting to get worried about Boone. There was still no sign of him, and his last text had sworn that he had one more errand. Then he was on his way.

Several more minutes ticked by and I was thinking of texting Boone again to check on him when he finally arrived. I had already let my father and Hannah leave, so I waved Boone to the soda fountain stools and turned my attention back to the trio of silver-haired ladies debating the purchase of matching cupcake earrings.

The women were the last customers in the store but seemed in no hurry to finish their shopping. My patience was about worn out by the time they settled on the earrings with the blue cupcake liners versus the pink ones. Gritting my teeth in a lockjaw smile, I herded them over to the register and rang up their purchases. When the last octogenarian handed over her twelve dollars and fifty-three cents, I escorted the threesome to the exit, thanked them for their patronage, and restrained myself from pushing them out the door.

As soon as they cleared the threshold, I turned the lock, flipped on the closed sign, and joined Boone. "Where in the hell have you been and where's your cat?"

"Hello to you, too," Boone said, not at all disturbed by my impatience. "Tsar's therapist decided he was ready for a playdate with my folks, so he's staying with them for a couple of hours."

"I'm glad Tsar is doing so much better," I said sincerely, then eagerly reached for the yearbook that Boone held protectively cradled to his chest. As we played tug-of-war with the annual, I demanded, "What did your friend say about Kizzy?"

"Jeffrey was gone by the time I got there, but he left a note with the yearbook saying that Kizzy and her clique reigned over the school like Marie Antoinette and her court." Boone continued to resist my efforts to pry the volume away from him and added, "He wrote that even the teachers were intimidated by her and her friends."

"Aha!" I finally managed to wrestle the book out of his fingers. "So Kizzy's claim to Chief Kincaid that she was loved by all was a lie."

"Shocker." Boone waved his hand in front of his face. "A popular girl who was mean. Could you get any more cliché than that?"

"Fine." I started paging through the yearbook. "Have you looked at this?"

"I haven't had time." Boone crossed his legs. "And I wasn't sure exactly what to search for. I mean, we can't talk to the entire senior class. We need to figure out how the yearbook can help us narrow down who hated Kizzy."

"Yeah. And the killer might not even be someone who was in her grade. It could be anyone in school with her at the time," I mused. *Shoot!* What *were* we looking for? I thought about it and said, "Maybe the activities pictures or the seniors' last will and testament or the section where the seniors' futures are predicted will give us a clue."

"Those are as good places to start as any." Boone reached over and flipped pages until he came to the group photos. "Wow. Kizzy was in almost everything. She was the captain of the cheerleading squad, and here she is singing the lead in the all-school musical, and here she is again on the debate team. Hell, she was even a member of the FHA."

"There was a Federal Housing Administration club?" I raised a brow. Now I'd heard everything. "What did they do, loan out lunch money?"

"Once a financial consultant, always a financial consultant," Boone snickered. "FHA is Future Homemakers of America," he clarified. "According to their banner in the photo, they are the family, career, and community leaders of America." He tilted his head. "That's probably where Kizzy got interested in baking."

"Or her interest in baking was why she joined the organization," I said. "Although Harlee did say she and Kizzy had planned to marry their high school boyfriends and live next door to each other, so maybe Kizzy just wanted to learn to be a good homemaker."

"Could be," Boone murmured. "How ironic. I see Kizzy only came in second place in the FHA cooking contest. Odd it doesn't say who came in first. I bet Kizzy was ticked off at the winner."

"No doubt." Having been around Kizzy for the past four days, I felt it safe to assume that she would regard second place as first loser. "The cupcake queen would not take being defeated well."

"It looks as if Harlee was in all the clubs and activities, too." Boone pursed his lips. "But she was always in Kizzy's shadow. She was the lead's sister in the play and the assistant captain for the cheerleaders and a floater for the debate team."

"We definitely need to have another talk with Harlee," I decided. "She avoided my question about why she and Kizzy left town so abruptly and why, after being best friends, they didn't keep in touch."

"That is suspicious." Boone nodded, then said, "Oh, here're the senior prophecies."

"And?" I was curious to see what Kizzy's classmates had predicted for her future.

"According to this, Kizzy and Harlee will marry their high school sweethearts and live next door to each other in matching mansions." Boone made a face. "They will each have two adorable children—a boy and a girl—and become president and vice president of the CDM."

"I'm sure Noah's mother would have had something to say about that." Nadine had been the supreme ruler of the Confederacy Daughters of Missouri for as long as anyone could remember.

"If Kizzy Cutler had gotten married and stuck around Shadow Bend, I have a feeling Nadine might have had a run for her money." Boone smirked.

"Any mention of who the girls' sweethearts were?" I realized we hadn't figured out any of the other members of Kizzy's posse.

"There are a lot of pictures of Kizzy, but it seems that anyone with her in those photos is in the shadow and their faces are hard to see."

"Crap!" I bit my lip. "We have to get Harlee to identify the rest of the crew."

"Put that question on the list," Boone ordered, then added, "Here's the seniors' last will and testament. Kizzy leaves her overwhelming popularity to no one."

"Wow." I marveled at the sheer audacity that it took to put something like that in writing. That was quite an ego, even for a teenager. "How about Harlee?"

"I don't see anything for her." Boone ran his finger down the page, then shook his head. "Nope. Either Harlee didn't write her will or the yearbook editor left her entry out."

"Who was the editor?" I asked, fairly sure I knew the answer.

Boone turned to the listing in front of the book. "Kizzy, of course."

Having come to a dead end, we examined the yearbook again, this time going page by page. At the very back, stuck between the end pages and the cover, was a yellowed newspaper article. I placed it gently on the marble countertop and read the faded print.

> A white Cadillac DeVille driven by 16-year-old Marla Parrett was struck Saturday night by a train on the outskirts of Shadow Bend. Police report that the accident happened on the railroad tracks near First Avenue. Investigators said the girl was killed instantly. Police continue to investigate. The victim's family refused to be interviewed, saying they are too grief-stricken to comment.

"I wonder why your friend Jeffrey kept this clipping," I mused.

"Let's go over to his house and ask him," Boone suggested. "I texted him that I'd return his yearbook this afternoon, and he responded saying that he'd be home all day."

"Perfect." I got up and started shutting off the lights. "I need to put in an appearance at the dinner, but even if we spend an hour talking to your friend, we should be able to get there in time to grab a bite to eat before the award announcement."

I locked up and we headed over to Jeffrey's place. A few minutes later as I pulled into the driveway of the nineteen twenties brick bungalow, I was glad that Shadow Bend was so small and that most of the cupcakers were probably already over at the Methodist church, staking out the best tables. A couple of miles between most destinations and no traffic to speak of made me thankful to live in my little hometown.

We walked up a short ramp to the front porch and I admired the four redbrick pillars supporting the sloping roof. The exterior was in pristine condition, but the vintage feeling of the house had been retained. Jeffrey greeted us at the door, and after Boone introduced me, his friend invited us inside. We followed Jeffrey's motorized wheelchair as he led us into the living room and waved us to a seat on the brown leather sofa.

"You have a lovely home." I gestured around me. "The earth tones and walnut floor really complement the brick. And I love your wrought-iron chandelier and candleholders. It feels so cozy in here."

"Thank you. I've tried to restore it to what I imagined the original owners might have had." Jeffrey positioned his chair facing us. "Can I get you something to drink? I've got a fresh pot of coffee on."

"No, thanks," I answered for us both. "We need to get over to the cupcake dinner before the awards, so we're in a little bit of a hurry."

"We won't keep you, but we have a question about an article we found in your yearbook." Boone handed the clipping over to his friend. "We wondered why you had saved this particular piece."

"Ah." Jeffrey examined the yellow paper carefully. "My first love."

"Marla Parrett was your girlfriend?" I asked, then said, "I'm so sorry."

"Not my girlfriend." Jeffrey smoothed the clipping. "We were in occupational therapy together. She had a visual-motor learning disability and I was there because of my cerebral palsy." He shook his head. "But she was a sophomore and I was only a freshman, so I never asked her out." He gestured to his wheelchair. "Plus, I wasn't sure how any girl would feel about this."

"So you admired her from afar," Boone said. "Her accident must have been a horrible shock for you and everyone else in the school."

"It wasn't an accident." Jeffrey's lips thinned. "And

for most people in our school, Marla's death wasn't even a blip on their radar."

"Oh?" I asked, not quite sure how a train hitting a car could be anything but an accident. "Are you saying Marla was murdered?"

"You could say that." Jeffrey sighed. "Marla was bullied to death by Kizzy Cutler and the Cutthroats, which is what we called her clique. They didn't physically abuse her, just tore her to shreds with their words."

"You mean Marla committed suicide?" I asked, wanting to make sure I understood his meaning. "But that wasn't what the article said."

"Her family and the school worked together to hush it up, but witnesses said that Marla drove her car onto the tracks, shut off the motor, and just sat there as the train crashed into her." He closed his eyes. "And no one cared enough to make sure the truth came out."

"Why is that?" I asked, then answered myself. "Because no one wanted to admit that some poor girl had been tormented so badly by the popular kids that she'd decided that death was the only answer."

"Precisely. The adults couldn't acknowledge that a girl was persecuted to the point that she was afraid to walk down the hallway." Jeffrey scowled. "Marla's parents were already ashamed of their less-than-perfect daughter. She had a learning disability, she wasn't socially adept, and she had no interest in makeup or hairstyles or the latest fashions." Jeffrey tapped his fingers on the arm of his chair. "She was quiet, sweet, and loved to cook. Not exactly what most teenagers, or even grown-ups, admire."

"What I don't understand is why Kizzy would target a mousy sophomore." I tried to recall what I knew about bullies' motives but drew a blank. Making a metal note to call one of my sorority sisters who was a school psychologist, I refocused on Jeffrey.

"It all started that fall when Marla won the FHA baking contest with her vanilla-rosewater cupcakes," Jeffrey explained. "She had come up with this amazing honey lavender icing, and her entry beat Kizzy's by a mile. Besting Kizzy in that competition invoked the wrath of the Cutthroats."

Something about Jeffrey's answer rang a bell in my head, but before I could figure out why, Boone said to his friend, "You didn't mention this in the note you left me in the yearbook."

"I hadn't thought of Marla or what happened to her in nearly twenty years." Jeffrey looked at Boone. "Last night when you texted me about Kizzy, I was in such a hurry all I could recall was how popular she was." Jeffrey stared at his lap, then buried his head in his hands. "No. That's not true. I just didn't want to relive it. I felt guilty. I had been so afraid that if I spoke up and tried to stop them from bullying Marla, they would turn on me."

"I very much doubt that you could have done anything to change what happened." Boone got up and hugged his friend. "If anyone should feel ashamed for not intervening, it should be the teachers."

"No," I said sharply, and both men looked at me strangely. "If anyone should feel guilty about Marla's death, it should be Kizzy and her friends."

CHAPTER 23

"We need to talk to Harlee," I said, checking my watch as I slid behind the wheel of my Z4. "Let me call her and see if she's home."

"Won't she be at the supper?" Boone asked, buckling his seat belt.

"I bet you're right," I said. "Since the little chat I had with her after the fashion show about people commenting about her absence at the cupcake events and the importance small-town folks put on socializing, Harlee has attended all the festivities."

"It would be more productive to surprise her than to phone her and give her time to come up with answers," Boone suggested.

"Absolutely," I agreed. Harlee was a smart cookie, and I had a feeling she'd avoid the subject of Marla's suicide if she could.

I glanced at my watch. We'd spent fifteen minutes with Jeffrey. It took only five more to drive to the Methodist church, so dinner was still being served when we arrived. I spotted Poppy as soon as we walked into the banquet hall. The mayor had her cornered by the punch bowl. When she saw Boone and me, she jerked her head, indicating that she'd join us as soon as she was free.

Harlee was sitting at a table with several women business owners I knew from the Chamber of Commerce. She seemed to be having a good time and I hoped that I wasn't about to ruin her evening for nothing. When I caught her eye, I motioned for her to step into the hallway. With a puzzled expression, she nodded her agreement, then excused herself and stood.

"What's up?" Harlee asked as soon as we were in the corridor.

"Do you know my friend Boone St. Onge?" I asked, ignoring her question.

"Yes." Harlee smiled at Boone. "He represented me when I purchased my store."

"As I recall, you did all the hard work." Boone beamed back at the shopkeeper. "You negotiated a great deal for that building."

"Well, Boone and I were best friends all during school," I said before the conversation got sidetracked into real estate law. "Sort of like you and Kizzy." I leaned a hip casually against the wall. "Except, of course, that Boone and I have remained close."

"How nice for you." Harlee's tone cooled. "But you two stayed in Shadow Bend."

"True," I conceded. "Though geographical proximity is just one part of friendship. There's also all the shared secrets and nicknames. Sometimes our friends know too much of our past to ever really untangle our lives." I allowed her to process what I had said, then added, "Like being part of Kizzy's clique. Once a Cutthroat always a Cutthroat, right?"

"I see you've been talking to someone from the old days," Harlee said, frowning.

"That's the problem with a small town." I stuck my

hands in my pockets. "Long memories." I paused, then said, "Especially when a girl takes her own life rather than face one more second of bullying."

"I—" Harlee flinched as if I had slapped her, but she lifted her chin and said, "I don't have any idea what you mean."

"Let's not drag this out." The more I thought about Marla's torment, the less patient I became. "Because Kizzy couldn't stand to come in second in anything, let alone a baking contest, the Cutthroats harassed Marla Parrett until she drove her parents' Cadillac onto a railroad track, shut off the motor, and waited for a train to wipe her off the face of the earth." I stared at Harlee. "There's no way you weren't a part of Marla's mistreatment. Birds of a feather flock together. Then they crap all over the ugly ducklings."

"I . . . I . . ." Harlee tried to speak, then buried her head in her hands. Finally, she wiped the tears from her cheeks and choked out, "Poor Marla. There isn't a day that goes by that I don't regret what we did to that girl. Regret that I decided to stick with my friends rather than put a stop to Marla's persecution . . ." Harlee trailed off, then said, "The psychological damage Kizzy inflicted with her bullying was only a game to her. She reveled in the chaos it created. But the night Marla died, I vowed never to allow anyone else to be terrorized."

Before I could respond, Boone squeezed my arm and shook his head. I closed my mouth and waited. I still wasn't sure how this all connected to the attempts on Kizzy's life, but I was beginning to see a glimmer of possibility. If I could just nail down the thought that was floating in the back of my consciousness.

"I joined the service the next day," Harlee continued. "And I worked hard to make sure wherever I was stationed or whatever I was assigned to do, the people of that country and the soldiers around me were protected." She straightened. "I'm not sure I can ever forgive myself for what my friends and I did to Marla, but I severed all ties with Kizzy and the others. I had no idea what had become of her until Ronni came up with this Cupcake Weekend extravaganza. I don't eat sweets, so I'd never heard of Kizzy Cutler's Cupcakes until Ronni told me about her plan to bring the competition to Shadow Bend."

"When did you decide to murder your old friend?" I asked, even though there was something bothering me about Harlee as the killer.

"Never!" Harlee yelped. "I'm not the one who's been trying to kill her."

"Can you prove it?" I asked. "Because from where I stand, you're the best suspect." I ticked the points off on my fingers. "First, Kizzy made you do something that has haunted you ever since you were eighteen. Second, instead of going to college, you ended up in the army. Third—"

"I have an alibi for the time of the hit-and-run attempt," Harlee interrupted me. "I was within the sight of my clerk and all the models for the fashion show from six p.m. until the show was over." She sighed. "If you don't believe me, ask Chief Kincaid. He interviewed my assistant and the models this morning and was satisfied that I was innocent."

"Oh." Evidently, the chief had listened to me after all. But that meant my last suspect was in the clear. *Hell!* My chance of solving the mystery and claiming the reward Lee had offered was fading faster than a cheap T-shirt. "Are any of the other Cutthroats still in town?"

"Not as far as I know." Harlee sagged against the

wall. "Kizzy told me the other night that her boyfriend and mine went on to college, married other women, and live halfway across the country." Harlee twisted a strand of hair. "The four of us were the core of the group. The others were mostly hangers-on. I haven't heard that any of them stuck around Shadow Bend after high school. Since there are so few jobs here, most kids who go to college don't seem to come back."

"Damn!" I chewed on that information for a while, then said, "I wonder if Marla's parents are still here." I pursed my lips. "Probably not. I don't remember anyone named Parrett in the area."

"The family's name isn't Parrett," Harlee said. "Marla was Mr. Bourne's stepdaughter. You know the guy who owns the Savings and Guaranty? Mrs. Bourne was a widow with a one-year-old daughter when they got married. They had Gwen three or four years later."

How had I not known that Gwen had a half-sister who had died? Probably because I would have been only nine or ten at the time of Marla's death. Maybe I had heard about the train crashing into a car, but probably not too much about the victim or the circumstances of the accident. Afterward, everyone involved would have wanted to let the matter drop and forget the ill-treated teen existed.

I had to swallow the lump in my throat that had formed for the forgotten girl before I could speak, but I finally said, "Mr. and Mrs. Bourne live in Florida now." I recalled the buzz around town a couple of months ago. After an incident with the president of his bank, Mr. Bourne had hired a new manager—a position he'd offered to my father, who had turned down the job—and retired from actively running the Savings and Guaranty. The Bournes had then given their big fancy house to their daughter and moved away. "So neither

Mr. nor Mrs. Bourne is around here to go after Kizzy to retaliate for Marla's suicide. Not that they would, considering that they reacted to the poor girl's death by hushing up the whole thing."

"How about Marla's sister?" Harlee asked. "Gwen would have been eleven or twelve when she died. Want to bet that her folks never told her the real story?"

"Sorry." I shook my head. "I can't afford that kind of gambling loss."

"Marla's death might explain a lot about Gwen's personality," Boone said. "It had to be devastating to lose her sister like that."

"It must have been horrible for her." I felt a little bad about how I'd treated Gwen in the past, then remembered that when I virtually lost both my parents during my teenage years, she'd been none too nice to me, either. Still, maybe I'd cut her some slack from now on—unless, of course, she was the murderer. I turned to Harlee. "You're suggesting that Gwen discovered what really happened to her sister, and when Kizzy came to town, she decided to avenge Marla's death?"

"Anything's possible." Harlee shrugged. "It's hard to tell how people will react to discovering a secret from their past. A twelve-year-old might have felt protective of her sister. Marla's differentness made her vulnerable. And even though she was the older sibling, she was the one who the parents didn't treat very well. Gwen might have some guilt over being the favorite."

"Maybe Gwen found something when she took possession of the family home that made her question the circumstance surrounding her sister's death," I speculated. "Then talked to someone like we did. Someone who was able to tell her the true story of Marla's so-called accident."

"Someone who remembered how badly Kizzy reacted to Marla's winning the FHA baking contest," Boone added. "And told Gwen about the bullying."

"That's it!" The fragment of an idea that had been niggling at me since we talked to Boone's friend finally crystallized. "Kizzy's original cupcake, the one she founded her company on, was a vanilla-rosewater combination with lavender honey frosting. Which, according to Jeffrey, was the flavor of Marla's first-prize creation."

"Oh. My. God." Harlee slid to the floor as if her bones had turned to water. "Kizzy not only tormented Marla to death, she appropriated her recipe and made millions from it."

"And that is more than enough motive for Gwen to want revenge," I said. "Gwen has a real thing about possession and ownership." I turned to Boone. "Look how she is about Noah. He took her out once, and now she thinks I stole him from her and hates me. She might have been upset to find out about the bullying, but profiting from a recipe that belonged to the Bourne family would push her over the edge."

CHAPTER 24

"So you never realized that Kizzy stole Marla's cupcake recipe?" I asked Harlee, trying to keep the skepticism out of my voice.

"Remember, I told you that I had never even heard of her company until Ronni told me about it." Harlee took a deep shuddering breath. "So I had no idea what kind of cupcakes she sold."

"I'm surprised someone from town didn't figure it out." Boone frowned.

"Except that Kizzy didn't start her company until several years after Marla won the contest," I reminded him. "By then, who would think about a high school bake-off recipe?"

"Especially since the winner was dead, and everyone involved wanted to forget the incident," Harlee added, with a grimace.

"Sadly, true," Boone agreed.

"What are you going to do now?" Harlee stared at me. "Your theory that Gwen is the killer is all supposition."

"First, I need to think over some stuff." I paced up and down the hallway. "Once I have it all straight in my mind, I'll call Chief Kincaid, tell him what we figured out, and turn the entire matter over to him."

"Let me know if you need me to corroborate anything to the chief," Harlee said. "I'm going to head home. This stroll down memory lane has ruined my appetite." She sighed. "I need a stiff drink a lot more than a heavy dinner."

After the door closed behind Harlee, Boone asked, "Now what?"

"Before we go to Chief Kincaid, I want to make sure Gwen doesn't have an alibi for any of the incidents. I can't figure out a way to check her whereabouts for the time of the package delivery to Fallon on Thursday, but I know I saw her at the dime store just before Kizzy arrived on Saturday, so she definitely could have snuck upstairs and bonked the cupcake queen over the head. Setting my store on fire would have been a twofer for her, considering how much she dislikes me." I chewed my lip. "Gwen was also at the Friday night dinner, but I don't remember if she left before we did. She would have had to leave at least ten minutes or so before our group in order to have time to get her car and try to run Kizzy over."

"Didn't you tell me Vaughn Yager was her escort?" Boone asked. "Certainly, he'd know how long she stayed at the supper."

"Right." I strode over to the banquet hall entrance. "That's a good place to start. I saw him inside, sitting with his aunt. Let's go ask him about his date with Gwen."

Vaughn greeted me, shook Boone's hand, then said, "You look like a couple on a mission. Is there something I can do for you two?"

"What made you decide to ask Gwen Bourne to go with you to the dinner Friday night?" I asked immediately, too impatient to ease into my questions.

"Actually, she phoned me." Vaughn gave me a shrewd look. "I was sort of surprised."

"Did you pick her up and drive her to St. Saggy's?" I asked.

"No," he answered slowly. "She said she might be running late, so asked me to meet her in the foyer. Funny thing. She was there before me. Why?"

"I'll explain everything later, I promise," I assured him, then asked, "Did you go to the fashion show together afterward?"

"We were supposed to," Vaughn said, crossing his arms, "but she said she had an early day and was too tired, so she cut out from the supper right after you saw us together." He wrinkled his nose. "I didn't believe her excuse, but by then I was glad to get rid of her, so I bid her a fond farewell and finished my chocolate cream pie in peace." He curled his lip. "I don't mind a little wickedness, but I draw the line at malicious, and that woman is spiteful with a capital *S*."

"Thanks!" I kissed Vaughn on the cheek. I took Boone's hand and hurried him away.

Once we were back in the hallway, Boone said, "So Gwen had her own car Friday night and could have used it to try to mow down Kizzy."

"That's two attempts she could have made on the cupcake queen's life—the hit-and-run and the fire." I leaned against the wall and crossed my arms. "I just wish I knew how to find out about where Gwen was Thursday evening."

Before Boone could respond, Poppy came rushing out to the banquet hall and said, "They're about to start the award ceremony. You guys better get inside."

"Did you save us a seat and something to eat?" I asked, taking a step to follow her.

"Would I let you guys go hungry?" Poppy asked.

"Three of the ladies on Mom's committee pooped out on her, so I came early to help set up and snagged a table by the stage."

"There are perks to being a dutiful daughter," I said.

"Definitely. Those church women move the heavy tables around like they're made of Styrofoam." Poppy held open the door for us. "And I got a good giggle when I saw Gwen sneak in. I've never seen her such a mess. She usually looks like she just fell off a charm bracelet, but today she had her hair shoved up in a baseball cap and wore sunglasses. I guess she didn't have time to do her usual full war paint."

"Gwen was here prior to the church hall opening up to the public?" Goose bumps popped up on my arms and I shivered.

"Right after Mom and I unlocked the door. We were in the storage room counting out chairs, but my phone rang, so I stepped out into the corridor to get a better signal and I saw Gwen disappear into the banquet room." Poppy frowned. "She had a gift-wrapped box, so I peeked through the door's window to see what she was going to do with it."

"And?" Boone asked.

"She put it on the floor by Kizzy's chair," Poppy answered. "Who would have guessed that Gwen was a Cutler's Cupcakes groupie?"

"Call the police," I ordered, pushing past her through the door. "I think Gwen might be trying to poison Kizzy again."

"Again?" Poppy asked. "You mean Gwen was the one who poisoned Fallon?"

"That's our current theory," I shouted as I darted inside the banquet hall.

I found Kizzy and Lee chatting with the mayor and finishing their desserts. A large brightly wrapped package was sitting on the floor by Kizzy's feet. Neither of the women seemed the least bit sick, and if I recalled correctly, Fallon had felt ill almost immediately. I skidded to a halt, wondering if my suspicion of Gwen was totally off base.

Not wanting to look like a hysterical fool, I thought quickly. If I could remove the box and turn it over to Chief Kincaid when he arrived, I wouldn't have to risk falsely accusing Gwen of murder.

Pasting a smile on my face, I said, "Kizzy, Lee, how's everything going?"

"Fine," Lee answered. "We're about to announce the contest winner."

"Great." I beamed. "The cupcakes all looked fabulous when I saw them this afternoon. The judges must have had a tough time deciding."

"I'm sure," Lee agreed.

"I see someone gave you a present, Kizzy." I edged toward the box. "Would you like me to put it in your car for you so you don't have to worry about it later? It looks sort of unwieldy."

"Sure." Kizzy narrowed her eyes at me as if wondering why I was being so helpful, then pursed her lips. "But I'm still going to remember that you wouldn't lend me a hand to carry stuff up to the display room yesterday."

"Sorry about that," I said, forcing out the insincere apology. "I don't know what got into me."

"Hmm. Our car is the white 1960 Lincoln Continental." Kizzy jerked her head toward Lee. "Give her the keys."

"Thanks." I tucked the ring Lee tossed to me into my pocket, then realized that I didn't want to touch the package. Maybe poison took longer with some people than with others. Grabbing two napkins, I used them like potholders to pick up the box.

When I noticed that Lee and Kizzy were staring at me, I said, "The wrapping is so pretty I don't want to get it dirty."

Kizzy lost interest and turned back to the mayor, but Lee raised a brow and I shrugged. Hurrying back into the hallway, I rejoined Poppy and Boone in the foyer.

"Chief Kincaid should be here any second," Boone reported. "I see you got the gift. Did Kizzy seem sick?"

"Not at all." I put the box on the floor. "Maybe we're wrong about Gwen."

Before Poppy or Boone could answer, Chief Kincaid marched through the front door, pointed toward the package at my feet, and demanded, "Is that the box in question?"

"Yes." I nodded, then explained how I had gotten it away from Kizzy.

"So Ms. Cutler didn't appear ill?" Chief Kincaid asked me. When I shook my head, he turned to Poppy and asked, "Did Gwen have gloves on or did she carry the package up to Ms. Cutler bare-handed?"

"I'm pretty sure I would have noticed gloves." Poppy paused, then nodded to herself. "She was definitely bare-handed."

"If Gwen is the killer—"

Chief Kincaid interrupted me. "When Boone explained your theory of Gwen's motive to me, I checked to see what kind of vehicle she drives. That information, along with what I learned not fifteen minutes ago, has left me strongly suspecting that Gwen is indeed our murderer."

"Why?" Boone asked. "You told Lee Kimbrough that you thought she did it."

"Ms. Kimbrough was the prime suspect in our investigation, but now we have new evidence," Chief Kincaid informed us.

"Which is?" I asked.

"Mr. and Mrs. Wells are back. They're the folks who live across the street from Veronica Ksiazak's B and B in that big Gothic revival house. The ones who left town to avoid the Cupcake Weekend crowds," Chief Kincaid said, then looked at me to see if I was following his explanation. When I nodded, he continued. "I was interviewing them when Boone called. The husband told me that he was out walking their dog Thursday evening and saw a package being delivered to the guesthouse."

"The package Fallon had stayed back to wait for," I murmured. "He saw the delivery service that you could never find?"

"Correct. And according to the witness, Thursday evening someone wearing jeans, a hooded sweatshirt, sunglasses, and gloves parked a yellow Mercedes-Benz about a block away from the B and B. The driver got out of the car and walked to the guesthouse." Chief Kincaid took a small notepad from his pocket and read, "Mr. Wells stated that he was behind a hedge with his Labradoodle. The Mercedes driver didn't notice him, but Mr. Wells watched this person ring the bell at Ronni's place. Then when the door opened, the delivery person tried to back away, but the young woman who answered the door yanked the large padded envelope from the Mercedes driver's hand."

"By then, Fallon must have been in a hurry to get to the restaurant," I murmured. "She was probably starving."

"The delivery person snatched the envelope back and took off running," the chief continued.

Now that I thought about it, when Fallon called, she'd said the package had shown up, but not that she had it in her possession. I wish that I had figured that little detail out sooner. For a nanosecond, I wondered why Fallon hadn't said that the delivery person had grabbed back the envelope. Then I realized that Kizzy would have had a hissy fit that her assistant had failed to retain the mysterious package and Fallon was probably already feeling too sick to deal with her employer's wrath.

Poppy interrupted my musings when she stated, "Gwen Bourne drives a yellow Mercedes."

"One of only two in the entire county," Chief Kincaid confirmed.

"So most likely, Gwen *is* the killer." I thought for a moment about the progression. Gwen had started with poison, moved on to hit-and-run, then tried to burn Kizzy up. It seemed to me that Gwen was getting more violent with each failed attempt. "Gwen has never repeated any of her methods, so maybe the gift isn't poisoned." I stepped away from the box. "Maybe it's a bomb."

"Look at the tag." Poppy pointed downward. "It says, 'Do not open until midnight.'"

"When Kizzy would most likely be alone," Boone said.

"That must mean it doesn't have a detonator that sets it off when the package is lifted up." I knew way too much about stuff like that. I really had to stop watching *CSI Miami* reruns with Gran. "But rather a remote one on a timer."

"Good thing for you since you carried it out here," Poppy pointed out.

Chief Kincaid squatted next to the box and sniffed, then muttered, "Ammonia with a slight burning plastic smell." Immediately, he stood, backed away from the package, and said, "I don't want to operate my radio near this thing. It could set it off. I'm going to find the minister's office and telephone my dispatcher from the church's landline. She'll contact the Kansas City ATF office and request their bomb squad, then call in all police and fire personnel and have them report here." We nodded our understanding and he continued. "Go into the banquet hall and start evacuating through the kitchen exit. Make sure no one uses their cell phone."

"What do we tell them?" I asked.

"Suspected gas leak," the chief snapped. "Now go!"

As we hurried away, I heard Chief Kincaid mutter to himself, "We need to pick up Gwen Bourne ASAP."

Thankfully, the winner must have already been announced, because people were getting ready to leave, or I didn't think we'd have been able to get the crowd to vacate the building. As it was, the church ladies were none too happy to abandon their kitchen before cleaning up the mess.

I noticed both GB and Lauren seemed subdued and I assumed that meant they didn't have the ten-thousand-dollar check in their pockets. Later I overheard chatter that the kumquat cupcake with the royal icing hyacinth flowers took the prize, but I didn't recognize the name of the baker who made it.

When the police and firefighters arrived, they took over clearing the building. Once everyone was outside, most got into their cars and drove away, but Poppy, Boone, and I relocated a few blocks away to a strip mall parking lot to view the proceedings. Our choices were limited since the new Methodist church was near the highway and there weren't any other houses or stores nearby. On a positive note, that would be a good thing if the bomb exploded.

The L-shaped strip mall contained a dental practice, a chiropractor's office, and a dry-cleaning business on the long leg, and a pawnshop along the short one.

Poppy had three canvas folding chairs in the back of her Hummer, and she, Boone, and I set up camp to watch the goings-on at the church. As we settled in to observe the scene, I glimpsed a flash of yellow near the dentist's office.

I casually got up and strolled toward the pawnshop's front window. As I walked, I could see a car parked in the crook of the L-shaped lot, and the emblem on the grill of the vehicle was the Mercedes logo.

As I dug my phone out of my pocket, Poppy and Boone joined me. I jerked my head in the direction of the car and whispered to my friends, "Don't look, but I think that's Gwen's Mercedes."

Poppy pawed through her purse, pulled out a compact, and peered into it. "You're right."

Boone snatched the mirror from Poppy's hand and added his confirmation, then said, "You'd better call the cops."

Once I got through to Chief Kincaid and informed him of his suspect's possible whereabouts, Poppy asked me, "But why would Gwen stick around with all the police presence?"

"She probably was watching from here to make sure that Kizzy carried the gift out with her," I explained. "Then when the cops showed up, she couldn't risk leaving and being seen."

A split second later, several squad cars zipped into the parking lot. Now that there was no need to remain concealed from Gwen's view, the three of us moved nearer, watching the cruisers surround the Mercedes. In retrospect, getting closer to Gwen was stupid. What if she'd had a gun? But at the time, we were all caught up in the excitement of catching the murderer.

A nanosecond later, car doors slammed and we heard Chief Kincaid's voice amplified through a megaphone. He ordered, "Gwendolyn Bourne, put your hands on your head and get out of the vehicle."

He repeated the command several times and finally we saw Gwen emerge from the Mercedes. Poppy had been right about how bad she looked. I had never seen the socialite in public anything but Barbie-doll perfect before. Whatever had caused Gwen to snap had played hell with her appearance. She looked more like the Unabomber than a member of one of Shadow Bend's wealthiest families. Gwen had always reminded me of an egg. I knew she was going to crack one day, just not when she was going to take that inevitable leap into the sizzling pan.

As Chief Kincaid put her in the backseat of the squad car, Gwen screamed, "I would have stopped after that poor girl died, but Kizzy just had to keep bragging about *her* wonderful, original cupcakes. That's Marla's recipe, not hers. She shouldn't have been profiting from what she did to my sister."

The whole time the chief tried to get Gwen seated in the cruiser, she continued to shout her justification in trying to kill the cupcake queen. I had never liked Gwen, but a part of me felt sorry for her. Kizzy had tormented Marla to death, and because of that earlier bullying, Marla's little sister's life was destroyed as well.

Still, instead of wreaking her revenge on Kizzy, Gwen had killed a girl who had barely been out of diapers when the incident took place. I sighed and shook my head. There really was no excuse for Gwen's actions. Our past may influence who we are, but in the end, we're responsible for who we become. Violence and vengeance never do work out the way the instigators plan. And it's always the innocents who are caught in the crossfire.

CHAPTER 25

From the moment that I opened the dime store on Monday at noon, Gwen Bourne's arrest, confession, and subsequent mental breakdown were the only topic of conversation. The rumor mill confirmed my speculation that when she took ownership of the family estate, Gwen had cleaned out the attic and found her sister's diaries.

According to the grapevine, Marla had painstakingly chronicled each of Kizzy's verbal assaults. A second journal had contained all of Marla's original recipes, and once Gwen realized how her sister had really died and who was behind Marla's suicide, she vowed to get revenge.

Gwen was claiming that she had only aimed to make Kizzy sick with Thursday evening's poisoned delivery, not kill her. But then when Fallon died, and the cupcake queen went on with the weekend, Gwen's rage grew. She had set off the tornado siren during the opening ceremonies because she couldn't stand to see the whole town kowtowing to the woman who had bullied Marla to death, then stolen her recipe to become rich and famous.

With every failed attempt to kill Kizzy, and each of the cupcake queen's public appearances, Gwen's thirst for vengeance grew. Then when Kizzy hired a bodyguard, Gwen got desperate. Since the cupcake queen was no longer accessible, Gwen decided a bomb was the only way to finish her off for good. Gwen alleged that she never meant to hurt anyone else and only intended to detonate the bomb when she was sure Kizzy was alone in her room at the B & B. Her plan was to climb onto the suite's balcony and wait until she saw Kizzy start to open the package before setting off the explosive.

As I collected money and bagged purchases, I learned from my customers that Gwen's parents had hired a private plane, flown into Kansas City late last night, and were already in residence back in Shadow Bend. I also found out that Gwen was being held on Triple Creek Hospital's locked psychiatric ward. Evidently, Mr. and Mrs. Bourne had hired a criminal attorney from California who was famous for getting wack-job celebrities off with a slap on their wrists. This was the same lawyer who while defending a strung-out superstar had stood up in open court and said, "If the lunatic has a fit, you must acquit."

I overheard a lot of the gossip regarding Gwen from the Knittie Gritties—a club that met at my shop every Monday afternoon. As they knitted and pearled, they speculated about the details of Gwen's crime spree. Some bigmouth at the PD had already spilled his guts and the whole town knew way too much about the case.

It was hard to do, but when the Gritties questioned me about my part in Gwen's arrest, I kept quiet. Chief Kincaid had played fair and square with me, and I wanted to return the favor by not disclosing any facts that hadn't already been leaked.

The chief had been grateful to me for the information that I had provided him that allowed the police to not only apprehend the killer, but also prevent another murder. He showed his appreciation by letting me know that the search warrant for Gwen's house had turned up dieldrin—a chlorinated hydrocarbon insecticide—in her garage, and that the ME was certain it would be a match for the substance that poisoned Fallon.

They also found signs of bomb making. Then there were Gwen's fingerprints on the bomb itself, as well as the dime store's smoke detector and back doorknob. Chief Kincaid's theory was that Gwen didn't bother to wear gloves while she was assembling the explosives because she believed any fingerprints would be destroyed in the blast.

It was good to know that the police had physical proof. Gwen's lawyer would probably get her confession thrown out on the grounds that she wasn't rational at the time. But it would be hard to convince a jury she wasn't guilty as each piece of solid evidence was uncovered.

Shortly before the store's closing time, Lee dropped off the five-thousand-dollar check she'd promised me for solving the case. It was a shame that the Cupcake Weekend was technically over by the time that I figured out that Gwen was the killer or I could have collected twice that amount. Still, even after donating half to the animal shelter in Boone's name, I had enough left to pay a couple of months of health insurance premiums for Dad and me, and Gran's Part B Medicare.

After handing over the reward, Lee said, "Kizzy wanted me to thank you for saving her life. She had to return to Chicago early this morning for an important meeting, or she would have come by to express her gratitude in person."

"My pleasure." I took Lee's statement regarding Kizzy's appreciation with a grain of salt the size of Ayers Rock, but tried to sound gracious. "I understand that business comes first."

"Speaking of business"—Lee dug a sheaf of papers from her purse—"Kizzy would like to offer your store exclusive distribution rights of Cutler's Cupcakes for the Kansas City area."

"Wow." I was stunned at the generous gesture. Maybe Kizzy's gratefulness *was* sincere. She certainly put her money where her mouth was. An exclusive distribution deal like that could be worth thousands of dollars. "That would be fantastic."

"Great." Lee smiled. "Look over the agreement and return it at your convenience."

"Thanks." I placed the contract on the shelf under the register, then asked, "How is Kizzy taking Gwen's claim that the Cutthroats bullied Marla to death and that she stole the poor girl's recipe?"

"As per her usual worldview—the one where she's the center of the universe—Kizzy denies both accusations." Lee shrugged. "She says it was all good-natured teasing, and although the recipe is somewhat similar, she made significant changes and improvements, so that it is no longer the cupcake with which Marla won the contest."

"I wonder if the Bournes will try to sue." I had no idea if a recipe could be copyrighted.

"Kizzy's meeting today in Chicago is with our attorneys." Lee leaned a hip against the counter. "My guess is we'll offer a trade. No civil action against Gwen for the harm she caused to our company due to her interference with the Cupcake Weekend, and the Bournes sign away any claim to the recipe. I've also suggested that we donate a portion of the profits from the sales of that particular cupcake to an antibullying foundation."

"Good idea." I'd have to make sure everyone in Shadow Bend bought lots of that flavor when I started selling the cupcakes in my store.

"I'd better get going." Lee turned to leave. "It's a long drive back."

As I walked her to the door, I said, "I'm curious about the fight you, Kizzy, and Fallon had Thursday night. Do you mind telling me what it was about?"

"Fallon wanted to work for me since she had had it with Kizzy." Lee ran her fingers through her hair. "And when Kizzy found out, she felt betrayed by both of us. But Fallon was resigning as Kizzy's assistant whether I hired her or not. I explained that at least this way she would still be available as Kizzy's photo double, which was all Kizzy really cared about, so the matter was settled amicably."

After saying good-bye to Lee, I locked the dime store's front entrance and went into the back room to change into the clothes I'd brought with me from home that morning. Once I was dressed and my hair combed, I took out the bag of dinner stuff from the mini fridge, then headed to Coop's apartment to make him the meal that I owed him. I had tried to talk Ronni into accompanying me since I thought she and the handsome firefighter would be a good match, but she'd claimed to be too busy.

After I rang Coop's bell, I stared at my reflection in the window beside the door. Why had I dressed up so much? The flirty gray-and-white skirt paired with a sleeveless pink blouse looked too much as if I thought this was a date. What had I been thinking?

Coop showed me around his apartment, which was the typical bachelor pad. A king-size bed dominated the bedroom, a weight-lifting system took up most of the living room, his refrigerator contained only beer and condiments, and his cupboards were practically bare. Fortunately, I didn't need much equipment to fix our meal or we would've been out of luck.

We discussed the attempted bombing as I cooked, and I asked, "Did you hear how that bomb was made? I mean, how in the world did a small-town socialite figure out how to make an explosive device?"

"The Internet," Coop answered. "It's pretty damn simple to make a homemade bomb."

"Seriously?" I placed the pan of lasagna in the preheated oven. I had prepared the dish that morning before opening the store at noon. Once it was baking, I turned my attention to the salad. "But where would she get the components?"

"It's all fairly common stuff." Coop attempted to snatch a cherry tomato from the bowl and I slapped his fingers away. "Glass jars, salt substitute with potassium chloride, instant cold packs with ammonium nitrate, sugar, coffee filters, water, tin can, a few plastic measuring cups, and a scale."

"That's it?" I was shocked.

"Pretty much." Coop took two bottles from the fridge, twisted off the caps, and handed me one. "You just take the ammonium nitrate and—"

"Stop." I held up my hand. "I really don't want to know the exact recipe for making a bomb. If I have that knowledge, I might be tempted to use it the next time someone ticks me off."

"Gotcha." Coop took a slug of beer.

"Okay. Gwen figures out how to make the explosive part, but the detonator has to be more difficult. Right?"

"Not really." Coop succeeded in snitching a crouton from the salad and grinned in victory. "A bomb can be ignited using any simple electronic device. A digital watch, garage door opener, cell phone, kitchen timer, or even a nine-volt battery and Christmas lights."

"Well, that's disturbing." I finished assembling the salad and moved on to the garlic bread. "I love technology and all, but the idea that any lunatic can put together a bomb in their garage using stuff from the grocery and hardware store sends chills up my spine."

"Life is risky." Coop moved closer. "That's why we shouldn't put off having a good time." He stared into my eyes. "We need to kick the tires and start the fires."

My mouth was suddenly dry. What do you say when a sizzling-hot guy tells you to leap into the flames with him? I so wished that Ronni had come with me. She and the hunky fire chief would make such a cute couple. Before I could come up with an answer to his challenge, "Torn Between Two Lovers" started playing from my skirt. Fishing my cell from my pocket, I edged away from Coop. He opened his mouth to object, but I made a face that dared him to comment.

When he held his hands up in surrender, I rushed into the bathroom. Closing the door, I swept my finger across the phone's screen and demanded, "Jake? Are you okay?"

"I'm fine." His smooth baritone filled my ear. "Sorry I couldn't call sooner. We caught the Doll Maker, but it took a couple of days to locate Meg. During that time, things were pretty hairy around here."

"Is she all right?" I hoped the maniac who had kidnapped his ex-wife hadn't harmed her. His MO was to carve his victim's face and body into his twisted idea of the perfect woman.

"Meg wasn't sliced up," Jake assured me. "Evidently, he was saving that until he was able to capture me, too. He wanted to re-create Rodin's *The Kiss*."

"Yikes!" My heart sank, at the thought of both Jake being hurt and him being in an eternal embrace with his ex. Yes. I am that petty. And the irony of where I was and whom I was with wasn't lost on me. Clearing my throat, I asked, "But the Doll Maker is back behind bars and Meg wasn't hurt?"

"He's locked away so tight this time even a search-and-rescue dog couldn't find him." Jake's voice exuded satisfaction. "That freak will never see the light of day again."

"Thank God!" I paused, then took the plunge and said, "Are you coming back to Shadow Bend soon?"

"I'm about three hours away," Jake answered.

He murmured something, but it didn't make sense, so I asked, "What did you say?"

"Nothing." Jake's tone was odd. "It was probably the radio. Look, it'll be late by the time I get home. How about tomorrow I come by the dime store at closing time and take you to dinner?"

"Great," I agreed. We said our good-byes and I wondered why Jake sounded so funny. And what radio show broadcast the words "You're safe, honey. Go back to sleep?"

EPILOGUE

Jake dropped his cell back into the cup holder. He'd been relieved to catch the Doll Maker for a lot of reasons. Not the least of which was that in the back of his mind, he'd feared that once the serial killer got bored with Meg, he'd somehow find out about Jake's relationship with Devereaux and target her next.

Speaking of Meg, Jake glanced over at the passenger seat. His ex-wife's eyes were closed, but even dozing, she twitched and jerked, making frightened mewling sounds as she fought the demons in her dreams. Bringing her to Shadow Bend was going to cause a lot of problems. Tony hated Meg and he'd be infuriated that Jake intended to install her in the spare room.

Hell, Jake didn't like his ex-wife very much, either, and he wasn't sure why he'd stepped in to help her. Except she had nowhere else to go and no relatives or even friends willing to take responsibility for her.

Meg had been virtually catatonic since they found her strapped to a cot in a self-storage locker. The doctors had said that there was nothing wrong with her physically, but that she needed rest and time to recover emotionally. If Jake hadn't volunteered to bring her home with him, she would have had to be put in a nursing home. She would have been at the mercy of strangers, with no one to make sure the staff was treating her okay.

Jake looked at his ex. She was a shell of the woman he'd divorced. Always petite, now she was emaciated. She moaned, and Jake patted her knee. His touch seemed to calm her.

Swinging his gaze back to the road, he wrinkled his brow. Surely, Devereaux wouldn't hold Meg's presence against him. Jake smacked his forehead with his palm and groaned at his own stupidity. What girlfriend would understand when the guy she was dating brought his ex-wife home to live with him? Meg could very well cost him his future with Devereaux. And wouldn't that be a kick in the pants? The woman who dumped him when he was injured in the line of duty might once again ruin his life.

Skye Denison Boyd adjusted the straps of her bathing suit, then kicked off from the edge of the swimming pool. Her goal was to make it to the other end without losing her breakfast. Not that a couple of soda crackers and a cup of tea was much of a meal, but that was all she'd been able to tolerate in the mornings for the past month. And some days, even the saltines didn't stay down.

Refusing to think about tossing her cookies—or to be more specific, crackers—Skye concentrated on improving her butterfly stroke. Seven years ago, when she first returned to her hometown and started working as a psychologist for the Scumble River School District, she had swum most weekday mornings and often on Saturday and Sunday as well. In the summer, she used the local recreational club, a lake formed from a reclaimed coalmine. And when it was cold, she'd do laps in the high school's highly debated pool.

Due to the source of its financing, the swimming pool was a hot topic among the Scumble River citizens. A while back, the district received some extra tax money from the construction of a nearby nuclear power plant, but instead of buying more up-to-date textbooks or employing additional teachers, the school board had spent the funds on athletic equipment and a pool.

The board members had been hoodwinked by a fast-talking salesman and a group of parents with their own agendas. It was the one time in anyone's memory that the board president, Skye's godfather, Charlie Patukas, had lost a vote. Because of that, she'd always felt a little guilty when she used the facility.

Those ambivalent feelings had helped her make excuses to skip her daily swims until she rarely, if ever, swam at all. But a couple of months ago, after returning from her honeymoon, Skye had vowed to get back to her previous exercise routine. And a little bit of nausea was not going to stop her. Besides, the doctor had said that swimming might actually help the morning sickness.

Which reminded her, when she wiggled into her maillot at home, she'd noticed a definite baby bump. Up until now, because of her already generous figure, there hadn't been much danger that anyone would notice the three or four extra pounds she was carrying. Evidently, that anonymity was about to end. She and her husband, Wally, would have to make some kind of announcement soon or speculation would sweep the town. Scumble River's main drag wasn't known as Blabbermouth Basin Street for nothing.

Skye and Wally's motives for keeping mum about the blessed event were due in part to Wally's concerns about revealing the pregnancy prior to the completion of the first trimester. Furthermore, they hadn't wanted to take the spotlight away from Skye's brother and sister-in-law's baby shower, which was scheduled for Saturday.

However, the most compelling reason for them to

keep quiet as long as possible was Skye's mother. May had a tendency to be a bit overbearing, okay, a lot overbearing. And as soon as she found out her daughter was pregnant, she would try to take over her life. Compared to May, DB Cooper was an amateur hijacker.

Skye's mother had waited a long time for grandchildren. Both Skye and her brother, Vince, had married relatively late—Skye had been thirty-six and Vince nearly forty—which meant May had been ready to be a grandmother for close to twenty years. And although Skye hoped her mother would be distracted by Vince's baby, she was pretty darn sure May would find the time to drive her daughter crazy as well. As an equal opportunity meddler, May would make sure neither of her children felt neglected. She wouldn't want either of them to think the other was her favorite.

Wincing at the thought of her mother's reaction to her pregnancy, Skye reached the opposite end of the pool. Performing a perfect flip turn, she started back, happy that she felt less queasy and determined to put May out of her mind.

Willing herself to relax and enjoy the sensation of the water sliding over her skin, Skye focused on her dolphin kick. Because the butterfly was one of the most exhausting strokes and she hadn't yet rebuilt the strength to swim more than a few lengths of the pool before having to rest, she wanted to put the time she had to the best use.

March in Illinois had been chillier than usual, but in the heated pool, Skye could pretend that she was back on her honeymoon. Even though the cruise had been full of surprises, including a dead body, she and Wally had both been able to unwind from their demanding lives and have an unforgettable trip.

Wally, as the chief of the Scumble River Police Department, had been badly in need of a break. Although the town's population was just a shade over three thousand, between the devious mayor and several murders, the community in no way resembled Mayberry. Which meant Wally's work was no Andy Griffith kind of job.

Skye's position as the sole mental health professional for the entire school district kept her stress level in the head-about-to-explode range as well. Add planning a wedding during the frantic Christmas holidays and her psych consultant contract with the PD, and she, too, had been more than ready for a vacation.

Their honeymoon had been wonderful, but now that they'd been back for two and a half months, Skye had a feeling that their downtime was about to end. This was the final week before spring break, which in Skye's world meant frazzled teachers and students with cabin fever.

For Wally, kids out of school required preparing his officers for hordes of unoccupied teens with way too much time on their hands. Not many Scumble River families could afford to take off from their jobs and jet off to Florida or the Caribbean. So while they were busy making a living, their offspring were often left unsupervised and looking for something to do.

Skye finished her fifth lap, and as she rested against the side of the pool, she checked the clock on the far wall. It was only six thirty. Staff was required to be on duty at seven twenty, while students started their school day at ten to eight. Allowing half an hour to style her hair, slap on some makeup, and put on her clothes, she had fifteen minutes before she had to get out of the water and start to dress.

Because of her nausea, Skye had been up an hour before her normal time, and she'd gotten to the pool much earlier than usual. When she turned into the school's driveway, there hadn't been a single car in the parking lot. Even the custodian's old red Silverado pickup wasn't in its usual spot by the Dumpster yet.

She'd used her key to enter the back door of the empty building and made her way to the gym. The only way into the pool area, except for an alarmed emergency exit, was through the student locker rooms. As she passed through the girls' side, she'd stripped off her sweat suit and placed it and her duffel on one of the benches. The locked bag held what she would need to get ready for the school day, as well as her purse and the tote bag full of files she'd brought home on Friday to work on over the weekend.

Most mornings there were other staff members using the pool, but because she'd arrived so early, the place had been deserted. At the time, even though Skye knew she shouldn't swim without a buddy, she'd been happy to have the water to herself. It was nice not to have to worry about colliding with another swimmer or slowing someone else down. But now, it felt as if she was no longer alone. Had someone else arrived to take a pre-workday dip?

Skye glanced from side to side. Almost the entire wall of the pool enclosure was made up of frosted blue safety glass. She squinted. Was that someone peering through the partition? She called out a greeting, but no one answered. That was odd. Maybe whoever it had been had gone into the locker room. Her imagination must be getting the best of her.

She shoved her swim goggles up on her head and looked around for a second time. With the exception of a couple of safety rings and a pole with a hook on the end leaning against the wall, the area was empty. Taking a deep breath, she tried to calm her racing heart, but the scent of chlorine overpowered her. *Uh-oh!* Now she felt queasy again.

Swimming over to the ladder, Skye had just begun to climb out of the pool when she thought she heard retreating footsteps. A chill ran up her spine. Had someone been watching her? *No!* That was silly. Why would anyone spy on her? Was pregnancy making her paranoid?

Skye shook her head at her own foolishness and heaved herself out of the pool. She hurried into the locker room and peeled off her swim cap. Catching a glimpse of herself in a mirror, she sighed. While the cap kept her hair dry, it also left it a snarled mess. Bending over, she ran her fingers through her long chestnut curls in an attempt to fluff out the strands.

She was busy trying to work out a particularly stubborn tangle when a hand descended on her shoulder and someone snapped, "You need to leave immediately."

Skye screamed.